W9-AXT-278

Skating on Thin Ice

A *Murder, She Wrote* Mystery

Skating on Thin Ice

A *Murder, She Wrote* Mystery

A NOVEL BY
JESSICA FLETCHER & DONALD BAIN

Based on the Universal television series created by
Peter S. Fischer, Richard Levinson & William Link

AN OBSIDIAN MYSTERY

OBSIDIAN

Published by New American Library, a division of Penguin Group (USA) Inc., 375 Hudson Street, New York, New York 10014, USA • Penguin Group (Canada), 90 Eglinton Avenue East, Suite 700, Toronto, Ontario M4P 2Y3, Canada (a division of Pearson Penguin Canada Inc.) • Penguin Books Ltd., 80 Strand, London WC2R 0RL, England • Penguin Ireland, 25 St. Stephen's Green, Dublin 2, Ireland (a division of Penguin Books Ltd.) • Penguin Group (Australia), 250 Camberwell Road, Camberwell, Victoria 3124, Australia (a division of Pearson Australia Group Pty. Ltd.) • Penguin Books India Pvt. Ltd., 11 Community Centre, Panchsheel Park, New Delhi - 110 017, India • Penguin Group (NZ), 67 Apollo Drive, Rosedale, North Shore 0632, New Zealand (a division of Pearson New Zealand Ltd.) • Penguin Books (South Africa) (Pty.) Ltd., 24 Sturdee Avenue, Rosebank, Johannesburg 2196, South Africa

Penguin Books Ltd., Registered Offices:
80 Strand, London WC2R 0RL, England

First published by Obsidian, an imprint of New American Library,
a division of Penguin Group (USA) Inc.

First Printing, April 2011
1   3   5   7   9   10   8   6   4   2

Copyright © 2011 Universal City Studios Productions LLLP. *Murder, She Wrote* is a trademark and copyright of Universal Studios.
All rights reserved.

OBSIDIAN and logo are trademarks of Penguin Group (USA) Inc.

LIBRARY OF CONGRESS CATALOGING-IN-PUBLICATION DATA:

Set in Minion

Bain, Donald, 1935–
Skating on thin ice: a murder, she wrote mystery: a novel/by Jessica Fletcher and Donald Bain.
p.   cm.
"Based on the Universal Television series created by Peter S. Fischer,
Richard Levinson & William Link."
ISBN 978-0-451-23234-2
1. Fletcher, Jessica (Fictitious character)—Fiction. 2. Women dectectives—Fiction.
3. Women novelists—Fiction. I. Murder, she wrote (Television program) II. Title.
PS3552.A376S57   2011
813'.54—dc22   2010052156

Printed in the United States of America

Without limiting the rights under copyright reserved above, no part of this publication may be reproduced, stored in or introduced into a retrieval system, or transmitted, in any form, or by any means (electronic, mechanical, photocopying, recording, or otherwise), without the prior written permission of both the copyright owner and the above publisher of this book.

PUBLISHER'S NOTE
This is a work of fiction. Names, characters, places, and incidents either are the product of the author's imagination or are used fictitiously, and any resemblance to actual persons, living or dead, business establishments, events, or locales is entirely coincidental.
    The publisher does not have any control over and does not assume any responsibility for author or third-party Web sites or their content.

The scanning, uploading, and distribution of this book via the Internet or via any other means without the permission of the publisher is illegal and punishable by law. Please purchase only authorized electronic editions, and do not participate in or encourage electronic piracy of copyrighted materials. Your support of the author's rights is appreciated.

To Dick Button,
with thanks for his many hours of figure skating
commentary, and for not only teaching us
the technicalities of skating but also
sharing his love of the sport.

ACKNOWLEDGMENTS

The wonderful folks at the Danbury Ice Arena run a first-class operation and made our research glide smoothly. In particular we'd like to thank assistant manager Patrick McGannon, Jr., for his insights into rink operation; skating director Karla Jones, for her information on staffing and figure skating schools; and especially instructor Alan Helms for his knowledge of skating and his patience with and encouragement of the only student over seventeen in his "adult" class. We're also grateful to the lovely lady at the International Skating Center of Connecticut in Simsbury, who answered our questions but hung up before we could get her name.

Thanks, too, to Pete Nevin of Far West Ranch and Cattle Sales and Management for his real estate advice and for not hanging up when the cell phone reception became spotty.

All the people we consulted were generous with their time and expertise. Any errors are solely ours.

Skating on Thin Ice

A *Murder, She Wrote* Mystery

Chapter One

"What on earth are you doing?"

I was on my knees with my head buried in the attic closet when I heard Seth Hazlitt's voice behind me. I turned sharply, bumping into a carefully piled column of books. "Hold on," I called, putting up an arm to keep the column from toppling—again—and further fraying my already ragged nerves. Moments earlier I'd accidentally knocked an old mop to the floor, and the snap it made when it hit the wood had given me a real start. That was when the top rows of the leaning tower of literature had started cascading down, bopping me on the head one volume at a time like something out of a Saturday-morning cartoon show.

"I know they're here," I said.

"What's there?"

I scrunched down, ignoring the indelicate picture I must be presenting, and poked one hand deep into the recesses of the dark closet, pushing aside my old snowshoes and trying to grab hold of the purple canvas bag behind them. "I knew it!" I said, looping a finger into the handle and dragging it with me as I carefully backed out, hoping the books would stay put and my head would be spared another landslide.

I sat up, clapped the grime off my hands, and smoothed down the back of my hair, which stood on end thanks to the static electricity created when I brushed against the hems of sweaters hanging above. "See?" I said.

"What I see is a slightly mussed mystery writer with a smudge on her nose. May I ask what occasioned this archaeological dig into the bowels of the attic?" Seth asked, extending a hand to help me to my feet.

I took his offer and, once upright, dusted off the knees of my blue jeans. "I really must bring up the vacuum," I said. "It's been far too long." I leaned the mop in its place, picked up my purple prize, and headed for the stairs. "How did you know where to find me?"

"The back door was unlocked. I called out your name, but you didn't answer."

"I didn't hear you."

"But I heard you. At least I heard something upstairs falling over—thump, thump, thump—followed by some muffled cursing."

"I wasn't cursing. Those were expressions of frustration," I said, closing the door to the attic steps.

"I figured you were in some kind of difficulty, so I came to the rescue."

"No rescue needed, but thank you for the intent," I said. "I've been meaning to box up those books and take them over to the library for its book sale. What just happened was a physical reminder that I've neglected them for too long. But," I added, "I found what I was looking for."

We made our way to the ground floor and through the living room to the kitchen. I rested the purple canvas carrier on a chair and took two mugs from the cupboard.

"And just how long are you going to keep me in suspense?" Seth said.

"Coffee or tea?"

"Coffee," he replied, pulling out a chair and easing into it. "Now, what is that?" He pointed to the object of my search.

"My ice skates."

"Your ice skates! I assume that you intend to donate them to some deserving teenager."

"Actually, I was planning to see if they still fit."

"You've done some foolish things in your life, Jessica Fletcher, but now I've heard it all. You can't possibly mean to start ice-skating at your age."

"I'll ignore the last part of that comment. And I'll thank you to know I was second runner-up to the queen of the winter carnival in seventh grade. My talent was figure skating."

"It was, eh?"

"Yes," I said, pouring the coffee, and then taking milk from the refrigerator. "I was pretty good at stroking, had mastered the left crossover—the right was still a bit wobbly—but I could do a three-turn and was working on my Mohawk."

"Isn't that a hairstyle?"

"No. A type of turn." I took the top off the cookie jar. "Snickerdoodle?" I asked.

"Just one. I'm trying to take off a pound or two."

I fished out two cookies, one for him and one for me, and set the plate in front of him. My good friend and Cabot Cove's favorite physician had a weakness for cookies— actually, for good food of any kind. He cautioned his patients about overeating but wasn't very good at following his own recommendations, although he made an effort every now and then. Apparently this was one of those times.

Seth picked up the cookie and took a small bite, savoring the cinnamon and butter flavor, and changed the subject. "I suppose having the old ice arena refurbished and reopened has prompted this bit of folly on your part."

"Having a nice place to skate is appealing, Seth. Half the town is talking about it, and I'm no exception."

He grunted before saying, "You do know, don't you, that Coddington only decided to fix up the place in order to sell it?"

"Did Eve Simpson tell you that?" I asked, referring to one of Cabot Cove's leading real estate brokers.

"Ayuh. My point is, Jessica, that all the excitement about the arena probably won't last long. Whoever buys it from Coddington will probably turn it into a factory, or another of those mini-malls. Lord knows we don't need more of those."

The Cabot Cove Ice Arena had once been a center of social activity for the town. But it fell on hard times. Skaters sought more modern facilities, such as the rink installed in a mall down the coast that had the added benefit of being surrounded by stores. Without celebrity skaters to bring attention to the sport, our ice arena seemed to fade in the public imagination. Paid hours on the ice, either for pure recreation or for classes, dwindled to the point where the owner, Eldridge Coddington, had closed it down, and the assumption was that he'd find a buyer for the building. But Coddington surprised everyone, including me, when he decided to invest money to renovate the skating center using a hefty portion of a considerable inheritance from his uncle, who'd made his fortune in the halcyon days of the lumber industry. Coddington's plans were impressive. In addition to modernizing, he added a second rink to accommodate the growing popularity of hockey and was angling to bring in a semipro team. He had the name all picked out—the Cabot Cove Lobsters, according to Evelyn Phillips, the editor of the *Cabot Cove Gazette*. On top of that, he let it be known that he was going to open a world-class figure skating school and was casting about for a star coach to bring attention to the program. He found one in Brian Devlin, a former gold medalist, who agreed not only to head up the school, but also to bring in elite athletes to burnish its reputation. You can imagine the excitement that announcement created; Cabot Cove was all abuzz.

But that was almost a year ago. Devlin's arrival unfortunately coincided with the start of the recent recession, prompting Coddington to scale back some of his more ambitious plans for the renovation. But that didn't impact the general skating sessions that took place twice a day at the rink, or the revitalized hockey program. The vast space above the new hockey rink was colorfully decorated with large banners displaying every school with a hockey team in Maine, a blatant bid to draw playoff games to the arena, plus other flags representing the semipro teams Coddington hoped would play there. Lilting music poured from the new public address system, the concession stand was open and doing a brisk business, and there always seemed to be enough staff on hand to handle the skaters, who ranged in age from toddlers to senior citizens and covered the gamut from rank beginners to veteran skaters who didn't want to let go of what for many was a lifelong passion.

I'd stopped by the rink on a few occasions, not to skate but to watch. Each time I went, I thought of my skates in their purple bag hidden deep in the recesses of my attic closet, and I knew that the lure of being on the ice would eventually trump what my dear friend Seth Hazlitt would undoubtedly term common sense. Of course, that's exactly what happened, much to his chagrin.

My most recent visit to the arena was with Jim Shevlin, Cabot Cove's popular mayor.

"I suppose you've heard the rumors," he said to me as we watched the skaters glide by.

"No," I said. "What rumors?"

"The way I hear it, Coach Devlin has been venting his anger about some of the promised renovations not being completed, or even started. He claims that the pairs couple he's training isn't happy with the facility. At least that's what he told Susan when she met him at a luncheon." Susan was Jim's wife and the town's leading travel agent. "Devlin told her that the gym has never been completed, only has one weight-lifting bench and a few donated barbells. He complained that the ballet bar hasn't been installed, and she said he was particularly irked by the lack of some contraption, a kind of harness rig to help figure skaters learn to jump. I'm really not sure of all the particulars, Jessica, but Susan says Devlin was really hot under the collar. And I've heard that he and Coddington have had some heated shouting matches lately."

"I'm sorry to hear that," I said, meaning it. Having a potential world-class pairs team training in my hometown was cause for celebration, and I hoped that nothing would erupt to taint it.

The situation that Jim Shevlin had mentioned wasn't the only controversy surrounding the rink, and this one wasn't dependent upon the town's keenly honed rumor mill for verification.

Luc Beliveau, the hockey coach and head of the youth hockey program at the arena, had made a series of statements to Evelyn Phillips at the *Gazette* in which he dismissed the importance of having figure skaters training at the facility: "Let's face it," he'd told her—and she dutifully reported—"a hockey team will draw audiences to our town and be a huge boost to the local economy. That's something a few figure skaters who haven't even competed together can't do."

Devlin was reportedly miffed at Beliveau's comments and fought back by organizing a figure skating exhibition scheduled to take place following the upcoming youth hockey league game against Bangor. It all appeared to be a good example of healthy competition between the town's hockey lovers and figure skating fans, but I wondered whether it might blow up into something more divisive.

Evelyn and the *Gazette* took full advantage of the spat between Devlin and Beliveau. Circulation was up each week. Not only was there the possibility of a semipro hockey team to report on, but Devlin's past glories on the ice, and the young skaters he was training at his new headquarters, provided material for a wealth of stories.

But Evelyn certainly didn't have an exclusive. Other papers in the state ran articles on what was happening in Cabot Cove now that it might get a hockey team and already boasted a successful former figure skater and coach who was preparing a new pairs team for big-time competition. *Sports Illustrated* and the *Boston Globe* sent sports reporters to write about these big happenings in formerly sleepy Cabot Cove, and a Russian television crew had arrived to film a feature story on the pairs team—the unique pairing of a mixed-race American woman and a Russian male skater who'd abandoned his former partner in Moscow to skate for Team USA.

Seth watched me suspiciously as I removed my skates from the bag and examined them. "They're old," I commented.

"Exactly my point."

I changed the subject. "Mara said most folks in town would prefer that Coddington not sell," I said, passing along the gossip I'd heard at Mara's dockside luncheonette, a source of Cabot Cove news that rivaled the *Gazette*.

"Why's that?" he asked. "He's never been a popular sort. He's moody and mistrustful and squeezes the last drop out of a dime if he spends it at all. I imagine that's why he hasn't made an appointment for his physical in years. Doesn't want to pay for it."

"I suspect it's a case of the devil you know being better than the devil you don't know," I replied. "They don't like the idea of someone coming from out of town to take over one of our few winter recreational opportunities. And that's assuming that whoever buys it would keep it an ice arena."

" 'Few winter recreational opportunities?' What's wrong with ice fishing, and sledding, and cross country skiing, or just taking a walk? There's plenty to do when there's snow on the ground."

"I should have said *organized* recreational opportunities, something our youngsters and teens can do indoors when it's cold outside."

"Seems to me young people's time is too organized as it is. They all need someone to tell them what to do. When I was a boy, we left home in the morning and didn't get home until suppertime. There were no cell phones, and our mothers never worried where we were. If we weren't in school, we were playing with our friends. Simple as that."

"Well, evidently it isn't that simple anymore," I said, hoping to head Seth off before he launched into one of his tirades on how spoiled today's young people were. While I didn't always disagree, his rants raised his blood pressure and upset his stomach.

"Anyway," I said, "the last time I spoke with Eve, she told me that Eldridge Coddington had stopped fixing up the arena, at least for now, and Mayor Shevlin heard it, too. Eve thinks he's changed his mind about selling."

"I bet the coaches were none too happy to hear that," Seth said.

"To hear what? That he changed his mind about selling?"

"No! That he's stopped fixing up the place."

"Both Jim Shevlin and Eve said that Devlin was furious. He's been counting on the renovations to draw more top-ranked students into his program."

Seth pointed to the second Snickerdoodle.

I broke it in half and put the rest back on the plate. "I'm wondering what all this is going to mean to the girl from California and this Russian partner of hers who came here to train with Devlin."

"Well, all they need is a pair of skates and ice, and Devlin's got plenty of that."

"He must have promised a lot more than ice to convince her father to move them across the country," I said. "Devlin has a lot to live up to for that pair. They're both supposed to be good, but they haven't skated together for very long."

"If Devlin's as all-fired wonderful as everyone claims, that pair should be on their way to the Olympics in no time."

I shook my head. "Pairs skating is more complicated than that, Seth. It'll take time for them to adjust to each other's styles. They need to see how they measure up in skills, and work together to match their steps so their movements are in unison."

"How do you know so much about pairs skating?"

"Television, of course," I said. "I love watching the competitions on TV. It's more than a sport; it's also an art. Everything I know I learned from Dick Button. And from Peter Carruthers. He and his sister Kitty were Olympic silver medalists."

"You going to finish that cookie?"

I shot Seth a look. "Go ahead," I said, taking my coffee cup to the sink. "It's your diet."

"I have a theory about that."

"About what?"

"Diets. If you starve yourself, you lose a little weight at first, but then your body adjusts to the new regimen and stops burning calories as effectively as it did in order to conserve energy. You stop losing weight. But if you give your body a jolt by eating something sweet, like this cookie, it says, 'Oh, it's all right to burn those calories again,' and you continue to lose weight."

"Did they teach you that in medical school?"

"You don't learn everything in medical school. You hone your knowledge with years of experience and practice."

"Exactly why pairs skaters need to skate together for years before they're ready for competition."

"We're back to them again, are we?" Seth rinsed his mug in the sink. "I had a hunch you'd feel you'd have to go down there to look around once you heard the rumors the rink was having a run of bad luck."

"Running out of money to fix up the rink may be bad luck," I said, "but a strange man hanging around the girls' locker room is not."

Some of the casual female skaters had complained to staff that a young man had been lurking near the entrance to the ladies' room. No such person was seen when the staff and a security guard went to investigate, and the incidents, two of them, were quickly forgotten.

"It was probably just some hormonal adolescent with a crush," Seth opined. "You know how these things get blown out of proportion."

"Perhaps. But what about the person who scattered screws on the ice? That is something else entirely. There are a lot of children who skate there. Wasn't the young woman from San Francisco injured?"

"Her fall was not the result of a screw on the ice," Seth said. "Her father claimed that someone purposely pushed up the rubber mat in a place where she would trip on it. But if you ask me, that's just the overreaction of an overindulgent parent protecting his coddled youngster. I suggested as much."

"Seth, you didn't."

"'Fraid I did."

"I'm sure that went over well."

"He already thinks I'm a dinosaur. Said so, in so many words. Referred to Cabot Cove as a 'hick town.'"

"That must have been quite an office visit."

"I got my licks in. Bottom line is, apart from a couple stitches, the girl wasn't badly hurt. Just to be sure, I recommended she take it easy for a day or two, but I'm told she was back on the ice that afternoon. So much for following my good medical advice."

"Youngsters are resilient, but I'm not sure I like how these athletes play with pain," I said. "It can't be healthy."

"You're changing the subject, Jessica. We were talking about your skating, not Christine Allen's."

"Well, I'm going to do it. I want to see if I can still skate."

"You may say that you want to take up ice-skating again, but I know better."

"You do?"

"You want an excuse to spend more time at the rink and poke your perpetually curious nose into what's happening down there."

"Well, maybe a little of both. All the news articles about the arena have inspired me. I want to see the pairs skaters train."

"You don't need your ice skates to snoop around, Jessica. Besides, don't you have a book to write?"

"Seth, aren't you always telling your patients to get lots of exercise?"

"Of course, but exercise appropriate to their age and condition."

"Well, I'm not going to argue with you about my age, but I'm in pretty good shape. I still jog when it's not too cold, and I certainly get in plenty of walking and bike riding."

"You do. I never said you were out of shape, just too . . . let's say 'along in years' to begin skating again. You'll fall and give yourself a concussion, if not a broken bone. How are you going to write with your arm in a sling?"

"My goodness, you are certainly predicting dire consequences if I get back on the ice. But I'm willing to take the chance. Besides, I think it's going to be fun."

"If you fall, don't say I didn't warn you."

"I won't," I said.

And I didn't. But he found out anyway.

Chapter Two

"All right. Do it again. This time focus on soft, deep knees; feel like you're sinking into the ice on that outside edge. I want to see a long ride-out. From the back crossovers. Let's go. Deep knees. That's better. On three, the double axel. Hold that back outside edge. One . . . two . . . three."

Brian Devlin clapped his gloved hands and pivoted on the ice as the two skaters passed him and executed a side-by-side jump. "Better! But check that rotation, Alexei. You have to be in control of your shoulder. Chris, watch when his right leg comes around, and match your timing to his. Let's try it with music." Devlin pulled a paper from his pocket and consulted its contents. "Cue the exhibition program, Lyla," he yelled to his assistant coach, who was in a booth beside the rink.

The two members of the pairs team Devlin was coaching had arrived in Cabot Cove separately several months ago. Christine Allen was a pretty eighteen-year-old with a halo of curly black hair that she'd inherited from her African-American father, and dark almond-shaped eyes, a legacy from her Korean mother. She had moved from San Francisco to train with Devlin. According to a feature article in our local newspaper, she'd skated at the Yerba Buena Ice Skating and Bowling Center, training home of famed Olympic gold medalist Brian Boitano. She now was living with her father, William Allen, a banker, who had taken up temporary residence here in a rented house downtown, at least until he was confident that his daughter had settled in. Her mother, who had stayed home with a younger daughter, planned to visit at a later time.

Christine was lithe but muscular, and she looked petite standing next to her partner, who was broad shouldered and at least a foot taller. With a shock of blond hair falling in his eyes, Alexei Olshansky seemed the more self-assured of the pair. The newspaper had quoted him as saying he was from Moscow and had come to Cabot Cove after he and his previous skating partner Irina Bednikova had parted ways. I had never seen the Russian pair interviewed on TV, but from what I gathered in the article, Alexei's English must have been more than adequate, which was fortunate for him. As far as I knew, no one in Cabot Cove spoke fluent Russian. Certainly, Coach Devlin didn't.

I leaned against the boards, watching the young couple practice. They had been skating together for only a short time and were working to develop the seamless unity required to compete at the highest levels.

Alexei skated a circle around Christine, showing off with fancy footwork. He pretended to lose his balance, rocking back on his skates and wheeling his arms, catching himself at the very last moment to lean forward into a low bow. I couldn't hear what they said to each other, but their laughter carried over the ice.

Strains of Rimsky-Korsakov's "Scheherazade" came over the loud speakers.

Alexei smacked his palm to his forehead with exaggerated exasperation. "*Nyet! Nyet!* Not that again," he cried.

Devlin ignored his histrionics. "We'll listen to new music this weekend," he said. "Please, Alexei, let's not get into a squabble over the music. I want to see you skate around the rink together." They took off across the ice. "Switch sides, please. Alexei, you have to be on the outside. *She's* on the inside. That's it. Match your strokes. Signal to each other when to start the crossover. I want to see you in unison."

"Isn't he dreamy?" a voice to my left said.

Marisa Brown leaned her elbows next to mine on the railing and stared out across the rink.

"Which one?" I asked.

A puff of air escaped her lips. "Brian Devlin, of course," she said, her brows disappearing under her brown bangs as her eyes met mine. "You couldn't think I meant Alexei."

"Well, he's attractive, as well," I said, smiling at the teenager who'd been hired to staff the front desk. A homegrown skater with a lot of potential but not a lot of capital to support her passion, Marisa was paying for her lessons by working part-time at the rink.

"I suppose Alexei is nice-looking in an adolescent sort

of way," she said, "but Brian is gorgeous. He has such sultry eyes. Doesn't he remind you of George Clooney? Everyone says so."

"Everyone?"

"All my girlfriends."

Devlin was considerably older than Marisa and sported two days' growth of stubble on his chiseled jaw—by design, I thought—and possessed the sort of dark, brooding looks so many men in Hollywood cultivate these days. I could see how he would appeal to the local teen population.

"How old is Alexei?" I asked.

"Twenty-four, twenty-five, something like that," she said, waving a hand around. "He doesn't even have a beard yet."

"He's mature enough to have traveled halfway around the world to further his skating career," I said.

Marisa shrugged. "True," she said. "He's traveled a lot. But he still lives with his mother when he goes back to Russia. That's what the skating magazines say. Anyway, travel doesn't make him a man. From what I've seen, he still acts like a kid. Carries on whenever he doesn't get his way."

"Ah," I said, taking another look at Christine Allen's new partner.

Devlin's assistant coach, Lyla Fasolino, overheard our conversation. "If he's rude to you again, Marisa, please don't complain to Jeremy," she said. "There's enough bad blood between them. Just let *me* know."

"Okay."

"Don't you have some work to do for me in the office?"

"I already typed up the list of students for the exhibition."

"You may have typed it up, but I haven't seen it," Lyla said, turning Marisa toward the door and giving her a gentle push.

"All right," the younger woman said with a sigh. "I'll go print it out and put it in your mailbox."

"Along with the new hockey schedule, please. And we have rehearsal later. We'll see you on the ice at five. Don't be late."

"How is she doing?" I asked Lyla as the girl walked away.

"She's a great kid. Works really hard and has a lot of talent. She took first place last fall at the regional competition and just missed the podium at the sectionals. I'm sure by next year she'll be ready for the junior ladies championships."

"You must be very pleased," I said.

She shrugged. "I am. I guess." She nervously played with a gold chain around her neck, and I gathered she was less than thrilled with the prospect.

"Why do I hear a 'but' in there?" I asked.

"Marisa needs to focus," she said, tucking the chain into the neck of her shirt. "She's been thinking about competing in pairs. One of the other coaches, Mark Rosner, has matched her with Jeremy Hapgood. He works here, too. You may have seen him on the Zamboni."

"I have. That's exciting. Won't being a singles skater help with her pairs skills?"

"Without doubt, but she'll also be doubling her chance of injuries by participating in both pairs and singles, and she won't be giving full attention to either discipline."

"It's been done before, hasn't it?"

"That's what Mark argues. But the decision should be based on what's best for Marisa, not because Mark wants to compete with our star over there by coaching another pairs team." She nodded toward where Brian Devlin continued to work with Christine Allen and Alexei Olshansky.

"Can we get a little speed up there?" I heard Devlin yell at Christine and Alexei as he clapped to set the pace. "Move, move, move, move. You're skating on ice, not mud. The judges want to see action."

Lyla turned to me. "So, what brings you down here, Mrs. Fletcher?"

"Just looking around; I'm planning to start skating again soon."

"You are?"

"It's been years since I've been on the ice," I said, "but I used to be a pretty fair skater. I'm going to give it a try. We'll see what happens. I'm hoping it's like what they always say about riding a bike when you haven't ridden for years, that the skill will come right back to you."

"I hope so," Lyla said, looking doubtful, "although it's not quite the same. But it's a great sport. Remember, we have skating chairs for beginners, if you need one."

"Skating chairs?"

"Metal chairs you can push around the ice to give you something to hold on to, to keep you from falling. We don't allow them on the weekends when it's crowded, but you could use one during the week until you get your skating legs back. It might be a little low for you, though. We have them for the children."

"That's a new wrinkle to me. There have been so many

changes here since I last skated. I was reading about them in the newspaper this morning. Oh, and here's the man responsible for it all. Good morning, Eldridge."

Eldridge Coddington strode past us without acknowledging my greeting, his eyes trained on the trio on the ice. He was a tall, spare man with pale blue eyes and a fringe of white hair sticking out from under his olive green flat cap. A deep vertical line was etched between his eyebrows thanks to his usual scowl, and no one would chalk up the channels that bracketed his mouth as being caused by excessive smiling. He and his wife, Bella, had been childless, and though he'd always been an irritable man, she had softened his edges and pushed him into social and civic activities. When he'd lost her to a flu epidemic a decade ago, he'd retreated into solitude, rejecting all offers of sympathy and sinking deeper into depression. Nothing seemed to interest him. The town had seen his recent efforts to fix up the ice arena as a positive sign, evidence that he was emerging from the doldrums. The word around town was that the leopard was changing his spots. But I was not so sure.

Coddington leaned over the boards, waving a copy of the *Cabot Cove Gazette* in the air. "Devlin!" he roared. "I've got a bone to pick with you."

The coach didn't bother turning around. He pointed to his pairs team and waved his hand in the air, indicating for them to continue practicing.

Alexei and Chris began skating backward.

"Devlin! Did you hear me?" Coddington boomed again.

The skaters stopped where they were, confused about what to do.

There was a moment of silence before Devlin slowly rotated on his skates. "*I* am giving a class right now," he said in clipped tones. "*You* will have to wait."

"How dare you talk to that reporter about what we discussed? Those were privileged conversations."

"You are interrupting my lesson and wasting my time. We can discuss that later." Devlin turned his back on Coddington and continued talking with his students.

"It had better be sooner than later," the rink owner shouted, his face red. "I'll be in my office. And I want some answers."

"Oh, dear," I said to Lyla as Coddington stomped out. "He's not very happy today."

"Mr. Coddington is never very happy," Lyla whispered. "I'm used to his ways, but Brian isn't. Big-time coaches can have big-time egos. They like to be stroked. Mr. Coddington is not very good at stroking."

"Evidently," I said. "I wonder what he was so angry about. I thought it was a wonderful article."

"This is the second week in a row that he's become apoplectic over something in the paper. Last week, it was the police report."

"Oh, yes. I saw that," I said. "He must have been upset about screws being deliberately dropped on the ice."

"He was more upset that it was mentioned in the paper. It wasn't that many screws, really. They probably slipped out of someone's pocket. I don't think it was intentional. But Jeremy made a big fuss with Mr. Coddington about how it could have damaged the Zamboni, not to mention causing skaters to fall. Anyway, Mr. Coddington called in the sheriff. Frankly, I think he was more worried about the machine than the skaters, but that's just between us."

"You really think so?"

She nodded. "Of course, when Christine tripped over the rubber mat here and hurt herself, I heard him tell Marisa to check his liability insurance. Christine's father, Mr. Allen, gave the old man a heck of a tongue-lashing and threatened to sue, but I don't think he will. He's counting on Brian Devlin making his daughter a star. Anyway, she wasn't badly hurt. Skaters fall all the time. They're used to it."

"But they usually fall *on* the ice," I said, "not off."

"She's tough. And it looks like we're settling into a good routine now."

"I'm glad to hear it."

Lyla Fasolino had come home to Cabot Cove after a career as a professional skater. She'd joined Holiday on Ice right out of junior college and stayed with the touring show for five years, performing all over Europe. But she'd never made it into the featured ranks. Tired of travel, she'd come home to run the figure skating school, only to have the rink close for renovations. But it was back now, and so was she, giving group and private lessons and administering the program.

"How do you like working with Devlin?" I asked.

"I won't lie," she said. "It was a bit rocky at first, you know, having to get used to another coach who demands a lot of attention and who's more important than I am. Mr. Coddington has Devlin addressing the local business organizations to get their support. He never asked *me* to do that.

But I'm warming to Brian. He can be charming when he wants to be. And he's not hard on the eyes."

"Marisa certainly seems to agree."

"I have to admit that his movie star looks haven't hurt business. We've gotten a gaggle of teenage girls signing up for classes. Sold out this season. Of course, they were all disappointed when it wasn't Brian who showed up to teach, but they seem to be content with glimpsing him from afar."

"Did I hear my name being bandied about?" Devlin said, leaving the ice by the gate next to which we'd been standing.

"I'm only saying good things," Lyla said playfully, "but you'd better be nice to me."

"I'll be extra nice to you if you lend me a twenty," Devlin said, slipping rubber guards over his blades. "I left my wallet at home, and I'm starving."

"Likely story," she said, "but I'll do it if you promise not to lose it all on the ponies."

"Very funny," he said. "Excuse us," he said to me, and walked with Lyla out of the rink.

Christine and Alexei came over to the gate and stepped down from the rink to the rubber mat.

"You didn't have any problem with your skates today," I heard Christine say.

"I fix them. But I will always have them where I can see them from now. I make sure to keep your boyfriend's hands off."

"For the last time, Alexei, he's not my boyfriend. And he didn't do anything to your skates."

"He wants to be the boyfriend, yes?"

She rolled her eyes and sighed as they picked up the guards for their blades, which they'd left on the railing, slid them into place, and traipsed toward the door with wide, rocking gaits. I followed them out.

Christine glanced over her shoulder at Alexei, who was winding a long red scarf around his neck. "Mr. Devlin wants us to do the star lift in the exhibition," she said. "Think you're ready?"

Alexei flexed his biceps and pounded on his chest with his fists. "Strong peasant man," he said with a grin as he came alongside her.

His partner laughed.

Alexei leaned over and swatted her on the backside. "But you must make your weight lower. No more sweets. I don't want to lift baby elephant."

"Keep your hands to yourself and off my daughter, Olshansky."

Christine's father, a middle-aged black man, stood outside the glass door to the rink. Dressed in a long, camel-colored cashmere topcoat over a charcoal gray pinstripe suit with a white shirt and a regimental tie, he scowled at the young Russian coming toward him. "Change into your shoes and street clothes, Christine. You have dance class in an hour."

"Oh, Daddy," she said, "he didn't mean anything."

"I want him to treat you with respect. You deserve that. You *demand* that." He pointed to Alexei, who had dropped back behind Christine. "You hear that, young man? I didn't pay for you to come all this way to abuse my daughter."

"He didn't mean any disrespect, Daddy. He was just kidding around."

"He's here for business, not to kid around. Come on, I want to check your computer before the class. You got another one of those e-mails again."

Alexei whirled around and walked toward the concession stand, chin tucked into his chest, cursing in Russian, his voice low.

"What's the matter?" Devlin said, grabbing Alexei's arm as the young man stormed past him.

"You keep that—that—that *person* away from me," Alexei said, wrenching his arm free and pointing at Christine's father. "He does not own Alexei. I spit on his money. I am better skater than his little brown bird. I make the team good. The audience, they love me. Her jumps are weak. You see double axel? Nothing to mine. I can do triple."

Devlin poked a finger into the skater's chest and leaned forward. "Listen to me, buddy," he said between clenched teeth. "This team isn't any good unless you're *both* good. You hear me? Her jumps are damn good, as good as yours. I didn't come here to train a self-centered artiste. You're both going to work your tails off for me or I'll ship you home to Russia so fast your head will spin."

Alexei's eyes widened. He put his hands up, palms forward. "Yes, boss."

"Don't 'yes, boss' me. Just follow my instructions and keep your mouth shut. I don't want to hear a whisper of a scandal like what surrounded you and Bednikova back in Russia. If Mr. Allen knew about that, you wouldn't be here now."

"Not my fault."

"I don't care whose fault it was. You have a second chance here. Don't blow it."

"Ah, yes . . . boss. But the same can be said of you. No?"

Devlin glared at him before saying, "I don't know what you're talking about," and walking away, a troubled expression on his handsome face.

Chapter Three

"Eve is telling everyone how handsome the new coach is," Loretta Spiegel said as she fluffed the back of my hair at her beauty salon.

"He is, I guess, if you like them tall, dark, and unshaven," I said.

"Sounds good to me. Virile and sexy."

"Well, he isn't my type," I said, "but I'll give you the virile part. And he's attracting quite a few teenaged fans. Lyla Fasolino said her after-school classes filled up quickly this year."

Loretta ran a comb down the back of my head. "It doesn't look too bad, if I say so myself," she said, "but you really could use a haircut, Jessica. It's been four weeks."

"I know, Loretta, but I don't have the time today. I just came in for a manicure. I don't know how you talked me into a wash and style."

"It's the Tuesday special—a styling is half price when you have a manicure."

"It's definitely a bargain," I said, glancing at my watch. "Now, tell me what I owe you. I'm going to be late if I don't get going."

I was standing at the desk paying my bill when Eve Simpson hurried in.

"Well, speak of the devil," Loretta said. "I was just telling Jessica what you said about the new skating coach. She doesn't think he's that handsome."

"Now, that's not exactly what I said, Loretta."

"Forget Brian Devlin," Eve said. "I've got to get ready to meet Harvey Gemell. Loretta, can you fit me in right now?"

"You just got a haircut last week, Eve," Loretta said.

"I know, but I want to look my best."

"Who's Harvey Gemell?" I asked.

"*Who's Harvey Gemell?*" Eve said, her eyes flying to the ceiling. "Just the man who will make my fortune, and if I'm really good, perhaps my future, as well."

"Take a seat at the sink," Loretta directed her, pulling a fresh cape from the shelf and shaking it out.

"His name isn't familiar," I said.

"Is he from around here?" Loretta asked.

"No, *mes amies*. He is not from around here. He is the most sophisticated, urbane, brilliant businessman—and too, too wealthy, if I don't miss my guess. He's an entrepreneur, the president and CEO of Gemell Capital Investments of Greenwich, Connecticut. Isn't that impressive?"

"Is he good-looking, too?" Loretta asked, whipping the cape around Eve's neck and snapping it in the back.

Eve hesitated. "Well, he looks nice in his picture, although he said it was taken a few years ago, but who cares if he's good-looking if the deal goes through."

"You haven't met this paragon of business?" I asked.

"Not face-to-face, but I know all about him. We've talked on the telephone a lot, and his profile online was so exciting. I just knew he'd be the perfect one."

"What profile?" Loretta asked.

"The perfect one for what?" I asked.

"The perfect one to buy the ice arena," Eve said as Loretta pressed her seat back against the sink and turned on the water.

"Didn't you tell me that Eldridge Coddington changed his mind about selling?" I said.

"What did you say, Jessica?" Eve said. "I can't hear with the water running. Loretta, just wet me down. I washed my hair this morning."

I raised my voice and repeated my question.

Eve waved a hand in front of her. "Doesn't matter."

I waited to respond until Loretta turned off the taps and began drying Eve's hair with a towel.

"Why bring a buyer all the way up here from Connecticut," I asked, "if the seller isn't interested in selling? Doesn't seem fair to me."

"Jessica, I'm surprised you're so naïve," Eve said, peeking out from under the towel.

Loretta energetically rubbed Eve's hair and rolled her eyes at me.

"Everyone has his price," Eve continued. "Coddington will sell if the right buyer comes along and offers enough."

"Well, you know your real estate customers better than I," I said, glancing up at the clock on Loretta's wall. "Oh, my heavens," I said. "Is that time right, Loretta?"

"Don't worry. I keep the clock ten minutes fast," Loretta said, leading Eve to a seat in front of the mirror.

"Why on earth do you do that?" Eve asked.

"People like it that way. When they think they're late, they're really on time."

"Thank goodness for that," I said. "I really have to go."

I had dropped off my skates at Charles Department Store that morning. In addition to selling street shoes, snowshoes, sneakers, hiking boots, and ice skates, Charles Department Store sells just about anything else you think you need, and even more that you've probably forgotten you need. It always amazed me that no matter how exotic the item I requested, the proprietors, David and his brother, Jim, not only had heard of it, but could produce it, or at worst have it in stock by the next day.

David was running his annual skate inspection for his customers and graciously offered to have his expert check over my old skates to make sure they were safe, tighten any loose screws, and sharpen the blades. I could have had the skates sharpened at the ice arena or at the sporting goods store in the mall outside of town, but David said those places were better for hockey blades. His guy was a specialist in figure skates.

The bell jangled as I opened Charles's door. It was ten minutes to closing. Jim was at the register ringing up a roll of duct tape and a package of clothesline for a young man in a ski jacket. "Go on in the back, Jessica. Mr. Klingbell is finishing up for the day."

I walked around the showcase of fancy cookware, past a display of tea kettles and a hanging rack of halogen lightbulbs, to the small workroom in the rear. A wizened man wearing a Red Sox ball cap set backward on his head was sitting on a stool, eyeing a skate blade under the glare of a lamp clipped to a shelf over his shoulder. He ran a thick finger gently over the edge of the blade and nodded. "Should do."

David stood nearby, wrapping a pair of skates in craft paper. He marked the bag into which he slid them with the name of the owner and set them on a shelf. "Perfect timing," he said. "Jessica Fletcher, meet Aaron Klingbell. Aaron is looking over your skates right now."

"How do, Mrs. Fletcher," the man said, lifting his cap to reveal an irregularly shaped, completely bald head.

"Nice to meet you, Mr. Klingbell. Will my skates last me another twenty years?"

"They will if you don't skate on 'em, but these don't look too bad to me. The boot is a little scuffed, but the blade hasn't had too much wear."

"I'm going to start skating again after a long time off the ice."

"Take it slow at first. Might even try walking around in the skates at home. Either way, your anklebones will be a little sore at first."

"My anklebones?"

"Secrets of the trade," he said with a small smile.

"C'mon, Aaron," David said. "Will you share your secret if Jessica promises not to write about it in any of her books?"

"Mebbe," Klingbell said, looking from my skate down to my feet and back. "These skates are the kind that conform to the shape of your foot, but it takes a while. You got to break them in. When the skates aren't worn for a long time, sometimes they go back to their original shape. I put a bit of lamb's wool inside the left one. Stuff it around your ankles when you put on the skates, and that should help ease the pressure until they fit right again."

"Thank you," I said. "I never had a problem with weak ankles. You always hear people complain about them."

"No such thing," Klingbell said. "Just weak skates. You're not going to be doing any jumping, are you? These are fine for stroking around, but you need a tougher boot if you want to jump."

"If I had to guess, I'd say my jumping days are over, Mr. Klingbell. Not that I ever really jumped before."

"Never can tell these days. They have adult competitions now, you know. Seniors, too. Even for old coots like me."

"Have you entered a competition?"

"Nope."

"Why not?"

"Don't skate."

David hid a smile as he wrapped up my skates. I bid him and Mr. Klingbell good evening and took my package to the register. Jim was just turning over the OPEN sign to CLOSED when a woman in a long silver fur coat, and holding a tiny white dog with a jeweled collar, pushed inside, closely followed by two linebackers in black overcoats with somber expressions.

"We're about to close," Jim told her, nervously eyeing the men, who appeared to be her bodyguards.

"I need for the hair, this thing," she said with a heavy accent, using one hand to hold an imaginary hair dryer over her head while clutching her dog to her chest with the other. "You have this? Must have tonight. Please."

"I'm sure I can help you, but I'm with a customer now."

"I can wait, Jim," I said.

"Are you sure, Jessica?"

"Go ahead. I'll just browse these holiday ornaments you have on sale."

"All right, miss. Come this way." Leaving the two men posted on either side of the door, the woman followed Jim to a display of hair dryers and styling wands. "Is this what you're looking for?"

"*Da!*" she said, a satisfied smile on her lips.

Jim held out his hands. "Would you like me to hold your dog?"

The woman contemplated his offer for a moment, cocked her head at her pet, then thrust the tiny dog into Jim's arms, shrugged off her fur coat, threw it over a tray of socks, and began examining the dryers, lifting one after the other, and inspecting the plugs.

I was surprised to see how slim and how young she was. In the coat, she had appeared to be bulky, but she was built like a miniature doll with platinum blond hair peeking out from under her fur hat. Her perfume filled the room.

A bemused Jim looked down at his fluffy charge, then

up at me. "Cute, huh, Jessica? I wonder what kind of dog it is."

"It looks like a toy poodle," I said.

The dog watched Jim closely, but when he tried to put his nose near the dog's snout, we heard a low growl.

"Pravda!" its owner said, scowling at her pet.

The dog slunk down in Jim's arms and whimpered.

"This will work in U.S. of A., yes?" she asked, holding up a box.

"Guaranteed," Jim said.

She looked confused and Jim corrected himself. "Yes. This will work."

"*Spasibo!* Thank you."

She put on her coat, took back the dog, handed the box to Jim, and followed him to the register. It was difficult to say how old she was since she wore heavy eye makeup and bright red lipstick, but I guessed she was in her twenties. She nodded at me. "*Izvinite*," she said, as she walked past. "*Scusi.* Uh, *pardonnez-moi.*" She stopped and shook her head. "*Nyet!*" Satisfied that she had found the correct language, she tipped her head to the side and smiled. "Excuse me."

"Certainly," I said, returning her smile.

She dug through an oversized alligator-skin purse and presented her credit card to Jim. When he'd completed the transaction, she signed the sales slip with a flourish, regally walked to the door with a dog in one arm and a shopping bag on the other, and waited while one of her bodyguards held it open for her.

"Wow!" Jim said, returning to the desk after locking

up. He waved a hand in front of him. "We don't have such glamorous customers every day."

"I'm sure you don't," I said, chuckling.

"I hope you're not offended, Jessica. I just meant—"

"I know exactly what you meant, Jim, and of course I'm not offended. She must be one of the reporters with the Russian film crew I heard was in town."

"How exciting. I never met a Russian before. Can't wait to tell my wife. Of course, I may leave out how pretty she was." He called out, "Hey Dave, you just missed a looker."

David poked his head out of the back room. "What did you say?"

Jim grinned. "Never mind." He handed me my skates. "Thanks for waiting, Jessica."

"Wouldn't have missed her for the world," I replied.

Chapter Four

The moment of my big day arrived.

I called the local cab company at which I had an account and arranged for a taxi to take me to the ice arena. I admit I had mixed emotions. On the one hand, I couldn't wait to lace up my skates and step out onto the ice. On the other hand, Seth's admonitions about being too old to take up skating again and risking injury stayed with me. I've always liked to consider myself someone who listens to others and benefits from their wise counsel. Seth had my best interests at heart, and there was no argument that what he'd warned of could happen. But I'm also a person who doesn't believe in losing out on the joys of life because of fear. That latter belief system overrode Seth's concerns, and I happily and enthusiastically got in the taxi, my arms around my skate bag, and the sort of smile on my face that you see on kids about to embark on an adventure.

The arena was busy when I arrived. I told the driver that I'd call when I needed a ride home, went inside, and took a seat at one of several round picnic tables arrayed in front of the concession stand, which hadn't opened yet. A half dozen other skaters were there getting ready to take to the ice, and if I'd been concerned that I'd be the only older person on the ice, I was quickly disabused of that notion.

At the next table was a woman with gray hair styled in a pageboy. She was easily my age, perhaps older, and wore black wool slacks and a pink angora sweater. She had already donned her gleaming white skates and was applying a lip balm over her pink lipstick. Next to her was a gentleman of an equally advanced age, who I assumed was her husband. His gray sweatpants were tucked into his black skates, and he had pinned his entry ticket to his zippered jacket. They smiled at me as they walked past and entered the rink.

I unzipped my carrier and pulled out my skates. I'd spent the good part of an hour the evening before trying, not entirely successfully, to polish out the old scuffs and smudges, and had tried out four pairs of socks before finding one that allowed my foot to squeeze into the skate without pain. I put guards on the blades and placed both skates on the floor in preparation for donning them.

Across from me was Jeremy Hapgood, the young man who worked at the arena. He was removing his socks while I was putting mine on. He picked up a hockey skate and, after liberally shaking baby powder into it, shoved in his bare foot.

"You skate barefoot?" I said, shaking my head.

He heard me, smiled, and nodded. "Oh, hi," he said. "Best thing to do if you forgot to bring socks or brought the wrong ones. The powder makes the inside of the boot slippery, makes it easy to get your foot in."

"But aren't your feet going to freeze without socks?" I asked.

"When you get moving, you warm up everywhere," he replied. "Thick socks help only if your skates are too big and don't fit properly. A thin sock isn't going to make that much of a difference anyway. Besides, I like to feel the texture of the ice, and you can do that better when the only thing between you and the ice are your boots and blades."

"You've been skating for a long time, I take it."

"Since before I was four. My dad bought my first hockey stick when I was born." He laughed. "You think he had plans for me?"

"And do you play?"

"Sure! Sometimes. When I can get a little time off. Actually, I do more teaching than playing. I've got team practices. Coach Beliveau has me leading the drills for the mites and squirts."

"Sounds like an infestation."

"The little-kid hockey leagues. I like hockey, but I don't play all that much."

While we'd talked, he'd powdered and put on his second skate, laced up both of them, and shrugged on an oversized brown down jacket with CABOT COVE ICE ARENA across the back in block letters, and his name, JEREMY HAPGOOD, in small letters on the front.

A man in a matching jacket clapped him on the back. "Hey, Jer. Will I see you guys later?"

"Sure, Mark, we've been working on our side-by-side toe loops."

"Great! Don't forget to change skates," the man said, walking toward the rink.

"Jeremy," I said, "aren't you the one who found the screws on the ice? I heard about that."

He acknowledged that he was. "Can you believe it?" he said. "Some jerk trying to make trouble. We finally get some excitement going in this town with the hockey teams and the skating school, and somebody wants to mess it up."

"Why do you think someone would want to do that?" I asked.

"Who knows why people do dumb things," he said. "Like the dork who drilled a peephole in the ladies' room wall."

My face mirrored my surprise.

"Yeah," he said, "Christine—she's training with Alexei Olshansky—she discovered it late yesterday and reported it to Security."

"Any idea who might have done it?"

He shook his head. "Some pervert, I guess. They patched it up." He stood. "You'll have to excuse me. I don't want to be late. He drew a whistle on a long cord from his pocket and looped it around his neck.

I was wondering whether the incident with the peephole had been reported to the police when music suddenly came from large speakers suspended from the ceiling. That hour's public skating session had begun.

I made my way unsteadily to the boards that encircled the ice and saw that the older couple was already skating and had been joined on the ice by two girls who skated holding hands; several men of varying ages in hockey skates; a young mother in a short dress with her toddler in a snowsuit; and a few other people who glided confidently around the rink. Jeremy, my barefoot-skating young friend, eyed all the skaters, perhaps counting them, and kept time to the organ music that blared from the loud speakers. At the far end of the rink, Lyla, wearing a big brown jacket like Jeremy's and Mark's, coached a woman dressed in a puffy white coat. *Maybe I should have arranged for some lessons before trying it on my own*, I thought as I removed my skate guards, left them on a bench, clumsily stepped through the swinging half door, and ventured out onto the ice, gripping the railing of the boards that ran around the periphery of the rink. The surface was a lot slipperier than I remembered. I held on tightly, wondering if maybe the skating chair Lyla had suggested wasn't such a bad idea. *Nonsense, Jessica; you've done this before*, I told myself.

Girding my loins, I slid forward, my arms out to the sides, but I stayed within grabbing distance of the boards. *One, two, three*, I silently counted as I stroked with first one foot and then the other. *Okay, not too bad*, I thought, moving a little farther into the rink. *I knew I could do it.* Then my blade caught a gouge in the ice and I gasped. I straightened my back, abruptly bent forward, and shuffled to the boards, one leg sliding out from under me just as I dug my fingers into the wood. Notwithstanding my awkward posture and heavy breathing, I was grateful I'd managed to stay on my feet and not land on my bottom. *Now I see what he meant by feeling the texture of the ice.*

While I stood by the boards trying to boost my confidence, I caught sight of Eve Simpson escorting a gentleman around the far side of the rink. She was gesturing with her arms as they looked up at the ceiling. My eyes followed their gaze, but I couldn't imagine what fascinated them up there. I watched for a few more moments, but when they walked in my direction, I turned my back, hoping they wouldn't notice me. If I was going to make a fool of myself, I preferred to do it in relative anonymity.

The older couple I'd noticed earlier did not skate together. Instead, she followed a circular pattern at one end of the rink, where large rings were painted on the ice, while he swiftly stroked down the length of the rink, leaning into the center and executing smooth crossovers like a speed skater. *If they can do it, I can do it*, I told myself. *Buck up, Jessica. It'll come back to you.*

Both inspired and intimidated, I started out once more, staying close to the boards, trailing the fingers of my right hand over the railing to assure myself that it was available should I stumble again. I worked my way around the oval, trying to sense the edges of the blades. Little by little, I remembered the feeling of skating. Counting the numbers of strokes, I tried to skate longer from foot to foot before resting on a glide. By the third time around the rink, my confidence had risen enough to allow me to give a slight wave to Lyla as I skated past her and her student.

"You're doing very well, Mrs. Fletcher," I heard her say.

The fourth time around, I was smiling, and by the fifth time, I was confident enough to stop and say hello.

"Are you enjoying yourself?" she asked.

"Very much. I had hoped skating would come back to me, and it seems to be happening."

"Good for you!"

"Yes, I'm so pleased," I said, twisting to watch the older woman skate smoothly by and for a second forgetting where I was.

It happened so fast I had no time to correct my posture. One moment I was standing. The next moment my feet slipped out from under me and I was flat on my back, my head snapping hard against the ice.

Lyla was at my side in an instant, helping me sit up. "Don't get up too quickly," she said. "Are you dizzy?"

I felt a spray of ice as Jeremy raced over and stopped just short of plowing into me.

"You okay?" he asked, bending over me.

"I'm fine," I said, rubbing the sore spot where my head had made contact with the ice and where a pulsating lump had already appeared. "I'm more embarrassed than hurt."

"Want some help getting up?" Jeremy asked.

I nodded. Jeremy swooped around behind, put his hands under my arms, and hauled me to my feet. "There you go," he said.

"Leave it to me to fall while I'm standing still," I said, brushing ice particles off my slacks.

"Happens all the time," Lyla said. "Are you sure you're okay?"

"Perfectly fine," I replied.

"You should go to the emergency room to be checked out," Lyla said as she guided me to the gate.

"No, that's not necessary." My hand came up again as the back of my head began to pound.

"Please," Lyla said, peering into my eyes. "I'm sure you're fine, but it's policy here that when someone is injured, they be seen by a doctor."

She didn't wait for an answer. Within seconds, a big, beefy man wearing the uniform of a private security guard extended a hand to help me off the ice.

"Joe will take you to the hospital," Lyla said.

"Happy to drive you there, Mrs. Fletcher," he said through a wide smile. "It'd be my pleasure. My wife, she's read every one of your books—says you're her favorite mystery writer. Come on. I'll get you there in no time, they'll check you out, and you'll be back here on the ice before you know it."

I didn't argue. With an ice pack provided by Lyla pressed to the back of my head, I left my skates in a locker, followed the guard to his car, and in ten minutes had checked into the emergency room and was sitting on a gurney being examined by a young female physician. Evidently I answered all her questions correctly because she decided that no serious damage had been done. "But I do want a CAT scan, Mrs. Fletcher, to make sure there's no internal bleeding."

I put up a feeble argument but found myself being taken to the room in which the radiology equipment was housed. Its operator was a young man in green hospital scrubs. Fifteen minutes later I'd been cleared to leave, with the recommendation that I wear a helmet if I planned to continue to skate.

Joe, the guard who'd driven me, had remained in the waiting room. He stood when he saw me and said, "Drive you home, Mrs. Fletcher?"

"Yes, I suppose so," I said. "I really appreciate this, and—"

"Something wrong?" he asked as I looked past him to one of the doors leading to the ER's treatment area.

"No, it's just that—oh, dear!"

"Jessica?" Seth Hazlitt said. "What are *you* doing here?"

"I, ah . . . I slipped at the ice arena and—just a bump on the head, Seth. Nothing serious."

Seth simply stared at me. He didn't have to say "I told you so." It was written all over his face.

"Oh, Seth, this is Joe. He's a guard at the arena. He was kind enough to drive me here and—"

"It was my pleasure," Joe said. "Happy to drive her home, too."

"Very kind of you, sir, but I'll take her from here," Seth said. "I'm leaving in a minute. Been here checking on a patient and stopped in the ER to say hello to a colleague."

Knowing the lecture I was undoubtedly about to receive, I would have preferred that Joe take me, but I knew that Seth wouldn't hear of it. I thanked the security guard profusely, and he left. I waited while Seth talked with one of the ER staff, then walked with him to where his car was parked in a spot reserved for doctors. He was oddly silent.

"I left my skates at the arena," I said. "I'd like to go pick them up."

"You should be home resting," he said.

"Seth, please," I said. "I know you're bursting to tell me

how foolish I've been trying to skate after all these years, and I'll admit I probably should have taken some lessons before starting again, but—"

He laughed, and I knew what was behind it. He'd made his point without saying a word. He didn't argue with me and drove me to the arena.

"I'm going to stay a while," I told him.

"Not to skate again," he said.

"No. My skating is done for the day. I've already arranged for a taxi to pick me up here. I'm fine, Seth, just fine. The doctor said I was fine. No need to worry." I climbed out of the car. "Thanks for the lift—and for the good advice."

Before he could debate it with me, I was headed for the entrance. I looked back once and saw him shaking his head as he drove off.

Joe, who was back on duty, greeted me. "Everything okay?" he asked.

"Oh, yes. My head is fine."

I didn't mention that my ego had been terminally damaged.

Chapter Five

"You should get back on the ice," Lyla said. "It's kind of like falling off a horse. If you don't get back up right away, you'll be afraid to do it again. You can use one of the skating chairs."

"I don't think so, Lyla. I'm sure it's good advice, but tomorrow's another day. I think I'll just spend a half hour or so moseying around. I've never really gotten to see all the renovations that have taken place."

My head still hurt but not nearly as much, and my ankles were sore, too—Mr. Klingbell had been right. I rewarded myself with a hot chocolate at the now open concession stand.

Warming my hands on the paper cup, I took a stroll to see the changes that had been made to the old building. Eve and her potential client were nowhere to be seen, and I tried to envision how he would assess the property as an investment. Catty-corner to the rink I had skated on was the hockey rink, where the Cabot Cove Lobsters would play if Coddington got what he wanted, and where the future skating exhibition would be held. The area was dark now, but I could see steel bleachers reaching almost to the glass windows that overlooked the rink from the floor above.

I circumvented the rink and arrived at a door that was ajar. I pushed it open and found myself inside what was obviously a storeroom. Stacked up on the right were floor panels used to convert the rink into a solid-floor arena when a traveling event, like a rodeo or circus, came to town. A small forklift was backed into a corner, next to trash bins.

Jeremy came through the door behind me.

"Hello," I said.

"Hi," he said as he strode past, cradling his hand. "You okay?"

"Just fine," I called as he pushed through another door marked ICE ARENA PERSONNEL ONLY.

I threw my empty cup into a trash can and turned to leave but noticed a few drops of blood on the floor leading to the door. I hesitated a moment, then followed.

"Jeremy?" I called.

"Out in a minute," he replied.

I was standing between two behemoth Zamboni machines in a cavernous, frigid room. The walls were cinder block and rose to at least thirty feet. Bare lightbulbs were strung across the gap overhead but offered only weak light. The sound of running water bounced off the concrete, making it hard to identify the direction from which it came.

I walked to the rear of the machines and found a large, mostly empty space with tall garage doors on either end.

On the right were rough wooden shelves holding an assortment of hardware. To my left, set into the concrete floor, was an open pool of water, partially covered by an ironwork grille. Perforated pipes on the wall spilled a continuous stream of water into the pool, which had a layer of ice floating on top. A shovel stuck out from a pile of snow that had been dumped on the metal grate.

Jeremy knelt next to the pipe and held his hand under the running water. "You're not supposed to be in here," he said, his back to me.

"Sorry," I said. "I just came in to see if you're all right. Seems to be a day for accidents." He removed his hand from the water and wrapped it in something white. "Did you injure yourself?"

"It's not too bad," he said as he attempted to tug a glove over his hand.

"What's on your hand?" I asked.

"Paper towels. Can't do much one-handed."

"Don't you have any gauze?"

"Probably some in that old first-aid kit," he said, cocking his head to indicate the wooden shelves on the far wall, where a rusted white metal case with a large red cross on the side was shoved in next to pieces of electronic equipment—switches, toggles, and push buttons. "I don't have time to wrap it right now. I have to get back on the ice. There are only two of us on duty."

"Let me see that," I said, reaching for his hand, which he extended to me. "Surely the rink can do without you long enough for you to get bandaged properly."

I pulled down the ancient first-aid kit. Inside I found a

roll of gauze, a pair of surgical scissors, and a brown bottle with a liquid inside. "I didn't know you could find this anymore," I said, setting the bottle aside.

"What is it?" Jeremy said.

"Tincture of Merthiolate," I said. "People stopped using it years ago because it has mercury in it. Throw it away and get the rink to buy you some iodine, and a new first-aid kit while you're at it."

"Like old man Coddington would spring for the money," he snorted.

"How did this happen?" I asked, carefully pulling the paper towels away from his wound.

"One of the guys skated into my hand when I was kneeling on the ice helping someone who fell. He couldn't stop in time."

I wound the gauze around his hand. "You'll want to show this to your doctor. You might need a stitch. By the way, what is that behind me?"

"You mean the pit? That's where we melt the snow that the machines collect when we clean the ice."

"How deep is it?"

"Six feet."

"And you leave it uncovered? That's dangerous. Someone could fall in."

"I know. But like I told you, you're not supposed to be in here."

"Have you ever fallen in?"

"Not yet." He laughed. "I've come close, but I'm pretty sure-footed. It's colder than a . . . Well, I wouldn't want to find out how cold."

"That should do it," I said, carefully tucking in the loose end of the gauze. I held his glove open for him.

He winced as he slid his hand in.

"Does it hurt a lot?" I asked.

"I'll pop an aspirin later, but Mark will be mad. We have some tricks scheduled for the exhibition we're supposed to practice. I only have a week to heal, but I probably can still do them if I tape it up good." He led me back between the Zambonis and out the door.

"What kind of tricks do you do?" I asked.

"Lifts, throws, that kind of thing."

We walked around the hockey rink toward the main hall.

"You're Marisa Brown's pairs partner, aren't you?" I said, referring to the young woman who also worked at the rink in exchange for skating lessons.

Jeremy stopped. "You heard about us already?"

"I've heard people mention it. I didn't think it was a secret."

"Hey, it's not a secret at all. It's just pretty recent. Mark Rosner is coaching us. This is my big chance, especially if Mr. Devlin likes what he sees. Maybe we could move up to him. Marisa is a terrific skater and we match up well. I hope it works out."

"Why wouldn't it?"

He gave a short laugh. "You wouldn't believe how expensive skating is. I asked Mr. Coddington to give me more hours so I can pay for the extra training. Chris—that's Christine Allen—she said her father is going to spring for more gym equipment for her and Alexei to use, and she said that Marisa and I can use it, too. That'll save us a bundle. I hope it's okay with Coddington."

"Why wouldn't it be?"

"Well, it's his rink, but it would be Mr. Allen's equipment. I don't know if Mr. Allen expects the arena to reimburse him, or if he would take it all away with him if he decides Chris and Alexei should practice somewhere else."

"I'm sure they'll work something out."

"I hope so. I'm really excited. Wait till you see us at the exhibition. We're going to be great. Hey, thanks for this." He raised his gloved hand. "Gotta get to work now. You'd better leave, too."

He hurried off, leaving me alone. How nice to see him so excited about skating with Marisa; I hoped his injury wouldn't spoil their program plans. I was pondering that when a movement in the second-floor window overlooking the rink drew my attention. I looked up in that direction and saw a figure silhouetted against the light. How long had he or she been there? My eyes scanned the rink to see if there was something or someone else that might be of interest. When I looked up again, the figure was gone.

Curiosity drew me upstairs. I ambled down the second-floor hallway. There wasn't much to see. One side of the corridor was the glass wall overlooking the empty hockey rink. Most of the doors were closed on the opposite side. I stopped at the first open one and glanced inside. It was the gym. Apparently, news of the coming hockey team had inspired more donations, or Mr. Allen's promise to install more equipment was already bearing fruit. I spotted a weight-lifting machine and a treadmill. I also saw Alexei

Olshansky's reflection in the mirror. Dressed in shorts, a thick gold chain glistening against his naked chest, he was watching himself, turning from side to side, flexing his biceps as he alternated lifting weights. He was speaking in a low voice. I couldn't tell if he was talking to himself or if there was someone else in the room with him. When he caught me looking at him, he set down the barbells and came toward me.

"Oh, hello," I said. "I'm Jessica Fletcher. I was just—"

He raised his eyebrows, gave me a silly smile, and closed the door.

Well, you didn't expect him to stop and chat, did you?

There wasn't anyone in the next room to shut the door in my face when I poked my head in. It was bare, only a folding chair in the corner with an old cassette player perched on the seat. One wall was covered in mirrors, and on the floor were rubber mats similar to those downstairs.

Raised voices down the hall caught my ear, and I debated whether to cut short my impromptu tour of the facility. But nosiness trumped my good intentions. I stood where I was and listened. I recognized Coddington's voice.

"I'm not accustomed to having to wait a day when I say I want to talk to someone, Devlin."

"And I'm not accustomed to being given arbitrary orders. What was so important you had to create a scene in front of my students?"

"I didn't bring you here to have you humiliate me in the press."

"I didn't say anything about *you* at all. All I said was that services and equipment were late in being installed, but that

I fully expected the arena would live up to its obligations. I thought I was being diplomatic."

"You call that diplomatic?"

I heard a newspaper being slammed down.

"Look, I didn't call the reporter. She called me. Don't give out my number if you don't want me talking to the press."

"We're trying to get some good publicity for the rink, Devlin. You're not helping," a third voice said.

"Don't give me that, Beliveau. You just want to boost your hockey program. I've already got ESPN interested in my top pair. We'll get more of that when we have a first-rate service to offer top skaters, like what was promised me. My reputation brings in the press. Big-time coverage, not some amateur story in your local rag."

"What do you have to complain about? I advanced you the money you wanted. You have everything you need here," Coddington said.

"This place is a far cry from the rosy picture you painted, Coddington."

"What's wrong with it?"

"Look around. It's a dump!"

"A dump! How dare you—?"

"Our contract called for a dance studio. Where's my spring floor? Where's my ballet bar, my Bose sound system? You call a couple of mirrors, some rubber mats, and a boom box a dance studio?"

"Has that baby Olshansky been complaining?"

"What's the matter, Beliveau? Has he been hitting on your girlfriends again?"

"Cut it out, you two," Coddington rasped. "I laid down a fortune to move you here, Devlin. When I see a return on my investment, we can upgrade the dance studio."

"You haven't had any 'return on your investment,' as you so nicely put it, with your hockey team, yet you managed to set up a shiny new locker room for Beliveau's players. I can't attract top-flight skaters with a second-rate facility. You live up to your promises or I'll—"

"Or you'll what? You have a contract, Devlin. If you think—"

"Mrs. Fletcher?" Lyla said from close behind me. "Is there something I can help you with?"

"Oh, you startled me. No, thank you, dear."

"Are you feeling all right? No headache from the fall earlier?"

"I'm fine, Lyla. I was just exploring, seeing the changes that Mr. Coddington has made."

"Well, let me show you around," she said, loud enough to be heard over the argument.

The voices fell silent.

Lyla walked in front of me. When she reached Coddington's office, she pulled the door closed. "I think they might like some privacy," she said. "Don't you?"

Chapter Six

The following morning I was in Mara's Luncheon-ette, a popular dockside restaurant in downtown Cabot Cove and home to the best blueberry pan-cakes in all of Maine, maybe all of the country. In addition to serving good food, Mara's was a prime spot in the town's gossip league, which also included Sassi's Bakery and the Cabot Cove Post Office. And, of course, there was always Loretta's Beauty Shop. Among them they regularly scooped the *Gazette* on local news, which was why Evelyn Phillips made certain to stop at each place on an almost daily ba-sis. On this morning she was detailing her plans for cover-age of rehearsals for the upcoming skating exhibition. She buttered her toasted bagel and tapped the lip of her cup to show Mara she wanted more coffee.

"Our regular photographer ran out on me," Evelyn said to me. "He's driving his daughter up to school in Mon-treal. He should be back in time for the exhibition, but in the meantime Richard Koser said he'd take pictures for me on Saturday. He's calling himself the paper's 'second-string photographer,' told me to order him business cards with that title. Smart aleck! But I need him. I'm going with a double truck of photos in the center of the issue. It's a slow news week." She took a bite of her bagel.

"What's a double truck?" Mara asked.

"That's newspaper talk for a two-page centerfold," I said, saving Evelyn from having to speak with her mouth full.

"Well, why didn't you just say so? 'Double truck' sounds like a tandem tractor trailer."

Evelyn swallowed and took a sip of her coffee. "I don't like to refer to a centerfold in the newspaper," she said. "People always get the wrong idea."

"You mean no naked pictures of Alexei Olshansky or Brian Devlin?" Mara said, chuckling. "Too bad. I kinda like that idea."

"See what I mean?" Evelyn said. "Who's the new waiter?" she asked, cocking her head toward a young man delivering two orders of pancakes to a table by the window. "Haven't seen him around before."

"I think I saw him at Charles Department Store the other evening," I said.

"That's Tommy Hunter," Mara replied. "Isn't he just the cutest kid?" She lowered her voice. "Came up from New York City. Told me he lost his folks a few years ago in a car wreck, poor thing. He's working his way through college."

"He looks too young for college," Evelyn said.

"He showed me his California driver's license. He's twenty-one."

"I thought you said he was from New York," Evelyn said.

"Must have moved there from California," Mara offered.

"How did you find him?" I asked.

"He found me," Mara replied. "He had breakfast here a few days ago, raved about my pancakes, paid his bill, then asked if I had any openings for work."

"Smart kid," Evelyn said. "He knew right away how to get around you."

"At least he paid his bill *first*," Mara said. "But he's been a big hit since he started. Real mannerly. A little shy. He offered to teach me how to use the computer for my accounting. I don't know if I'll take him up on it, though. Those machines scare me."

"Mara, you've had that computer for three years," I said. "You must use it for something. Don't you?"

"Just to e-mail my sister in Bangor."

"You could just as easily call her up," Evelyn pointed out.

"I do that, too. Anyway, Tommy said he'd show me what I need to do. I think he's a good addition to the staff."

"I'm sure he is," I said.

"Let me introduce you." Mara called out, "Tommy, come meet these ladies while I go refill this pot."

"I'll refill it for you, if you like," Tommy said. He was a slight young man with close-clipped sandy hair and a baby face.

"Isn't he sweet?" Mara said. "No, thanks, hon. The coffee is my job. How else would I learn about what's going on in this town if I didn't go table to table? Say hello to Evelyn Phillips and Jessica Fletcher. Mrs. Phillips is the editor of the town paper, and Mrs. Fletcher is our resident celebrity."

"Mara, please," I said.

57

"Well, you are, Jessica, and I like to brag about you."

"Wh-why are you a celebrity, Mrs. Fletcher?" the young man asked.

"You see, Mara, I'm not such a celebrity as you think."

The young man's cheeks turned pink. "Oh, I'm sorry. I didn't mean—"

"She wasn't a finalist on *American Idol*," Evelyn put in. "That's probably why you don't know her name."

"This is the famous J. B. Fletcher," Mara said.

"Stop that, you two." I turned to Tommy. "I write mysteries under the name J. B. Fletcher. If you're not a mystery fan, you wouldn't have heard of me. And even if you are, you might not have heard of me."

"Nonsense," Evelyn said. "If he reads mysteries, he knows your name."

"Um, I don't read much, I mean books, that is, actually. I'm kind of more of a sports fan," he said, looking nervous. "Can I get you anything? Mara has a terrific special, chicken noodle soup, perfect for a cold day." He pulled a black pencil from behind his ear and started scribbling on his order pad, clearly eager to make his escape.

"I'm fine," Evelyn said. "The bagel is enough, but I wouldn't mind more coffee." She eyed Mara's empty pot.

"Coming up," Mara said and went behind the counter.

"I'll have a cup of the soup," I said, "and some whole wheat toast."

"Speaking of a cold day," Evelyn said after Tommy went to fill my order, "it's supposed to snow like the dickens this weekend. I'm praying it won't interfere with the rehearsals. That's my lead story. That and the Russians in town. I bet their government is hopping mad that Alexei and Christine are going to skate for America in the next Olympics."

"They haven't even skated together in public yet. It's a little early to assume they'll make the Olympic team," I said. "And doesn't he have to have American citizenship first?"

"He does, I think. I'll ask Devlin. He's addressing the Cabot Cove Chamber of Commerce today. I'm going to stop by before I meet Richard at my office. Want to join me?"

"Yes, I'd like to hear his talk."

"Thought you might. How's the skating going? Heard you took a tumble."

"I was hoping no one would hear about that. Who told *you*?"

"Doc Hazlitt."

I sighed. "I have to admit that Seth cautioned me about falling."

"Lyla, the assistant coach at the ice arena, also mentioned it to me, but I don't plan to put it in the paper. I'm not that desperate for news."

I laughed. "I appreciate that."

"What made you decide to take up skating again?"

"You're partially responsible."

"I am?" Evelyn looked at me skeptically.

"I've been reading all your coverage of the renovations to the rink, and the excitement about the pairs program and the new coach. I guess I just got a yen to try it again."

"If you say so, Jessica, but I'm no lumper's helper. Sure you don't have some other motive, something else up your sleeve?"

I smiled. "You're looking for news where there is none, Evelyn."

"We'll see," she said, wrapping the second half of her bagel in a napkin and tucking it in her shoulder bag.

We left Mara's and walked over to Nudd's Bait & Tackle, where the chamber of commerce was meeting. Nudd's was the center of attention in the summertime, when Cabot Cove was filled with tourists and fishermen. Its barnlike interior was a popular stop, especially for children, who goggled at the huge fish mounted high on the walls and rafters, the small whale arched over one of the doors, and a fierce-looking shark over another. But business dwindled in the winter. Any fishermen going out had stocked up before dawn, the busiest time, and the remainder of the day for Nudd's was mostly long and empty. To fill his time and space—and sell the occasional item—Nudd volunteered his store for local gatherings. While the town's other fraternal organizations—the Lions, Moose, garden club, Rotary, and others—held their meetings at local restaurants, Cabot Cove's chamber of commerce chose Nudd's because he was an active member and to show its support for local businesses. He didn't charge a fee for using the space, which warmed everyone's thrifty Yankee souls; attendees paid only for the buffet lunch, which was catered by Mara's Luncheonette.

Folding chairs had been set up at makeshift tables toward the front, with several rows without tables at the rear for people who weren't interested in eating. All the tables were occupied when Evelyn and I arrived, and most of the seats in the front were, too. We took seats in the back near the door.

Tim Purdy, Cabot Cove's historian and the chamber's longtime treasurer, who'd also been elected president when no one else wanted the headaches, tapped on the microphone with his fingernail to make certain it was working. A screen on a tripod stand behind him showed a picture of Christine and Alexei in matching costumes and sporting big smiles.

"Our speaker is our outstanding figure skating coach, Brian Devlin, of the Cabot Cove Ice Arena," Tim said, rattling a piece of paper. "Mr. Devlin is considered—" Tim raised his chin to look down through the bottom of his glasses at the paper in his hand. "He's considered one of the best pairs coaches and choreographers in the country. He's a former gold medalist, a professional skater for many years before turning to coaching at the world-famous skating center at Hackensack, New Jersey. That means he's not a New Englander, but we won't hold that against him, I guess." There was laughter. "He's going to fill us in on what he does and explain his plans for the rinks. Let's give a warm Cabot Cove welcome to Brian Devlin."

There was a round of applause as Devlin stepped to the microphone. Without the bulky brown jacket that all the arena personnel wore, and without the added height provided by skate blades, he looked different than he appeared at the rink. He was shorter, of course, maybe just shy of six feet, and with a slender build, but his shoulders were broad under a tan wool sports jacket worn over dark blue jeans.

He had shaved for the occasion, revealing a dimple in his chin that his usual whiskers obscured.

"My, my, he *is* handsome," Evelyn whispered to me. "I can see why all the ladies are gaga over him."

"Are they?"

"Oh, yes. I hear they beat a path to his door. The older ones, that is. Some of the younger ones are smitten with Alexei Olshansky."

"Not Marisa, the young woman who works at the rink. She's crazy about Devlin, not Alexei."

"She's in the minority," Evelyn said. "Between the two of them, the ladies in Cabot Cove have a lot to talk about. Not so sure how the men feel about them, though."

Devlin cleared his throat. "Thank you all for coming today. I must say Cabot Cove has made me feel very much at home these past few months, and I thank you for that. My dad was in the military for twenty years, and we moved around a lot, ending up at Nellis Air Force Base before he retired. Having been a military brat, the opportunity to put down roots in as nice a town as you have here is deeply gratifying."

I looked around. He had everyone's ear.

"I want to tell you a little about figure skating and what we hope to accomplish at the arena, and leave you some time for questions. But I won't talk too long. By the way, I understand there's a nor'easter coming in this weekend. I'm not sure how my car will handle a Maine snowstorm. I hope there's at least one tow operator in the room."

There was a general chuckle.

"Al's Garage can help you out," someone at a front table said as he stood.

"Sit down, Witham," Tim said. "You don't have to advertise here. We all know who you are."

"Well, he asked, Tim. Just thought I'd be of help."

"Thank you, Mr. Witham," Devlin said. "I'll get your business card before I leave."

The picture behind him changed to a bar chart. "Just a few statistics to start off. I'm happy to see so many businesswomen with us today because women comprise the major portion of figure skating's fan base—seventy percent, in fact. It's the number one spectator sport of women and their teenage daughters. This will come as no surprise to the gentlemen here, but women prefer to watch figure skating on television than college basketball or football, tennis, or professional hockey."

"That's why I gotta fight my wife for the remote during the Super Bowl," said Al Witham.

"That's called counterprogramming, Mr. Witham," Devlin said. "The TV folks are no fools. They usually put skating on the schedule opposite a big sports event. You don't have to give up your Sunday game, but guys, if you want to woo your ladies, you should get tickets to the skating exhibition we're putting on the Saturday after this."

"We have some flyers up here on the counter," Tim put in. "Don't get up now. You can pick one up on your way out."

Devlin continued. "Americans love all kinds of skating—figure skating, speed skating, hockey—not just as spectators but as participants, too. Skating is great at any time of life, from toddlers through seniors. My mother put me on skates as soon as I could walk. I was skating as part of a pair by the time I was six, in competitions at nine. But you can start skating at any age. We have quite a few older folks taking up skating or coming back to it after a time away. I see a few familiar faces here." He looked to the rear of the room and smiled at me, causing heads to turn.

"I'm not the one," Evelyn said, looking up from her pad, where she'd been jotting notes. She shook her head and pointed a finger at me.

"Thanks, Evelyn," I said under my breath, straining to keep a smile on my lips.

"No problem."

"I hope to see more of you in this room enjoying yourselves on the ice," Devlin resumed, recapturing his audience.

The whole town would now know I was skating, and I had no doubt that news of my fall was a topic of conversation at the town's gossip centers.

"Skating as a recreational sport started in Europe, but it was actually an American by the name of Jackson Haines who first introduced the kind of figure skating we're familiar with today," Devlin said, pushing a button.

An old photograph, probably a daguerreotype, appeared on the screen. Haines's costume looked like something designed for an opera or ballet, with an elaborately striped, trimmed, and belted tunic over short pantaloons, with matching cap. The boots of his skates were high and topped with fur trim.

"At the time—we're talking the middle of the nineteenth century—his combination of skating and dance with a free-flowing style was at odds with the stiff and rigid movement people were accustomed to seeing."

"Nice legs," Evelyn murmured. "Obviously before Queen Victoria got everyone to cover up."

"His performances were not embraced here in the States, so Haines moved to Europe, teaching what came to be known as the 'International Style.' He was a sensation in Vienna, where he invented the sit spin, still one of our basic spins today. But the first competition here in the International Style didn't take place until many years after his death, in 1914, in New Haven, Connecticut."

Devlin moved to present-day topics and spoke for another ten minutes, detailing the many offerings of the Cabot Cove Ice Arena, even touching on Luc Beliveau's hockey program, although not with enthusiasm.

"Before we go, I'd like to introduce some of our stars of tomorrow," he said.

He extended his hand toward a table to his right, its occupants shielded from my view.

"Stand up and let them see you," he said. "Here's Christine Allen, Alexei Olshansky, Marisa Brown, and Jeremy Hapgood."

The four skaters stood and turned to the audience, waving and smiling, while the chamber of commerce audience applauded. Several people took pictures of them with their cell phones.

"These are pairs we are currently training for competitions. Marisa and Jeremy are local talents. They train with Mark Rosner. Christine and Alexei train with me. They moved here from far away, Chris from San Francisco and Alexei all the way from Moscow, Russia. We're hoping to make Cabot Cove a major training center for pairs skating in the U.S. There's another pair—exceptionally talented—who are weighing whether or not to come to Cabot Cove to join our program."

Both Christine and Alexei turned to look at Devlin. Apparently his announcement was a surprise to them. He waved the quartet back into their seats.

"That's why it's so important that the services we provide live up to the needs of our elite skaters. Skating is an expensive sport. It could cost upward of seventy thousand dollars for an elite skater to reach the Olympics. Skates alone can be a thousand dollars a pair. Throw in lessons, ice time, off-ice training, costumes, travel, and a host of other expenses. It adds up pretty fast. But you can help our American teams. If anyone wants to talk with me about sponsorship, I'll be here for a while after the meeting. Please support our skaters. Come to next week's exhibition and take advantage of the facilities and programs that the Cabot Cove Ice Arena has to offer. I hope to see you all there."

"I didn't realize they were up there at the table," Evelyn said to me, a look of consternation on her face. "I would've made sure that Richard came here to grab some shots."

"Perhaps one of those people who took pictures of them just now would be glad to share them with you," I said.

"A cell phone photo won't be sharp enough for the paper," Evelyn said. "Excuse me." She headed for the front of the room.

I lingered while the audience filed out. There was a small crowd around Devlin, mostly women, peppering him with questions, Evelyn among them. The athletes had wandered to the back of the store and were browsing the shelves.

They'd come with Devlin and were awaiting their ride back to the rink.

"Cut it out, Olshansky," I heard Jeremy bark.

I turned to see the two young men straining toward each other. Marisa was tugging on Jeremy's elbow. Christine had stepped in front of Alexei and was pushing him back, her hands on his chest.

Alexei let out a stream of Russian I was grateful I didn't understand, and spat in Jeremy's direction.

Devlin abruptly detached himself from his admirers and rushed to intercede. He stepped between them, pushed Christine aside, and grabbed a handful of shirt on each man, hauling them to his side. "If I see another squabble between you two, one of you won't take another step onto the rink, and I think you know, Hapgood, who that will be. As for you, Alexei, you're one step closer to getting on an Aeroflot flight home. You're both jeopardizing something I've worked a long time for, and I won't let it happen. You understand me?" His gaze switched from one to the other.

"Hey, you broke my necklace," Alexei complained.

Devlin relaxed his grip, and the skater's gold chain slithered to the floor.

"Fix it and bill me," his coach said as the Russian knelt to retrieve his jewelry.

"He better keep his hands to himself," Jeremy ground out. "He thinks he's above the law, and he isn't."

"What happened this time?" Devlin asked.

All four were silent.

"You want it that way, all right," Devlin said. He pushed Jeremy Hapgood away. "Find your way home."

"Why me? How am I supposed to get there? I drove here with you."

"You live in this town. Find someone to take you home. I don't want to see you at the rink until tomorrow."

"I'm on duty this afternoon, and we're supposed to rehearse tonight."

"Someone else will take your place. I'll tell Mark you'll rehearse tomorrow. Get out of here."

Jeremy shook himself and picked up his jacket. "Come on, Marisa. We're outta here."

"She stays," Devlin said, glaring at the younger man, daring him to contradict what he'd said. "You're on thin ice, Hapgood, no pun intended."

"Go on, Jer," Marisa said. "I'll call you later."

As Jeremy punched one arm into his jacket and stomped out of the store, Alexei slipped his hand into his pocket and then put something on a nearby shelf.

Devlin turned to Christine. "I want to know what happened, and I want to hear about it now."

She looked down at the floor and mumbled something.

Marisa jumped in. "It wasn't anything, Mr. Devlin," she said. "Alexei just bumped into me accidentally, and Jeremy, he . . . he thought it was on purpose. I tried to tell them that it was just a mistake, but they started to fight anyway. It's all over now."

Christine looked at Marisa, who avoided her eyes. She looked up at Alexei. His face was impassive, but he tapped his foot nervously.

"We're leaving," Devlin said. "Marisa, you sit up front with me. Go wait in the car. All of you."

Devlin turned. The chamber members were still gathered at the front of the store, silently watching. "My apologies," he said, walking toward them, "but I think we'd better break this up. You're welcome to come to the rink and talk with me anytime."

"What was that about?" Evelyn asked.

"A combination of youthful exuberance and too much testosterone," Devlin replied. "It's been a while, so I tend to forget how touchy they can be at this age. It explodes and it's over. They won't even remember it tomorrow. Thanks again for coming."

He walked out.

I went to the shelf to see what Alexei had placed there. It was a small piece of faux scrimshaw made of resin in the shape of a shark's tooth. A drawing of Nudd's Bait & Tackle had been etched on it. The label on the bottom said it was priced at twenty-five dollars. I gazed around. Similar scrimshaw carvings in Nudd's were displayed in a case against the wall. I took the piece and returned it to its rightful place, wondering all the while what it had been doing in Alexei's pocket.

Chapter Seven

"**A**re you skating again, Mrs. Fletcher?"

"I thought I would, Lyla. As you said, it's important to get back on the ice. But I came a bit early to watch the practice. Are those people press?"

"Uh-huh. They're from some celebrity Russian TV show."

A bright light lit up the side of the rink. A camera crew was interviewing Alexei Olshansky, but the person holding the microphone was not whom I expected. Instead of the glamorous young woman I'd seen in Charles Department Store, this reporter was a stocky fellow in a double-breasted black topcoat and black sheepskin hat. In his figure skates, Alexei loomed over the older man. The two conversed casually in Russian while a third man adjusted the focus of the large camera balanced on his shoulder.

Devlin paced impatiently, making a show of pulling up the sleeve of his down jacket to look at his watch.

The cameraman nodded, and the reporter spoke into his

microphone, then thrust it up to the mouth of the skater. Alexei appeared thoughtful and replied in Russian. Several more questions and answers followed, until the reporter's next question elicited a frown. Olshansky made a cutting motion with his arm. The camera kept rolling. There was a heated exchange; the only words I caught were a name: Irina Bednikova. She had been Alexei's former partner, and from what I knew, he'd severed their professional relationship and had come to the United States to skate with Christine Allen. But now I wondered if the customer at Charles might indeed have been his ex. And why would she be here?

"No more," Alexei said in English.

"What's going on?" Devlin asked.

"Nothing," Alexei said. "Let's get on with the practice."

"What did he ask you?" the coach demanded.

"He asks about Bednikova. She is history." Alexei removed his skate guards and entered the ice.

Devlin squinted at his student. "She'd better be," he said, following him.

Alexei slashed an arm behind his back angrily and glided to where Christine waited.

The cameraman shifted around to focus on the couple on the ice.

Alexei took Chris's arm, and they began to skate together. The rink was silent except for the grinding sound as their edges dug into the ice. Alexei pulled Chris in front of him, his hands firmly at her waist. They turned together. She put one hand on his wrist, crossed her skates, and bent her knees. In a smooth move, he lifted her, turned, and threw her in front of him. She rotated three times in the air, turning counterclockwise, and landed on one skate with her left foot raised behind her, arms stretched out to the sides.

Devlin watched for a few seconds, then cupped his hands at his mouth and shouted at the reporter's crew. "Okay, you got your shot. Now get out!" He turned to Chris and Alexei. "You two, wait for me over there." He pointed to the sound booth by the side of the rink where I stood with Lyla Fasolino.

"But you agreed we could shoot today," the reporter yelled. "You cannot change your mind now."

"No more. Your presence is disruptive. My skaters need calm. You got enough. Take your camera and go."

"I need another angle."

"You got all the angles you're going to get. I want you out of here. Do I need to call the cops?"

The reporter yelled something in Russian, followed by, "I am going to complain."

"Complain all you want. This is my rink when I'm teaching. Get out of here." He called to Jeremy Hapgood, who stood by the Zamboni, "Make sure they leave."

Jeremy, who was suited up for hockey, sauntered in the direction of the reporter and cameraman, swinging his hockey stick in front of him. He was tall and broad to begin with, but with the padding of his uniform and the extra height provided by his skates, he appeared to be enormous.

I looked to where Alexei and Christine stood and saw Alexei smirk. He pulled Chris into his side, wrapped his arm around her shoulder, tipping his head over to rest on hers, and wiggled his fingers at the departing camera crew.

The two men walked swiftly toward the exit. Devlin's eyes never left them, his expression furious. When he heard the sound of the heavy door slamming shut, he skated over to his students.

"That was quite a show," he said. "I don't recall telling you to practice the throw triple loop."

"We haven't practiced it," Chris said brightly, smiling up at Alexei, who grinned back. "That was our first time."

"You don't do any elements until I tell you to—especially not in front of a camera. Do I make myself clear?"

The skaters' smiles faded.

Devlin addressed Alexei. "You got away with it today, but what if she wasn't ready? What if she fell, was injured? Not only could you have scuttled your chances to make the next competition; your friends back in Moscow would have gotten quite a sight of your new American partner collapsed on the ice. That would have given some people we know satisfaction, wouldn't it?"

"But Chris did not fall. She did it perfectly."

"I say when she does it perfectly. Not you."

"Yes, boss."

Devlin narrowed his eyes. "Okay, big shots, you want to do throw jumps? That's what we'll practice today. But only a double. This time I want to see the entrance with a Mohawk turn."

Lyla nervously twisted the chain she always wore and said to me in a low voice, "Oh, boy, Mr. Allen is not going to like that. Chris just got the stitches out of her chin last night. If she falls facedown again, the wound might open."

"Do camera crews come here often?" I asked.

She shook her head. "Because this is a new program, we're getting a lot more attention. A sports writer for the *New York Times* arrived yesterday and wants to interview Devlin's students. Usually it's pretty quiet here, but having big names like Christine and Alexei changed things. I suppose the fact that he's Russian makes it an even better story. The Russians are irritated that Alexei is skating for America, calling him a traitor, although it'll be a couple of years before he can apply for citizenship."

"There was bound to be some reaction like that," I said. "Wasn't there a Japanese girl who skated for Russia? She was the victim of a lot of name-calling, as I remember."

Lyla nodded. "Well, this is complicated by the fact that Irina hasn't found another partner as good as Alexei. I haven't seen her, but there's a rumor around town that she's here gunning for him."

My second time on the ice was an improvement over the first—at least I didn't fall. But the skills I'd possessed in my youth did not return with the speed with which I'd hoped. I made a dozen circuits around the rink, sticking close to the boards just in case, after which I came off the ice and sat on one of the metal benches in the bleachers to catch my breath. Skating was hard work. Stroking around on a quarter-inch-wide blade meant constantly being aware of my posture, keeping my weight toward the middle or the front of the blade—not too far forward or the pick would scrape the ice, but not too far back either. That's how I'd fallen the last time, and I was determined to not allow it to happen again. Most important, I had to remember to breathe. I'd found myself holding my breath whenever I hit a rough patch in the ice, and there were lots of them. No wonder I was panting.

"You're doing very well out there today. Are you going to become a regular?" The speaker was the lady who'd worn a pink angora sweater the first time I'd skated. Today her sweater was powder blue. "May I join you?"

"By all means," I said, moving to the side, "although I warn you, this bench is icy cold."

"Oh, I'm used to that," she said. "My name is Muriel Charney. That's my husband, Larry, the speed skater." She waved at Larry as he streamed by, bent at the waist, left arm resting on his back, right arm swinging out in front of him.

"Nice to meet you. I'm Jessica Fletcher."

"Oh, I know who you are. Everyone in Cabot Cove knows you're a famous writer of murder mysteries."

"That's very kind," I said, "but right now I'm just another person trying to get her skating legs back. You and your husband are both wonderful skaters. Have you been at it long?"

"Larry's been skating for fifty years. He skated as a young man and never stopped. It's great exercise, and he loves it."

"And you? How long have you been skating?"

"Let me think. It'll be five years this May. That's how long Larry and I are married. So I've been skating for six years. How long had it been since you were on the ice?"

"A good twenty years, I think."

"It gets tougher as you get older. These knees and hips are not what they used to be."

"So I'm finding out," I said.

"But I do love it. Even with this gray hair, I get out on the ice and I imagine I'm an Olympic champion like Peggy Fleming or Dorothy Hamill. I'm dating myself, of course. They were from the sixties and seventies."

"Well, at least you didn't say Sonja Henie," I said, laughing. "That would be going back to the twenties or thirties when she won the title."

"Ooh, I loved her movies on television when I was a little girl. Have you had enough of a rest? Are you ready to go back on the ice?"

"That's a good idea," I said, "if only to get off this freezing bench."

"Whatever motivation it takes," she said, laughing.

We stroked around the rink together, and I found myself relaxing. Muriel was a talker as well as a skater. Just by trying to keep up with her, I was gaining more confidence as we circled the rink.

"Have you seen the any of the figure skaters that train here yet?" she asked.

"I watched Alexei and Christine for a few minutes this morning," I replied. "It's nice that they block some time for the public to watch."

"Christine Allen is lovely, isn't she? But he's a handful."

"What do you mean?"

"He gets into so many scrapes. Someone is always yelling at him."

"How do you know?"

"When you're here every day, you see things," she said, chuckling. "I don't know about you, but I find that the older

I get, the more invisible I am to younger people. They don't hesitate to speak or act out in front of me. It's as if I'm not there."

"I find it hard to believe that you're invisible," I said. "You're too pretty for that."

"You're a flatterer. Perhaps a better way to put it is that you become so familiar to the younger people around you, they don't pay attention to you anymore. Whatever it is, it allows me to be privy to conversations and arguments that, had they thought about it, they might have moved to a more private location."

"Who yells at Alexei other than his coach?"

"Well, he and Jeremy over there will never be best friends."

"Yes, I gathered they're not fans of each other's."

"I think Jeremy has a crush on Christine. That's what I told Larry. Alexei's probably afraid if Chris returns Jeremy's affection, it will jeopardize Alexei's position. So what does he do? He goes after Marisa, but not nicely, not flirting or anything. He teases her mercilessly. Tells her she needs to watch him and Chris if she wants to see what real skating is about. Just little taunts to undermine her confidence."

"Marisa certainly doesn't like him."

"I don't blame her. He makes her cry. Alexei obviously has a mean streak. He was called on the carpet for it yesterday."

"What happened?"

"I'm not sure of the exact circumstances, but Larry and I overheard Mark Rosner—he's one of Marisa's coaches—tell Alexei off. He threatened to report him, said his behavior was unbecoming and not gentlemanly. There's a code of conduct for skaters here. Lots of rinks have them, especially if they run freestyle sessions for competitive skaters. You could have several pairs on the ice at the same time. There's a need for rules, and respecting your fellow skaters is a big one."

"It's a good idea," I said.

"Well, Mark was hot under the collar. I think his re-marks went beyond the gentlemanly. The two of them went at each other."

"Physically?"

"And how. Mr. Devlin had to pull them apart."

"Oh, my."

"You said it. 'Oh, my,' indeed."

"I hadn't realized," I said.

"Stick with me, Jessica. You'll get all the gossip while you relearn to skate. See how nicely you're doing now? Come back tomorrow and we'll skate together again."

I happily agreed. I was gaining confidence with every turn on the ice. If I kept it up I might even invite Seth Haz-litt to watch me.

Chapter Eight

"You'll see a big difference with this pair," Lyla told me the next day as Evelyn Phillips and I watched her sift through a pile of CDs looking for the music for Marisa and Jeremy's exhibition program. Across the rink, Richard Koser focused his camera on the skaters.

"Are Christine and Alexei so much better?" I asked.

"Their skills are at a higher level, of course, but the real difference is in their styles. You'll see what I mean." She extracted one CD case, put it aside, leaned over the gate, and called to Mark Rosner, who was directing Marisa and Jeremy on the ice as the two ran through their program. "Let me know when you're ready for the music."

"A few more minutes," he called back. He turned to his students. "No lifts today, no throws," he said. "I want Jeremy's hand to heal before we put pressure on it."

A young man in a black ski jacket came through the rink door, tucking his bare hands under his arms.

"Hello, Tommy," said Evelyn. "Did Mara give you the day off?"

"No, ma'am. I have to be there in an hour," he said, hopping up and down. "It's fr-freezing in here."

Evelyn introduced Mara's newest employee to Lyla.

"Mara's great to work for," Lyla said. "I waitressed there when I was in high school."

"Yeah? She's nice."

"I think I've seen you here before, haven't I?" she said.

"Um, I might've been here once. I like to watch the skaters."

"Ever try it yourself?" I asked.

"No. I'm, um, I was raised on a ranch in Nevada. It never snows there."

"It snows in the mountains," Lyla said. "I skied at Lake Tahoe."

"Well, I'm from the southern part of the state, the flatlands."

"I thought you told Mara you were from California," I said.

"No. No. Only recently, when my folks moved West. Sold the ranch, the whole bit." His expression became sad for a moment. "Before they, um, before they died." He brightened. "But I'm a Down-Easter now. Isn't that what you folks say? Anyway, I came to see the famous skaters." He shivered and clapped his hands on his arms. "Where are they?"

"Yes, Lyla, where *are* Chris and Alexei this morning?" Evelyn asked. "I was hoping Richard could get some shots of them."

"They'll be back, but not for a while. They have the ice

booked after the lunchtime public session," Lyla said, looking at her watch.

"Nuts!" said Evelyn. "I was sure we'd catch them now. I
can't believe I have such bad timing."

"You mean I came here and they're not going to show
up?" Tommy said.

"Ordinarily, this is when they would be here, but they
switched practices with Jeremy and Marisa," Lyla said. "Mr.
Allen was planning to take them for final fittings on their
new costumes. They need to skate in them before the exhibition to make sure nothing binds them or flies up in their
face while they're moving."

"Aw! I was counting on seeing Christine," Tommy said.
"She, ah, I mean, I heard so much about her. She's a great
skater."

"I'm sorry you've missed them. I can let her know a fan
stopped by."

"No, that's okay."

"Why not stay and watch Marisa and Jeremy? They're
getting better with each practice session."

"Thanks, but I don't think so. I gotta get to work anyway." He walked away, yanked open the door to the rink,
and left it ajar.

"I guess they're not famous enough for him," Lyla said,
smiling.

Mark waved at Lyla, and she pressed the PLAY button.
The strains of the love theme from Tchaikovsky's "Romeo
and Juliet" filled the arena.

"What do you think?" Lyla asked after Jeremy and
Marisa finished the first run-through of their routine.

"They're terrific," Evelyn said. "Unless I can get a better shot of Allen and Olshansky later on, I'll block them in on the front page."

"I like the way they skate," I said. "They're not as sophisticated as Chris and Alexei, not as smooth, but their style is very lyrical. You certainly can see the talent, the potential."

Lyla sighed. "I know. They're going to be good. I'd still rather see Marisa stick to singles, but I understand why Mark was so eager to train them. Jeremy is a real natural. Some skaters just are."

I heard a sharp bark behind me and turned. A white ball of fluff came barreling through the open door to the rink. It stopped, turned in a circle, then trotted to my side and sat down, tail wagging.

"Hello, Pravda," I said, leaning down to give the dog a pat on its head.

Pravda's owner, wearing a fur jacket this time over skintight jeans and high-heeled boots, bustled inside and called to her dog in rapid Russian. She'd abandoned the fur hat she'd worn when I first saw her in Charles Department Store. Her blond hair was pulled to the side in a loose ponytail that came over her shoulder. She looked very chic and very young.

"I look for Alexei," she said, scooping up her dog and peering across the rink to where Marisa and Jeremy were practicing their spirals, a move in which they leaned forward on one skate, arms outstretched to the sides, the other leg elevated behind them, looking like children pretending to be airplanes. "Is not him," Irina said. She watched for a moment more and made a face. "Not very good. Free leg not high enough."

"Aren't you going to introduce her to us, Jessica?" Evelyn asked.

"We haven't been formally introduced ourselves," I said, "but I have a pretty good idea that this is Alexei's former partner."

"I'd know her anywhere," Lyla said coldly. She addressed our visitor directly. "You're Irina Bednikova. I hope you're not here to make trouble."

"Trouble? What trouble? I am here, speak to Alexei. Where he is? And where this famous coach is I never hear of? Devman? Devin?"

"Devlin," Lyla ground out. "You're too late," she said. "They were here early this morning but left about an hour ago."

"I am not finding him? Such bad. Alexei comes back, yes? I will wait. We must talk."

Richard Koser had made his way to our side of the rink and began to shoot pictures of Irina.

"Evelyn, do you have to?" Lyla asked.

"You're kidding, aren't you?" She addressed Irina: "Is this your first trip to the United States, Ms. Bednikova?" she asked, pen poised over pad.

"*Da!* I come only to take Alexei back. He runs away from home. Silly boy. But he knows he never find better partner than Irina."

"Does Alexei Olshansky know you're here?" Evelyn asked.

"I send word, but he hides from me like little baby."

"He's been at the rink every day this week," Lyla said. "I'd hardly call that hiding."

"I want he should come see *me*," Irina said, "but now I lose the patience. Is coming time to go home. Is enough stubbornness. He has plenty time for to see this Christine not as good as Bednikova. Is a little girl, no? Bednikova is a woman. I bring the heart." She pounded a fist on her chest, causing the dog to raise its head in alarm. Irina stroked Pravda's fur. "Alexei leave his poor mother at home. She is—how you say?—pinning for him."

"Pining?" Evelyn said.

Irina waved a hand dismissively. "Alexei's mother, she tells me, 'Irina, go bring my Alexei home. He is proud Russian, must not skate for U.S. of A., only for Russia. If not, I will be so embarrassed.'"

"Who will be embarrassed?" Evelyn asked. "You or his mother?"

"Both of us," Irina said, taking in a great breath. She let it out in a stream of impassioned Russian.

"English, please," Evelyn said. "We don't have a translator handy. Sorry."

"So tiring to speak the English," Irina said.

"How come Alexei speaks better English than you do?" Evelyn asked.

"He have cousin here. He visit when he was little boy. Bednikova has to study the other language. Not the same." She straightened to her full height, raised her chin, and looked down her nose at Evelyn. "But I speak the English some. You do not speak the Russian at all."

"*Touché*, Evelyn," I said. "She's got us there." I turned to Irina. "How long are you planning to stay in the U.S.?"

"I have booked flight for Sunday, but now it will snow. So . . ." She shrugged her shoulders.

One of the men I'd presumed to be her bodyguards leaned through the door and called to her.

"Who is that man?" Evelyn asked.

"My brother, Maxim Bednikov. He come help me. Together we convince Alexei is time to go home."

I had visions of Irina's brother and the other large man who'd accompanied her hustling Alexei into a car, tying him up, and forcing him onto a plane to Moscow. Perhaps that was what Irina had hoped to do. Apparently the potential kidnap victim was not cooperating.

"Ms. Bednikova, how long did you skate with Alexei before he abandoned you for America?" Evelyn asked. "And what did you argue about that made him want to leave?"

Evelyn must have been doing research on the Internet, I thought. But Irina was not fazed by the line of questioning.

"You follow," she said to Evelyn. "I have paper I give you. Explain everything."

"She comes with a press release," Evelyn said to me, her eyes merry. "Guess my timing's pretty good after all."

Chapter Nine

Mort Metzger stomped the snow from his shoes and energetically wiped his soles on the doormat before coming into Seth's kitchen. "Where's the doc?" he asked, sliding a box from Sassi's Bakery onto the counter.

"In the back with a patient," I replied.

"I didn't have time to bake, Jessica," Mort's wife, Maureen, said. "I hope that's okay."

"Anything Charlene Sassi makes is every bit as good as homemade," I said, quietly relieved we were spared one of Maureen's culinary experiments. Our sheriff's second wife was a lively redhead and an avid fan of TV cooking shows. She loved to tinker with recipes, but her enthusiasm far outweighed her skills. The results were unpredictable, sometimes wonderful, oftentimes dreadful. I'd been on the receiving end of both. "What's in there?" I asked, lifting the heavy box by the red-and-white string that was wrapped three times around it.

"Just some cookies and a few Danish pastries so Doc will

have something for breakfast tomorrow. I know he likes his sweets in the morning."

Well, there goes Seth's diet, I thought, but didn't say.

"Did you skate again today, Mrs. F.?"

"I did, and I'm improving each time out. I might even brave the weekend crowds tomorrow."

"Could be hard getting to the rink by then. It's snowing like a bandit out there," Mort said.

"What's the forecast?" I asked.

"More of the same," Maureen replied. "It's a real nor'easter."

"The last time I remember a snowstorm like this was when I was still in New York," Mort said. "The city was so quiet, it was like a Sunday in the summer. You'd think everybody packed up and left for the country. It was great. The bad guys stayed inside and the only people you saw on the street were the ones skiing down Fifth Avenue."

"That must've been quite a sight," I said as I lifted the lid of a pot on the back burner, picked up a long wooden spoon, and gave the contents a stir. "I don't remember it snowing that much when I lived there."

"It never lasts long in the city," he said. "Traffic turns it to slush by the next day, and it drains away." He leaned over the stove and sniffed. "Smells good."

"It's a recipe I had for lamb," I said, "but Seth is making it his own way, using chicken. It's got wine and garlic and tomatoes. I'm sure it'll be wonderful."

"I left the doc's number with my dispatcher. Hope he doesn't mind. It's not a good night for driving. We both might get some calls."

Seth had invited the Metzgers and me for dinner. We dined together every few weeks or so, alternating houses. Seth had become more adventurous in the kitchen and liked to share his special dishes with friends. While he was often critical of the sheriff and enjoyed giving this transplanted New York City policeman a hard time, he had a warm spot in his heart for Mort.

On his part, Mort let Seth's caustic remarks slide right off his back. "Doc's nothing compared to the junkies we used to roust from under the West Side Highway," he once told me. "They called me more four-letter words than were in the dictionary, and even some colorful names I'd never heard before."

"Is there anything I can do to help?" Maureen asked.

"Seth should be finishing up soon," I said. "Why don't we wait for him inside?"

We took seats in the living room and nibbled from a plate of diced cheese and oyster crackers while waiting for our host.

"Mort's been so busy this week, I've hardly seen him," Maureen said, smiling at her husband.

"Between the rink and the Russians, they've had me running," Mort said, rolling his eyes. "There's a news crew that seems to think the only thing my office is for is to smooth the way for them. When one of the coaches wouldn't let them film at the rink, they came whining to me."

"What could you do about it, honey?" Maureen asked.

"That's just it. Nothing. Then Craig Thomas from Blueberry Hill calls. Seems some skating fans showed up at his inn looking for autographs and were roughed up by a couple of guys the size of Mack trucks."

"Who were they?"

"A couple of Russian bears. At least they looked like bears. It was all over by the time I got there. Then I get a call from Mr. Coddington. Did I find who threw nails on the ice?"

"I thought they were screws, not nails," I said.

"Screws, nails, whatever. They were standard issue, get them in any home-center kind of store, nothing special about them. In fact, I found a box of them in the Zamboni garage. That kid Hapgood who works at the rink is a real electronics nut. He could stock a hardware shop with what he's got in there. Likes to tinker with remote controllers."

"Wasn't he the one who made the report?" I asked.

"Coddington did, but it was on Hapgood's say-so. He's the one discovered the screws in the first place."

"Maybe he did it himself," Maureen said.

"No, I doubt that," Mort replied. "He was so hot about it. But they don't keep the door to the garage locked. Anyone who worked there could have gone in and swiped a box off the shelf. For that matter, anyone who didn't work there could've done the same."

"But why would anyone want to sprinkle screws on the ice?" Maureen asked.

"Why do people put razor blades in Halloween candy, or tamper with pills and return the bottle to the store?" Mort said. "There's no accounting for some people."

We heard voices as Seth emerged from his medical office and escorted his patient to the door. "You call me if you get dizzy or nauseous or can't see clearly. No alcohol, no aspirin. Understand? Lots of rest."

"That's the hardest part," his patient said. She had a big bandage over her right eye.

"Lyla! Good heavens," I said, getting up and going to her. "What happened?"

"She sustained a cut over the eye," Seth said. "She'll be fine."

"One of the Plexi panels in the hockey rink came loose as I was walking past," Lyla said.

"And it hit you in the head?"

"No, but the puck it was supposed to stop hit me. Dr. Hazlitt thinks I might have a mild concussion, but I feel fine." She rubbed the back of her neck and smiled.

"See how you feel in the morning," Seth said. "And call me. Remember, rest. No excuses."

"But we've got the exhibition coming up. I have skaters to rehearse. Mr. Coddington will go crazy."

"I'll take care of that old fool," Seth said. "There are other coaches at the rink. Let him assign your duties to someone else. Rest! Have I said it enough times?"

"Is someone driving you home?" I asked.

"Brian's waiting in the car."

"Take care, Lyla," Seth said. "I'm going to close up back there and rejoin these good people."

Maureen nudged her husband and cocked her head toward the door.

"What, hon?" Mort said. "Oh!" He took Lyla's arm. "Let me walk you out, Ms. Fasolino," he said. "That bandage is big, and you might have trouble seeing. Besides, it's slippery out there."

"I can see fine," Lyla responded.

"Humor him, sweetie," Maureen said, holding the door. When she saw Mort open the passenger door of Brian's car, she whispered to me, "I think the rink is jinxed."

"What do you mean?"

"All the incidents, the prowler, the falls, and the nails and the screws," she said.

"But that was only once, Maureen. It was probably an accident."

"Well, it wasn't an accident last night."

"What happened?"

"Mort told me someone broke into the rink and turned off the compressor. If the alarm hadn't sounded, all the ice would've melted. You know what a mess that would've made?"

"I hadn't heard that."

"Mort said at first he thought it might have happened by accident, but the person who called it in insisted to the deputy that the door had been jimmied." She added in a soft voice, "And that hole some creep drilled in the ladies' locker room wall."

"You know about that?"

"Mort told me. Maybe he shouldn't have, but it's all over town. I'm surprised you haven't heard it."

"I have," I said.

"Whooee! It's coming down faster than the one train to South Ferry," Mort said, shutting the door behind him. He toed off his snow-covered shoes and padded into the living room.

"Please don't say anything," Maureen whispered to me. "I'm not supposed to talk about his business." She picked up a piece of cheese and popped it in her mouth. "Mmm," she said, winking at me. "Have some cheese, honey," she told her husband.

The phone rang as we sat down again. Seth walked in holding the receiver. "He's right here, Gladys," he said to the caller.

"I knew it," Mort said. "Every time I get a night off, the calls come pouring in." He took the phone from Seth. "Yeah. Okay, I understand. No. No. I'll be right there. Is anyone hurt? I'll check in when I get there. Thanks." He hung up and shook his head.

"What is it?" I asked.

"Got another complaint from the rink. Two of my guys are tied up with fender benders, the ambulance is on the way to a three-car pileup, and there's only one officer covering the jail. There's nobody else to respond to the call."

"Looks like I cooked for nothing," Seth said.

"Sorry, Doc, but you know how it goes."

"Yes, I certainly do."

"How about if we turn off the burner and we all go to the rink with you?" I suggested. "There's no point in our sitting around until you get back."

"Nah. You go ahead and enjoy your meal," Mort said. "I don't know how long this will take."

"You said the ambulance is tied up," I said. "If we go with you and someone is hurt, Seth can tend to them until the ambulance is free. We can eat later."

"Will the dinner hold?" Maureen asked.

"Easily," I said. "Dishes like this are even better the next day."

"Oh, I have a recipe like that. It's for meatballs coated in a lemonade mix and cooked in milk. It sounds strange, but it's really delicious."

"I'll take your word for it," Seth said.

"No, really, it was good. Wasn't it, honey?" Maureen asked Mort.

"It was an interesting combination, hon," Mort said, his expression pained. "Well, if the rest of you don't mind going out in the cold, I'd be happy for the company."

We piled into Mort's SUV, the perfect vehicle for the weather, and drove to the arena. The trip was slow, thanks to the heavy snowfall. Mort's radio crackled with reports of accidents—cars skidding through traffic lights near the strip mall outside town, complaints of stalled cars, an unfortunate encounter with a moose, and Mayor Jim Shevlin's call for residents to stay home and off the roads to let the snowplows do their job. The mayor's counsel notwithstanding, the parking lot was full when we arrived at the rink. Mort drove around to the main entrance and pulled into an empty handicapped spot, and we got out.

Thick white flakes fell steadily, frosting the trees and blanketing everything in sight. Most of the cars in the parking lot were caked with snow. It was going to take some folks time to dig out before they could get home.

"It's so peaceful out here," Maureen said. "Isn't it nice?" She tilted her head back, opened her mouth, and stuck out her tongue. She giggled. "We used to love to catch the snow on our tongues when I was a kid. You never really got enough for a taste of it, though."

Seth pulled out his medical bag and surveyed the parking lot. "What the devil are all these people doing here in the middle of a blizzard?"

"It's Friday night," Maureen replied.

He shook his head. "A good night to be home."

"I told you this was a popular place for youngsters," I said. "There's probably a hockey game tonight, or a rehearsal for the upcoming show."

"Let's see what all the fuss was about," Mort said, taking Maureen's arm.

We walked up the stairs to the entrance and trooped inside. The temperature wasn't much warmer than what we'd left outdoors, but the sound level was decidedly higher. It looked as if half of Cabot Cove had come to the rink, the younger half anyway. Children, from babies in strollers to teens in makeup, some in skates and some in sneakers or boots, occupied the entry hall from one end to the other. Every one of the round tables was occupied. Mothers and fathers wrangled with different groups of youngsters, trying to tie skate laces, zip up jackets, and snap on helmets. Others were carrying trays of hot dogs, French fries, and soda, or grabbing for sleeves as a child raced by. Clusters of teenagers, trying to ignore the younger children, gathered by gender and wandered in and out of the skating areas.

As I'd predicted, there was a game in progress on the hockey rink for the bantam division, a sign said, and a general session was taking place on the ice where I'd skated. Referees in black-and-white striped shirts directed the action in the hockey game, and rink personnel, some of whom I hadn't met before but who were easily visible in their big brown down jackets, manned the office and skate rental and patrolled the public skating rink.

Mort stopped at the counter in front of the office and showed Marisa his badge. "We got a call to come to the rink. What happened?" he asked.

"I didn't see anything unless it was the fuss made by Alexei's former partner. I caught a glimpse of her this morning, and she came back tonight, parading in here in a big fur coat looking for him. I told her that he probably went home, but she wouldn't listen. She had these two goons with her, and her dog wouldn't stop barking. She kept insisting Alexei was here and ordering me to go find him and bring him to her."

"Did you get their names?" Mort asked.

"The woman's name is Irina Bednikova," I said to Mort. "One of the men with her is her brother, Maxim. I don't know who the other man is." I looked at Marisa. "Do you?"

She shook her head.

"What did you do?" Mort asked Marisa.

"Nothing. I can't leave my post. Friday is a big night here. Besides, I knew that Alexei wasn't here. He and Chris had already rehearsed. I saw her here earlier, but she's probably long gone by now. They never hang around the rink when they can't use the ice."

"Who called the police?"

She shrugged. "Not me. Might've been Jeremy. The Russians were threatening to search the place."

"What Russians?" Mort asked.

"Alexei's former partner and those two big scary-looking guys with her."

"They're Russian?"

"Well, of course. Alexei is Russian, isn't he?"

"Do you know what's she's talking about, Mrs. F.?"

"I'll explain in a minute," I said. "What did you do?" I asked her.

"I told them to go talk with Mr. Coddington."

"Is he here?" I asked.

"I doubt it. He doesn't usually come in on a Friday night. I just said that to get them out of my hair. We were busy, and I was afraid those guys would scare some of the little kids. They scared me; that's for sure."

"When did they leave?" Mort asked.

"They might still be here for all I know."

"Where did you see them last?"

"Over there." She pointed to the staircase leading to the second floor.

I told Mort about the arrival of Alexei's former partner and her hopes to repatriate him.

"Must be the same people as out at Blueberry Hill Inn," he said.

We walked past a game room with an array of arcade machines, every one of them being played. The bells, whistles, and other sound effects added to the general cacophony in the building. Maureen covered her ears with her mittened hands, and feeling like a party of visitors exploring another planet, we climbed the steps to an empty hallway.

"How do those parents stand the racket?" Maureen asked.

"They're used to it," Mort replied. "Kind of like me and

the police siren. Doesn't hurt my ears anymore. It's just background noise."

"I don't know why I'm here," Seth said. "It's not as if anyone is hurt, and I've toted this heavy bag for nothing. I could be home by a nice fire enjoying my chicken à la Hazlitt, and so could you."

"I could eat it all myself," Mort said. "I'm about as hungry as a bear."

"I don't serve bears," Seth said stiffly. "The dish I made for tonight has a subtle blending of spices. It should be savored, not gobbled down."

"Whatever you say, Doc."

Our sheriff walked up and down the corridor trying the doorknobs. All the rooms were locked. He tried pounding on Coddington's office door, but there was no response.

"I don't think it's worth getting the keys," he said. "Sorry to get you all out for no reason. I'll talk with Gladys to see if she has more details on what the complaint was about."

"If we're finished up here," I said, "why don't we get back to Seth's house and enjoy that dinner?"

Mort hesitated. "Gimme a few more minutes," he said. "I'd better talk to that guy Jeremy and see if he's the one made the call."

"And give him a good dressing-down for dragging us out on a night like this," Seth grumbled as we headed off in search of Jeremy.

Chapter Ten

When we returned downstairs, both the hockey game and the public skating session had ended, and one Zamboni was already making its circuit on the ice. Skaters and parents crowded the hall. Seth had gotten waylaid by a mother with a question about her son's allergy medication, and a small circle had gathered around him. Seeing Seth occupied, Maureen, citing hunger pangs, had joined the line to get a hot dog.

"You know much about this guy Jeremy, Mrs. F.?" Mort asked as we approached the public rink.

"A little. He seems like a nice enough fellow. He has aspirations to become a top skater and works here to help that dream along. You've met him. What did you think?"

"Didn't spend much time with him. Seemed nice enough. Is that him out on the ice driving the Zamboni?"

I stood on my tiptoes and peered across the rink. "I believe it is," I said.

Mort and I walked toward the boards that separated

the ice from the rest of the rink area. A father with a child on his shoulders, and a few small boys who hung on the boards, watched the giant vehicle make its rounds as we moved closer to the gate.

When the Zamboni reached our side of the ice, Mort pulled out his badge and beckoned to Jeremy.

Jeremy put up his index finger, stopped the Zamboni, and fished around under the dashboard. He jumped off the machine, carrying what looked like a joystick for a video game, and slid his way over to where we stood.

"Hang on a second," he said as he stepped off the ice. "Hey boys, get your arms out of the rink," he called to the youngsters. The children reluctantly moved back from the railing. "Mr. Gervich, if you stay in here, you have to keep the kids off the boards," he told the father.

"Sorry, Jeremy. We were on our way out anyway. C'mon guys. Who wants a hot dog before we leave?"

A chorus of "me" followed him from the rink.

Jeremy turned to us. "What can I do for you, Sheriff?"

"What's that?" Mort said, waving at Jeremy's hand.

Jeremy looked down at the white tape on his palm. "It's just a cut. It's healing up pretty good."

"No, I mean what's that thing you're holding?" Mort asked

Jeremy lifted up the device. "This? It's a modified throt-tle quadrant."

"What in the heck is that?"

"It's a kind of controller. Originally they were used to run flight simulators. I use mine for Bessie over there."

"You name your Zamboni machines?" I asked.

"Sure. Doesn't everybody?"

"Show me how that works," Mort said.

"It's really not as complicated as it looks," Jeremy said, balancing the device on the railing and pushing several toggle switches. As he manipulated the controller, the Zamboni engine revved up and the machine lurched forward. "See, I use this joystick to put Bessie into her circuit, then flick this switch to hold her to the pattern. The Zamboni will follow the pattern of increasingly smaller circuits until it turns in a circle in the middle of the rink. At that point you have to stop it or it will keep circling itself until it runs out of gas or digs a hole in the ice."

"That's fascinating," Mort said. "Can I try it?"

"Sure. Just move this yoke to the left. Not too far; that's it. Now hold her steady. This one controls the speed."

I cleared my throat. "Mort?"

"Yeah?"

"Don't you have a question for Jeremy?"

"Huh? Oh, right." He handed back the controller. "That's pretty cool," he said, "but we need to talk to you about a call to the station that came in tonight."

Jeremy adjusted his levers, and the Zamboni continued on its route. "Sure," he said, his eyes following the machine. "What do you want to know?"

"Someone called my office to complain about a fight at the rink."

Jeremy swiveled to face us. "Sorry! That was me, Sheriff. I totally forgot about that."

"You *forgot*! You got me all the way out here for nothing?"

"I just forgot to call again when it was over. I'm really sorry. It's been such a crazy night."

"What happened?"

"I walk into the garage and find this guy sitting on Audrey. That's the other Zamboni. I told him he was in a restricted area and that he had to leave. He gives me some lip about lax security. Got really nasty. Wouldn't get down. I'm yelling at him to get off the machine. I'm responsible for those things; they cost a fortune to repair. And we've had so many things go wrong lately. He just sits up there taunting me. Finally, I go to pull him down, and he threatens me, says he's got a gun. I ran out of there and called your office."

"You saw the gun?"

"No, but he said he had one."

"Then what?"

"When I went back to tell him that I'd called the cops, he was gone. I looked around for him, but one of the staff grabbed me. The panel on the hockey rink that fell out earlier was loose again. Lyla got whacked in the head with a puck the first time it fell off. I didn't want anyone hurt again." Jeremy raised his hands and shrugged. "I'm sorry, Sheriff. I know I should have called again. I got so busy, it completely slipped my mind."

"Did you recognize this guy, the one on the Zamboni?"

"I've seen him around. Someone said he was thinking of buying the rink. It would be just my luck if he did."

Immediately I thought of Eve Simpson's real estate client, Harvey Gemell, and made a mental note to mention him to Mort when we left. If Mr. Gemell was walking around Cabot Cove wielding a gun, our sheriff ought to know it.

"Well, there you go, Mrs. F. That's what we missed dinner for," Mort grumbled.

"No harm done, Mort," I said.

I asked Jeremy, "While you were racing around tonight, did you happen to see the Russian lady and her two large companions? Marisa said they were looking for Alexei."

He shook his head. "After Lyla got whacked in the head with the puck and left, I've been honkin' all night. If Marisa hadn't filled in, I'd still be back in the skate rental. I'm basically running the show without the title or money, but please don't tell the old man Coddington I said so." He squinted at the Zamboni and pushed a button to stop its progress.

"Something wrong?" Mort asked.

"Looks like the blade is going to need replacing. Just what I need, another thing to do tonight." He looked at his watch, then used his controller to back the Zamboni up to the garage. "Any more questions, Sheriff?"

"A few."

"Mind asking them while I replace the blade? Actually, I could use a hand pulling the new one out of its case. It's heavy, but I can handle it once it's out."

Mort looked at me. I shrugged.

"Sure thing," Mort said. "Where is it?"

"In the garage. Down this way. Same place we talked last time."

"Do you mind, Mrs. F.?"

"Of course not. I'll come with you."

We walked down the narrow aisle along the boards to the area that housed the two Zambonis, and entered through the open garage door. With Bessie on the ramp of one rink, and Audrey on the ramp of the other—poised to go when its driver was free—the space inside appeared even larger and more ominous than it had the other day. A small hill of snow sat on the iron grillwork, a shovel thrust into its side.

"Shoot!" Jeremy said. "Who closed up the grille and turned off the motor?" He grunted against the strain of lifting a panel of the ironwork cover, leaned it against the snow pile, shoveled a fresh layer of snow onto the water, and flipped a switch on the wall, setting off the low hum of a motor. "I train people, but it's a lost cause," he said, walking across the garage to a tall door. "The blades are over here, Sheriff. We keep 'em locked up. They can cut a man's arm off if you're not careful, but they've got guards on them. It's heavy but not dangerous. If you'll take that end, I'll grab this one."

"Sure thing," Mort said. "Do you happen to know the name of the guy who was sitting on the Zamboni?"

"I don't, but I can try to find out."

"You do that and get back to me. I don't like the idea of someone wandering around here carrying a weapon."

"Like I said," Jeremy said, "I didn't actually see a gun. He could've been bluffing."

I wandered around the other side of the snow pile and peered into the pit. The perforated pipe that sprayed water on the melting snow wasn't operating, but whatever motor Jeremy had turned on was making bubbles in the corner of the pool, disturbing some of the snow that floated on the water. I noticed something colored at the edge of the snow. "What's in the pit?" I called out.

"Just water and snow," Jeremy answered. "If you can hold up that end, Sheriff, I'll pull it over here."

"Wait up a second," Mort said. "Let me get a better grip."

"There's something red in the pit, Jeremy," I said.

"Maybe it's a reflection from one of the lights."

"I don't think it's a reflection."

"Well, don't get too close. I'll take a look when we're done. Over here, Sheriff. Lay 'er down real slow."

I pulled the shovel from the snow pile and put it in the water, moving it from side to side to try to break up the coating of granulated ice on the surface. The red looked like a piece of fabric. Using the shovel, I pulled it closer to the edge of the pit, knelt down and reached into the frigid water. I gave it a quick tug, but it wouldn't come out. I let go and shook my hand to rid it of the painfully cold water. "I think it's a scarf," I said, "but it's stuck to something." I tucked my hand under my arm to warm it up.

"Watch your step, Mrs. Fletcher," Jeremy warned. "Don't you go falling in." He came up behind me. "We've had enough problems tonight."

I moved out of the way, and he crouched down to get a better view of the thing to which I was referring. "Didn't see this before," he said.

"What is it?" Mort asked.

"Looks like it's just what Mrs. Fletcher said, a scarf. Must be a long one. Someone either dropped it in, or one of the Zambonis picked it up when it came in from the rink. Happens sometimes." He put both arms in the water, grabbed hold of the scarf, and yanked. It wouldn't budge. "It's probably caught in the drain. Would you turn off that switch up there, Sheriff? Lucky it didn't gum up the Zamboni."

Mort turned off the motor. "Let me help," he said, squatting next to Jeremy. He put his hand on another portion of the fabric. "Ouch, that's cold," he said. "Okay, we pull on three. One, two, three."

The fabric gave, and both men fell backward, Jeremy catching himself with his free hand, Mort landing on his bottom on the wet floor.

"Oh, no!" Mort said, scrambling to his feet. "I just had these cleaned." He swiped at the seat of his pants. "You got any paper towels?"

"Sure. Over here, Sheriff," Jeremy said, running to pull a fresh roll of paper towels from a shelf.

"Mort?"

"Just a minute, Mrs. F. I'm soaked."

"Do you want more paper towels?" Jeremy asked.

"Mort, you need to see this."

"Can it wait, Mrs. F.? I'm freezing my butt off over here. Literally."

"I think you need to see this *now*."

I heard a sigh behind me, the shuffling of Mort's and Jeremy's feet, and then a low whistle from Mort and a gasp from Jeremy.

The three of us looked into the pit. A shock of blond hair was visible just below the surface of the water. Then the body rose and tipped to its side, and we could see the other end of the long scarf.

It was wrapped around Alexei Olshansky's neck.

Chapter Eleven

"What do you think, Doc?" Mort asked after we'd found Seth and brought him into the garage. "Looks like he took a misstep and fell in. Obviously a drowning accident, right?"

Alexei lay on the concrete floor next to the pit from which Mort and Jeremy had hauled him.

"Hard to tell," Seth said, kneeling by the body. "The scarf didn't leave any marks on the skin that I can see. No petechial hemorrhages in the eyes. That possibly rules out strangulation. More likely it's primary respiratory impairment from submersion in a liquid medium."

"Huh?"

"Drowning."

"Isn't that what I just said?" Mort grumbled, running his fingers through his hair.

"Face and lips are blue," Seth continued. "Course he could have had cardiac arrest from the hypothermia. We'll have to see if there's water in his lungs."

Jeremy stood as far away from the body as he could, his eyes roaming the room to keep from looking at the corpse. At Seth's pronouncement, Jeremy's teeth began to chatter, the sound reminding Mort of his presence.

"How many doors come into this room?" he asked Jeremy.

"One," Jeremy said, pointing toward the door to the rink I'd come through when first visiting the garage.

"Just one?"

"Yes. Uh, no, I mean, no," he stammered.

"Well, it's got to be one or the other."

"S-So sorry. There are . . . th-three, if you count the garage doors."

"Son, can you do something for me?"

"Yuh . . . yes, Sheriff."

"Listen carefully, please."

A shaken Jeremy pulled himself together as Mort issued instructions. "I want everyone cleared out of the building," he said, "except for the staff. Understand?"

Jeremy gave a sharp nod; his Adam's apple jumped in his throat as he worked to swallow.

"Get me a list of the names of everyone who worked here tonight, with their addresses and phone numbers," Mort continued. "Make me a couple of copies."

"S-sure, Sheriff. I'll have Marisa type it up for you."

"And get a pot of coffee going for us. Can you do that?"

"The concession stand is still open."

"Good. Wait for me in the office. After the public leaves, do not let anyone in the building without asking me first."

Relief flooded his face as Jeremy rushed out of the garage.

"He looked like he was about to faint," Mort commented. "Don't need any additional complications tonight."

"Won't you want to be questioning those people who are here tonight?" I tentatively asked, not wanting to challenge Mort's decision.

"Not right now," he said. "I don't want to set off a panic. Besides, they're all locals. I can catch up with them later after I know what we've got here. Anyway, we don't have enough officers available for all those people, and I can't pull the guys on duty away from the traffic accidents."

I agreed with his reasoning. It was highly doubtful that a casual visitor to the arena would have entered the Zamboni garage that evening; he was right in focusing on staff members, at least initially.

"Maybe Jeremy should use the mayor's announcement that asked people to stay off the roads as the reason for closing the arena," I said. "That way there will be fewer questions."

"Good idea, Mrs. F.," he said. "Tell him it's an order from the mayor."

I found Jeremy at the office arguing with Marisa.

"How did you get so wet?" she asked him.

"Never mind that. I need you to type up a list of everyone working tonight. Everyone. Understand?" Jeremy said.

"They're all up on the board over there. Look for yourself."

"Typed, I said."

"Why do you need it typed?"

"Just do what I'm asking, Marisa."

"You don't have to be rude about it."

"Forget it. I'll do it myself." He tore off his wet jacket and flung it across a desk. "And we've got to get everyone except the staff out of here. Now."

"You're full of demands tonight, aren't you? What's going on?"

I pulled Jeremy aside and told him about using the mayor's announcement as an excuse to instruct people to leave. "I know it's upsetting. Just take it one step at a time," I counseled. "We need you to be composed or you'll make others uneasy."

He closed his eyes for a moment, took a deep breath, and gave me a grim smile. Without revealing the real reason, he calmly told Marisa to clear the building. "It's because—because the mayor wants everyone off the roads during the storm. It's dangerous. The sheriff wants the mayor's order to be heeded. But we need the staff to hang around."

"If everyone's leaving, why can't the staff? I'd like to go home, too."

"Marisa, do I have to make the announcement or will you?"

A disgusted Marisa picked up the public address microphone and turned it on. "Hi, everyone," her perky voice came through the speakers. "Could I have your attention for a moment, please? We already have a good foot of snow on the ground, folks. The plows are working overtime. The mayor has asked us to close the rink and send everyone home."

A collective groan rose from a large group of the teen-agers.

"If you already bought passes for the late evening ses-sion, save your tickets and we'll honor them when you come back. Please take your time on the roads. They're very slippery. Drive carefully. Ice arena staff, please help empty the building, then wait for further instructions."

Marisa turned off the PA mike and eyed Jeremy, who nervously typed on the computer. "What's going on, Jer?" she asked. "Snow is usually no big deal."

"We'll talk about it tomorrow. Okay? Help get everyone out. Check the locker room, the restrooms, the upstairs hall, and ask the concession kids to see me."

"How late are we going to be here?"

"Just round up the staff and tell them to wait for me in the game room."

"Do you know what's going on, Mrs. Fletcher?"

"The mayor is worried about the snow," I said. I didn't like not being entirely truthful with her, but Mort was right. There was nothing to be gained by creating a panic. He needed time to sort things out.

While Marisa set off to usher any stragglers to the door and to gather the staff in the room containing the arcade games, I returned to the garage. Maureen followed.

"Why wouldn't you keep everyone here to question them?" she asked her husband upon learning of Alexei's death and Mort's order to vacate the arena. His expression said that he didn't appreciate being asked that question for the second time, but he checked his pique. "I don't want a lot of gossip about it," he explained. "It's better to clear the area and see what we've got here. I want to go about this methodically."

"Okay, hon. What can I do?"

Mort thought for a moment. "I already called for the ambulance," he said. "You can go help that kid getting me the list of the staff who worked tonight. And see if he put up a pot of coffee."

Maureen went to find Jeremy, leaving Seth, Mort, and me inside the garage with the body. The two ice resurfacing machines stood on the ramps outside the massive doors, like an enormous pair of guard dogs.

"Can you give us a time of death, Doc?" Mort asked.

"I can give you a guess, but it's going to be tricky considerin' the body's having been in ice water."

"He has a scratch on his nose," I said.

"What does that mean, Mrs. F.?"

"I don't know, but it wasn't there the last time I saw him alive. Have you checked his hands, Seth?"

"Not yet. They're swollen from the water. Might be some bruises and cuts. No rigor mortis yet. From the looks of the skin, I'd say he was in the water no more than three or four hours, Sheriff, but don't hold me to it. I'll need to examine the body more carefully to be sure."

"Any ideas, Mrs. F.? Looks like an accident to me."

"A good possibility," I said. "Or a suicide. Or murder. I'm sure you're not ruling out any of those possibilities."

"Of course not."

"I doubt that he would have killed himself, though. He

was a very confident young man, even overconfident. I can't imagine anything throwing him so much that he would take his own life, especially by drowning himself in ice water."

"Maybe he received some terrible news from home," Mort suggested, "something that would have made him feel miserable or guilty."

"Alexei had a very strong ego. He didn't strike me as a young man who would blame himself for anything—even if he *were* responsible."

"So we rule out suicide?"

"I'd say so."

"Accident?"

"Could be."

"What do you say, Doc? What would've happened if he just fell in? Could the cold water kill him?"

"Not immediately. Normal body temperature is around ninety-eight, ninety-nine degrees. People vary. Clinically, hypothermia starts when the core temperature is at ninety-five degrees."

"That's not much of a drop, Doc."

"No, it isn't. Even so, death from hypothermia usually takes a bit of time, even in ice water. What can happen, however—as the body temperature begins to fall, the victim is not always aware of it. He may become confused, make poor decisions, have difficulty performing tasks, not realize it's because he's losing heat."

"You'd think he would at least call for help," Mort said.

"I'm not sure anyone outside this room would hear him," I said. "The walls are concrete and the doors are steel. And you heard how noisy it was out there."

"Besides, if he swallowed some water when he fell in, he might've been straining just to breathe," Seth said. "Hard to yell under those circumstances."

"Alexei was very strong," I said. "If he simply fell in, he should have been able to pull himself out of the water even if he was short of breath."

"Ayuh," Seth said. "The body pumps out adrenaline when it recognizes danger. That would've helped him."

"How do you know how strong he was, Mrs. F.?"

"He and his skating partner, Christine, were talking about practicing their lifts. She must weigh around a hundred pounds, yet he was expected to lift her over his head."

"But his clothes would've been heavy from the water and pulling him down. He might not have been able to fight the added weight," Mort speculated.

We stopped talking for a moment, each of us contemplating the factors that might have contributed to Alexei's death.

"If he just fell in," I said, breaking the silence, "why was the grating covering the pit?" I walked to the snow pile and examined the ironwork grille, careful not to touch it. "It looks like it's pretty heavy, not something that would have tipped back in place easily. That suggests murder to me."

"I'd like to keep it considered an accident," Mort said. "If he grabbed at the grate to help pull himself out, it might've fallen back on him. If his calls for help couldn't be heard over the noise in the rink, and if he drowned before anyone missed him, he could have sunk to the bottom. Or someone could've just closed the grate the way Jeremy opened it and not noticed the body."

"That's possible," I said.

Mort studied my face. "But you don't think so?"

I shook my head.

"So, Doc, would you be able to tell if he was pushed into the pit?"

"Probably not," Seth said. "Any bruises he might have sustained could have occurred whether he fell or was pushed. If someone hit him on the head or another part of his body before he went into the water, we should see evidence of that. But unless the wound can be matched to a weapon, we couldn't be certain he didn't just hit his head on the corner of the grating or on the edge of the pool."

"But if that was the case," I said, "you'd probably find particles of concrete or shards of metal in the wound, wouldn't you?"

Seth nodded. "The autopsy will tell us more."

"I'd better call the medical examiner," Mort said.

"You're looking at him," Seth said. "Doc Foley picked this week to go to Florida. I'm filling in as ME."

Mort sighed. "Well, then, until you finish the autopsy, I'm reporting it as an accident. But I'll call in the evidence techs just in case," he said.

Worry was written all over our sheriff's face, and I shared his unease. I had little doubt that Alexei had been pushed into that frigid body of water, and the fact that he was a figure skater from Russia would undoubtedly raise the stakes where any investigation was concerned. Maureen Metzger's comment about the arena being jinxed now resonated. Murder represented the ultimate jinx.

"We'll have to find out if Olshansky made any enemies since coming to Cabot Cove," Mort said. "See if anyone disliked him. Enough to kill him, that is."

The door creaked open, and we all turned at the sound. It was Jeremy.

"The ambulance is here, Sheriff."

Chapter Twelve

Mort held the list of staff in one hand and a paper cup of coffee in the other. "I got thirteen names, but there are only nine of you here. Who am I missing?"

"Lyla got hit with a puck, and Mr. Devlin drove her to the doctor's," Marisa said. "They never came back."

"And two people went home when we emptied the rink," Jeremy said. "Apparently they didn't hear the part of the announcement directing the staff to stay." He glanced over at Marisa, who turned away.

Marisa and Jeremy sat on opposite sides of the arcade room now, on benches set up across from the coin-operated games to accommodate those waiting to play. Earlier, they had been standing with other staff members, watching some of their colleagues slip quarters into the pinball machine, when the evidence technicians had arrived toting a suitcase of equipment including still and video cameras.

"What's going on here?" Marisa had asked.

Jeremy hadn't replied.

Sometime later, when the EMTs wheeled the gurney holding Alexei's body past the door to the game room and out to the waiting ambulance, Marisa gave Jeremy a stunned look. "You know about this, don't you? Who is that?" she'd demanded.

"I can't tell you."

"Why not?"

"The sheriff asked me not to say anything."

"You can't tell *me*? I'm your partner. I tell you everything." He shook his head and turned away.

She now refused to sit next to him, moving as far away as she could.

Sitting between them were their coach, Mark Rosner, the hockey coach Luc Beliveau, the three officials in black-and-white striped shirts who'd called the bantam-league hockey game that night, and two teenagers, Joanne and Zack, who worked at the concession stand.

Once the ambulance departed, with Seth accompanying the body to the morgue at our local hospital, Mort began by telling the assembled group what had happened. It was a tragic accident, he'd said. Alexei had fallen into the pit in the Zamboni garage and drowned.

Marisa gasped, a hand flew to cover her mouth, and she started to cry. Mark slid closer and put an arm around her shoulder. Jeremy stared at the space between his shoes. Other than Marisa's whimpers, there was silence in the room.

"I'm going to ask you not to talk about this to anyone," Mort continued. "As much as we can, I'd like to contain the mountain of gossip that this is going to generate. Can I have your word?"

There were nods all around.

"Did anyone here see or talk to Alexei tonight?" Mort asked.

One of the hockey referees raised his hand. "I'd like to help you, Sheriff, but we don't even know what this guy looked like," he said, glancing at the other two officials. "Luc here can tell you. We came down from the next town over to officiate the game."

"That's right, Sheriff. They wouldn't know who Olshansky was," Beliveau confirmed.

"Actually, I saw the guy's picture in the paper," one of the officials said, "but I don't know that I'd recognize him if I ran into him."

"Maybe you could let these guys go home now," Beliveau suggested.

"Not just yet," Mort said, sipping his coffee. He studied the list of names as if it revealed some secret, but I knew he was just gathering his thoughts. "Let me start by asking if any of you saw someone—anyone—enter or leave the Zamboni garage tonight?"

"Only Jeremy," Mark Rosner said. "But I didn't pay any attention to him. That's his job." He shook his head and snorted. "There's going to be some lawsuit. Does Coddington know?"

"One of my deputies is calling him now," Mort said. "Did you see Mr. Olshansky at the rink today?"

"*Mr.* Olshansky?" Rosner said. "Yeah, I saw Alexei this morning." He shifted in his seat, taking his arm from around

Marisa, who'd been slumped against him and now wiped tears from under her eyes with a trembling finger. "He and Chris were rehearsing for the exhibition next week. I guess that'll be canceled."

Marisa's head whipped around. "It will?"

"Probably. I don't know."

"Mr. Rosner, I understand that you and Alexei had an altercation one morning this week," I said. "Could you tell us what that was about?"

Rosner squeezed his eyes shut, stretched his neck, and scratched his head.

"It was my fault," Marisa said.

"No, no, it wasn't," Rosner said, annoyed. "I hate to say ill of the dead, but truth is, he was a pain in the neck. Right, Luc?"

"Leave me out of this."

"Well, he was. Always testing the boundaries, seeing what he could get away with. He kept torturing her." He cocked his head toward Marisa. "I don't know what he thought he could accomplish—maybe break her concentration, weaken her confidence. Why? Who knows why Alexei did anything? Anyway, I ripped into him, and we got into it a bit. Brian broke us up. He apologized later. Alexei, that is. I told him to apologize to Marisa. Did he do that?"

Marisa shook her head. "No."

Rosner sighed. "Let's just say I'm not one of his admirers, Sheriff. But to tell the truth, it was so busy tonight, I don't even know that I would have noticed him if he were here. He might have gone into the Zamboni garage tonight, but I didn't see him. Did anyone else?"

"Are you kidding me? He never stepped foot in the garage," Jeremy said. "That was for the peons who work at the rink, not for prima donna skaters like him."

"He must've gone into the garage sometime today," Mort pointed out, "unless someone carried him in and dumped his body in the pit."

Jeremy flushed bright red and looked at the floor again.

"Coach Beliveau, you had a game," Mort said. "You must've been here a long time. Anything strike you as unusual this afternoon or tonight?"

Beliveau shook his head. "We had a panel fall out of the boards. That was the big news. By the way, I heard that Lyla's okay. Happy to hear it."

There were nods and murmurs of agreement.

"Did you see Olshansky at all today?" Mort pressed.

"Sure thing," Beliveau replied. "This morning when he and Christine practiced with Devlin. Look, Sheriff, he wasn't much interested in hockey, and I've never been known to give a hang about figure skating." He leaned forward and looked at Marisa and Mark. "Apologies to present company, but you know it's just not my thing."

"That's okay, Luc," Rosner said. "I don't give a hang about hockey."

"Anyway, I never let anyone put my head in a bucket," Luc said, using a colloquial Maine expression. His eyes went to Jeremy. "No Russian kid is going to turn me around."

Jeremy appeared startled. "He didn't turn me around. I knew what he was about. It was just that he was constantly looking for ways to put me down."

"Be specific," Mort said.

Jeremy shrugged. "He had it out for me. I don't know why. He was always accusing me of trying to mess him up, said I'd loosened the screws holding the blades on his boots or that I'd flattened a tire on his car. If anything bad happened to him, he'd point a finger at me."

"Why do you think he did that?" Mort asked.

Jeremy shrugged.

"Did you see him do that, Marisa?"

"Everybody did," she answered. "You can ask anyone here. Well, I mean those who are here all the time. The only people Alexei was nice to were Chris and Mr. Devlin, and maybe Lyla. He gave everyone else a hard time, but I guess he was afraid of being disrespectful to the coaches."

Mark snorted. "Except me," he said. "He had no compunctions about speaking disrespectfully to me. Then again, I wasn't *his* coach, just a coach at the rink."

"But he was meanest to Jeremy," Marisa put in. "He always picked on him—and me."

"Why do you think he picked on Jeremy?" I asked her.

"He was jealous," she replied. "He thought that Chris had a thing for Jeremy and that Jeremy wanted him out of the way."

"Was that true?" I asked Jeremy. "Does Chris have a crush on you?"

"How would I know?"

"Men usually can tell when a woman likes them," I said. "But what about you? *Do* you have a crush on Christine?"

" 'Crush' is such a weird word," Jeremy said.

"Answer the question," Mort said.

Jeremy stole a glance at Marisa, then looked away. "I like

Chris. She's a great girl, real pretty and always smiling." He shrugged. "But we don't, you know, we don't have a relationship or anything like that."

"That's not what Mrs. Fletcher asked you," Mort said. "She didn't ask if you and Chris had a relationship. She asked if you'd *like* to have a relationship with Chris, if you have feelings for her."

"So I like her," Jeremy said. "So what? That doesn't mean I'd kill her partner, for crying out loud."

"We didn't say that you did," Mort said. He let a moment pass before asking softly, "What kinds of things would Olshansky say to you that got under your skin?"

"He used to say that Jeremy would never be good enough to match up with the elite pairs skaters," Marisa said.

"I'm asking Jeremy the question, Marisa. I'd like *him* to answer."

"Well, like, he was boiled when Mr. Devlin included me as one of the 'stars of tomorrow' at the chamber of commerce meeting. Kept calling me 'a little fishie from Cabot Cove,'" Jeremy spoke in a high voice imitating Alexei's teasing. "He said I would have to 'swim fast' to make it even into novice competition. I couldn't walk past him without him getting in a dig." He gave Marisa a fast glance. "And he was mean to Marisa. She never did anything to him, but he ranked on her all the time."

"So, you really didn't like him," Mort noted.

"I hated him," Jeremy said, his eyes filling with tears. "But I wouldn't push him into the pit. I might have dreamed about doing it, but I'd never do it. I *didn't* do it."

There was a flurry of activity at the door. Mort turned

at the sound of voices. "I said to keep everyone out," he shouted. "What's going on?"

"That's what I'd like to know," Evelyn Phillips said as she barreled in with a deputy hanging on her arm. Right behind them was Richard Koser, carrying his camera.

"I'm sorry, Sheriff," the deputy said. "She insisted."

"I don't have enough to do. Now I have to deal with reporters," Mort groused.

"Ever hear of the First Amendment, Sheriff Metzger?" Evelyn asked haughtily. "Freedom of the press?"

"We're busy here, Mrs. Phillips."

"The scanner said there was a death at the rink," Evelyn said, looking around to take in who was in the room. "Once this story gets out, you're going to wish it was only me. You'll be inundated with press."

Mort nodded wearily. "That's what I'm afraid of."

The fact that there was nothing of interest for Richard to photograph didn't deter him. Mort wouldn't allow anyone into the Zamboni garage; he'd had the technicians seal off both rinks as well. Nevertheless, after Mort gave them a quick update on Alexei's death, Evelyn and Richard lingered in the hall of the arena, Richard shooting pictures of the block letters on the yellow tape: CRIME SCENE DO NOT CROSS.

"Why are you stringing up crime scene tape if the death was an accident?" Evelyn pressed.

"Because I don't have any yellow tape that says ACCIDENT SCENE on it," Mort replied. "We don't have any evidence that this was anything other than a tragic mishap."

"And if you did, would you tell me?"

Mort sighed. "With any death from other than obvious natural causes, there are procedures I have to follow. I can't talk to you before I at least notify the next of kin. You can understand that."

"I don't understand how he drowned. This is not a pond in the woods. The ice on the rink is maybe an inch thick, two at the most."

"I already told you he was found in the pool used to collect and melt the snow; it's level with the floor. The lighting is not the best. It could be easy to miss if you're not familiar with the room."

"There will be an autopsy, won't there?"

"That's the best I can do for you now. I'll issue a statement tomorrow."

"Has Eldridge Coddington been notified?"

"You'll have to ask him yourself," Mort said. "Now, please excuse me. I have work to do here."

Evelyn looked at me. "Jessica, care to comment for the record?"

"No, thank you, Evelyn."

"Thought as much."

Evelyn and Richard left the rink, and shortly afterward Mort dismissed everyone on the staff except Jeremy.

"Are you arresting me?" Jeremy asked.

"Is there a reason I should?"

"No, sir, none at all."

"Then let's talk someplace else where we won't be interrupted. I have to file an initial report and alert the other authorities. I don't know much about this guy. I could use your help."

"Whatever you say, Sheriff. I'll do anything to help."

"Good. Come with me."

Mort arranged for a squad car to be posted outside the rink to keep the curious at bay, and collected his wife, who'd been dozing off at one of the round tables near the concession stand. Jeremy unplugged the coffeepot, turned off the lights, and locked up the building. We all walked out to Mort's SUV.

Big white flakes were still softly falling, filling in the ruts in the snow that had been made by the tires of departing vehicles. The night was eerily quiet—and peaceful.

Too bad, I thought, that only Mother Nature was at peace at that moment in Cabot Cove.

Chapter Thirteen

The next morning, Saturday, was a gray, cold day. After a breakfast of oatmeal, half a banana, and a cup of steaming-hot coffee, I joined Mort Metzger at the rented home of William Allen, Christine Allen's father. I wasn't sure whether Mort would grant my request to accompany him as he began his questioning of parties of interest the day after finding Alexei Olshansky's nearly frozen body, although he had given me a copy of the staff list Jeremy had typed up. But to my surprise, he readily, perhaps even eagerly, agreed. "You were there when we found him, Mrs. F.," he said, "and you seem to have a pretty good handle on what's been going on at the arena. Happy to have you along with me."

Seth had called from the morgue the night before to say he wouldn't start the autopsy until the morning. In order to file an initial report and alert international authorities, Mort had driven to the sheriff's office after letting Maureen off at home. Jeremy and I had accompanied him.

The antipathy between Jeremy and Alexei was well-known; the two simply did not get along. Mort pressed him again in the station house. Jeremy was eager to list Alexei's offenses, all the while insisting he had nothing to do with Alexei's demise.

Hours later, Mort sent Jeremy home with instructions not to leave town. "Obviously, the Russian kid was a foul ball," Mort told me. "It's clear that he wasn't well liked, but I still think there's a good possibility that this was an accident."

William Allen sat in a wing chair in the living room. The table at his elbow held a pile of newspapers neatly refolded after having been read. Notwithstanding the fact that it was early Saturday morning, he was dressed formally, in a starched white shirt and maroon and green patterned tie. The trousers of his navy suit had a sharp crease in the center of his knee where it crossed his other leg. His shoes were polished. In contrast, his barefoot daughter huddled in a corner of the sofa, looking small inside an oversized gray sweatshirt and leggings. Her eyes were puffy and red. She clutched a pillow to her stomach as if she were in pain.

"We found him online," Allen responded to Mort's question of how he and his daughter came up with Alexei Olshansky as her pairs partner. "There's a Web site that specializes in matching pairs skaters. Alexei had recently separated from his partner and had put himself up there. We knew he was serious because he included a photo and video. Of course, we'd done our homework, watched as many videos as possible of his past performances, and read what we could find about him. On the part of the form where it asks if the skater will relocate, he said 'yes,' and where it asked his skating goals, he'd written that he wanted to find a partner in the U.S. to skate in senior competitions."

"What do you mean when you say you knew he was serious?" I asked.

Mr. Allen glanced over at his daughter. "Many pairs skaters are young and immature. Sometimes they'll get angry at their partner and want to hurt or scare them. They'll post that they're looking for a new partner before they've told their old one they're leaving. Usually, if you call their bluff, they'll back down. It's a foolish thing to do, and it doesn't happen often, but it happens. We looked for clues that he was sincere. He did have a reputation for being volatile."

"So you knew that going in?" I said.

"Oh, yes," he said, running his thumb and forefinger along the crease in his trousers. "But that went together with being fearless. Christine's former partner was too tentative. You can't make progress if you're afraid of making a mistake."

"Just out of curiosity," Mort said, "why would you choose to work with a skater from Russia? Wouldn't it have been easier to find an American partner?"

"Perhaps Christine would like to address this?" Mr. Allen replied.

Chris had been picking at a loose thread on her pillow. She raised her eyes, heaved a sigh, and coughed to clear her throat. "There aren't enough of them," she said. "There must be about a hundred girls for every American boy who wants to skate pairs."

"Why do you think that is?" I asked.

"I'm not sure. No one really wants to talk about it, but I have my own theory."

"Which is?"

"It's probably because in the States and Canada if a guy thinks he wants to skate, his parents push him toward hockey rather than figure skating. They think figure skating is for girls, or for guys who are gay."

"Why would they think that?" I asked.

"Because you have to be graceful as well as athletic. A lot of us study ballet. The men, too. I don't think that parents in Europe are as interested in hockey, most of them anyway. Russians love ballet and figure skating and don't think anything of men doing it. That's why I wanted a partner from Russia. They don't put labels on people like we do here."

"As far as you know," her father said.

"Yes. As far as I know." She dropped her head again. "Anyway, there just aren't that many senior male skaters available here, gay or straight," she mumbled.

Mr. Allen shifted in his chair, "Regardless of the reason, introducing foreign skaters has been a boon for the sport."

"How so?" I asked.

"The sport was dying from a lack of pairs making it to the senior levels. The International Skating Union wanted to loosen things up to bring more athletes into the picture. They changed the rules to allow a pair to compete so long as one member of the team held a passport from the country they were going to represent. They still have to sit out competitions for a year, but it's better than it used to be. They used to require them to sit out for two years. They've made it easier now if you want to find a foreign partner."

"It's still two years if their home country won't release them," Chris put in.

"Was that going to be a problem with Alexei?" I asked.

She shrugged. "We didn't know yet."

"I understand it's different for the Olympics," I said.

"Yes," Mr. Allen explained. "The Olympics require both members of a pair to hold passports of the nation they skate for."

"Did you consider that when you brought Alexei over to skate with Chris?" I asked.

"Those are hurdles you face when you get to them," he said, his eyes meeting mine for the first time. "First, you have to find a partner to skate with. Then you have to be good enough to attain the senior levels. Then you have to win competitions. We're talking years of training before the subject even comes up."

"But you assumed Alexei would be willing to become an American citizen if he and Chris achieved all those goals and were capable of making the American Olympic team."

"Mrs. Fletcher, I make no guesses as to what went on in that young man's head."

Chris raised her eyes to look at her father, then dropped them again. "It doesn't matter now, does it?"

"No, it doesn't matter now. We'll have to start the process all over again," he said, his disgust evident.

"Mr. Allen, when was the last time you saw Alexei Olshansky alive?" Mort asked.

"Yesterday morning, when he left the costume fitting."

"Was that the last time you saw him, too, Chris?"

She nodded but kept her gaze on the pillow.

"Did you practice every morning?" I asked her.

"Every day except weekends."

"Why not weekends?"

"We wanted to, but Mr. Coddington had the ice booked all day Saturday and Sunday, mostly for hockey games and public skating. Mr. Devlin tried to get him to give us more time, but he said we might have to wait for the end of the hockey season before he could free up some weekend ice for us."

"But you were scheduled to practice yesterday afternoon, weren't you?" I said. "Lyla told me the ice was reserved for you for after the noon public session."

"We didn't use it. We had booked the ice, but Alexei changed his mind about practicing."

"Why would he do that?"

"He knew his former partner was in town looking for him. He thought if he could avoid her a few more days, she'd go home."

"Then why didn't you use the ice time for yourself?"

"It was an unnecessary expense," Mr. Allen inserted. "They needed to work together at this point, not separately. I didn't want to waste the money."

"Marisa was working at the rink last night," I said. "She mentioned that she hadn't seen Alexei that evening but that she *had* seen you."

Chris shook her head vehemently. "I wasn't there. She

must've been mistaken. Maybe she mistook someone else for me."

"Were you with your father yesterday afternoon and evening?" Mort asked.

"Yes," her father answered.

"I'm asking Chris, Mr. Allen. I'd like her to answer for herself, please."

Chris glanced at her father and back to Mort. "Yes, sir, I was right here with my father all afternoon and evening. We watched a movie on TV and I did some schoolwork. I'm taking an online course for college credits, you know, on the computer."

"Speaking of the computer," I said, "why do you monitor her e-mail, Mr. Allen?"

"I don't know where you get your information, Mrs. Fletcher."

"That came from you, actually," I said. "I overheard you last week at the rink tell Chris you wanted to check her e-mail before you kept an appointment. I found that somewhat curious."

"Do you have children, Mrs. Fletcher?"

"I don't. But I have many friends with children, and I don't know too many teenagers whose parents keep an eye on their e-mail correspondence, although they're strict about what Web sites they visit."

"Perhaps if you had children, you would understand the need to protect them from strangers, from people who don't have their best interests at heart. We live in a dangerous world, Mrs. Fletcher. I protect my own. Anything else?"

"I did have one more question," I said. "I overheard Brian

Devlin say something about a scandal involving Alexei. Do you know anything about that?"

"My, what big ears you have," Allen said to me. "Do you listen in on everyone's conversations?"

He turned to Mort. "I don't mean to be rude, Sheriff, but these are a lot of questions for what appears to be a tragic accident. I told you that Christine and I were not at the rink. What more do you need to know?"

"We haven't determined yet if Olshansky's death *was* accidental, Mr. Allen," Mort said. "That's why we're asking questions, to help us make that determination."

"Do you think someone pushed him into the pit on purpose?" Chris asked me, her voice quivering.

"It doesn't matter what I think," I said. "The sheriff needs you to answer all his questions as truthfully as you can. Were you aware of any scandal surrounding Alexei?"

"Whatever it was, I'm sure it was nothing more than the usual adolescent high jinks," Mr. Allen said.

"Chris, had you heard about a scandal?" Mort asked.

Chris hesitated before replying. "There was a rumor that he might've gotten his girlfriend, Dariya, pregnant, and that's why he left her at home when he came here." She rushed to add, "But I don't know if it's true. He never said anything about her to me."

"Then I take it Alexei was not gay," I said.

"Is this relevant to your questioning, Sheriff?" Mr. Allen asked.

"It could have an impact on who his friends and acquaintances were," Mort replied, "and who we'd want to question about his death."

"In that case, yes, my understanding was that Alexei was heterosexual. Wouldn't you agree, Christine?"

She nodded. "He always had a lot of women around him. That's why Mr. Devlin tried to keep most of the practices closed, to keep him from getting distracted. I know he was upset when Mr. Coddington insisted that some of our practices were open to the public. Frankly, I didn't like having people there, but it wasn't my decision to make."

"Satisfied, Sheriff?" Allen said.

We got up to leave when I remembered something. "By the way, Chris, what movie did you say you watched yesterday?"

"Huh? I didn't say."

"You said you worked on your computer and watched a movie. What was the name of it?"

"Oh, just some silly old thing in black-and-white. I wasn't really paying much attention."

"Were you paying attention, Mr. Allen?"

"Not in the least. I was catching up with my newspapers." He patted the pile on the table.

We thanked them for their time and went to Mort's marked patrol car.

"Cold son of a gun, isn't he?" Mort said. "He doesn't seem too broken up about Alexei."

"He obviously didn't like him," I said.

"Then why pay for him to come all the way here from Russia?"

"He's a determined man, Mort. I think he was willing to overlook almost everything as long as it resulted in a world-class skating partner for his daughter. Parents will do strange things for a child. I think William Allen is a man who has made a lot of sacrifices to give his daughter her best chance to succeed at what she loves. Bringing a partner from Russia to skate with her is just one of those sacrifices. But aside from his personal dislike of Alexei, I don't think he was too happy with the results."

"But did he dislike him enough to heave him into the icy water?"

"He might have wanted to, but it doesn't matter. They gave each other an alibi. They were home together watching an old black-and-white movie that, conveniently, neither of them remembers. Where to next?"

"The victim's home, Mrs. F. Let's see what we come up with there."

Chapter Fourteen

Alexei's rented rooms were on the second floor of an old house down near the harbor. Built by a whaling captain in the nineteenth century, the house had been renovated twenty years ago to accommodate a downstairs gallery and shop, which represented local artists and was popular with tourists, especially in the summer, and an upstairs apartment with one large main room with an open kitchen, off which was a small bedroom and bath. The apartment was furnished with a long sofa, coffee table, and two bookcases flanking a window that overlooked the street and provided a partial view of the docks. A pair of tall stools drawn up to an island in the kitchen served as an eating area, and another table had been pushed against a wall to double as a desk.

Mort had given the landlord strict instructions not to allow anyone upstairs and had posted an officer there until the lock could be changed in case anyone else had a key to the skater's home. Unless Mort received alternative instructions, he assumed someone in Alexei's family would want his personal effects packed up and shipped back to Russia, but that step would await the autopsy results and any subsequent investigation.

"Did you speak with the doc this morning?" Mort asked as we looked around the apartment.

"Only briefly," I replied as I peeked into each of the kitchen cupboards. The apartment came supplied with dishware and pots and pans, all neatly stowed away. I wondered if Alexei ever used them. The refrigerator was almost empty except for a half-full six-pack of beer and a few containers of yogurt.

"Too bad about the dinner," Mort said, opening the desk drawer and pulling out an album. "I was really looking forward to that stew."

"Seth said it was delicious."

"Did he really eat it after it sat out all that time?" he asked as he flipped through the pages.

"I asked the same question. He said my comment about the recipe improving with age made him think there wouldn't be any danger."

"It was too hot to put in the refrigerator before we left, but it must've been a good four or five hours before the doc got back home, maybe longer. I don't know that I would have eaten it."

I moved into the living area and perused Alexei's bookshelves. "Seth blames me for leaving the pot on the stove. If I hadn't suggested we accompany you to the rink, the dish would have been eaten at the proper time and temperature. He said he figured if he got sick, it was my fault."

"What did you answer to that?"

"I told him I wouldn't be made responsible for his reckless behavior, and he said 'ditto.'"

"Ditto?" Mort looked at me quizzically. "What's that supposed to mean?"

"He thinks I'm behaving irresponsibly by skating again," I said. "He predicted all sorts of injuries I'm likely to acquire. After I fell and conked my head, he told me that if I really want to do myself in, I ought to take up hockey. He even said he knows a good dentist to see when I knock out my front teeth."

Mort chuckled. "That's quite a picture, you playing hockey."

"Thanks for the vote of confidence. I have no plans to play hockey, but it might be worth suiting up just to see the expression on Seth's face when I step onto the ice in a helmet and pads."

"I'd like to see that, too."

"I'll think about it. At any rate, Seth didn't get sick from the dinner, lucky for him. He refrigerated the rest of the casserole. I told him he took a greater chance than I did getting on the ice." I reached up and pulled down a package from Alexei's shelf.

"What's that you have there?"

"I'm not sure." I opened the cardboard carton to find a fabric-covered box inside.

"Anything of interest?"

"Just a souvenir from Charles Department Store," I said, lifting out a glass Christmas ornament in the shape of a globe with a gold star where Cabot Cove would be.

"How do you know it's from Charles?"

"They have a sale on holiday ornaments. I saw these on display the other evening. Besides, Alexei left the label on the box."

"Looks like he had quite a collection of souvenirs," Mort said, eyeing the bookcase. "I didn't figure Russians to be sentimental."

"I'm sure they're as sentimental as anyone else," I said.

"Think so? They always seem to me, at least the ones I see on TV, as cold."

"If they're cold, it might be the Russian winters," I said.

"Yeah, maybe that's it."

I smiled and continued to look over other items on the shelves, which included glass figurines, a kaleido-scope, a shot glass, a deck of cards, a tin of Boston mints, a pair of buffalo-nickel cuff links, and a New England Patriots snow globe. It seemed a strange assortment for a twenty-five-year-old man to have bought, and I voiced my thought.

"Maybe he planned to bring them home as gifts," Mort said.

"Or maybe he changed his mind and wanted to be able to return them," I said. "They're all still in their original packaging with the price tags on." I picked up the snow globe and shook it. "Of course, there's another possible ex-planation," I said, setting it down and watching the flurry of confetti swirl over the team logo and goalpost.

"Oh," Mort said. "You think he might've had sticky fingers?"

"It wouldn't surprise me," I said. "The other day at

Nudd's I saw him retrieve a piece of scrimshaw from his pocket and return it to a shelf."

"No kidding? I'd better check to see if there's been any recent report of shoplifting."

He held up the book he'd been perusing. "Take a look at this," he said.

"An actual photo album," I said. "How nice. Most young people today just post their pictures online."

"This album sure isn't new," Mort said. "Looks like a family album he brought with him from Russia."

It was as much a scrapbook as a photo album, with pictures of Alexei, both on and off the ice. In one boyhood photo he was flanked by two men, one of them possibly his father. In another, he sat on a sofa with a blond lady who must have been his mother, the resemblance was so strong. In addition there were articles featuring him from Russian newspapers and magazines, ticket stubs, program pages, and other memorabilia. There were several photos of him with different girls. One showed Alexei and Irina skating together as teenagers. From their smiles, it was clear that they hadn't always fought with each other.

"I didn't know he'd been here in the States before," Mort said. "Did you?" He handed me a yellowed clipping in English that had been tucked into the back of the album. It showed Alexei as a ten-year-old on skates and was captioned:

Alexei Olshansky from Moscow will skate in the Broadmoor Skating Club's Winter Ice Show.

"I just learned that myself," I said. "Irina, his former partner, mentioned that he'd come here as a child to visit a cousin. She said that's why his English was better than hers."

"Did she say how long he stayed in the States?"

"No, but this would seem to indicate that it was longer than a short visit. I imagine he had to have belonged to the skating club if he was participating in its winter show."

"Maybe this guy was a relative," Mort said, putting down the first clipping and picking up another, an obituary:

Colorado Springs businessman Paul Valery died in a one-car accident Tuesday. Mr. Valery, driving a vintage Alfa Romeo, failed to negotiate a hairpin turn on Mountain Road in Chipita Park and crashed into a stone embankment. The car flipped over the barrier and plummeted into the woods below, killing the driver. Police suspect suicide, although an investigation still continues.

No suicide note was found, but family members, citing recent financial reverses, said Mr. Valery had been despondent lately. His company, Deval Holdings, had been in the news for mishandling funds, leaving investors empty-handed when the firm closed its doors. Charges were pending against Mr. Valery.

Police said the road was clear and dry the day of the accident but investigation showed skid marks indicating the driver may have sped up approaching the turn. Police speculated the automobile was going over sixty miles per hour when it hit the stone wall.

A naturalized citizen, Mr. Valery was a native of Minsk in the former Soviet Republic of Byelorussia, now Belarus. He was active in several business organizations in Colorado Springs. . . .

"His name isn't here," I said, "but if Alexei was a distant relative, a cousin perhaps, he wouldn't have been mentioned among the survivors."

"I suppose not. Have you checked out the bedroom yet?"

"My next stop. Are you looking for anything specific, Mort?"

"No. Just getting a feel for his lifestyle in case the doc comes up with bad news. A toxicology report could take weeks to come back. I don't want to let that much time pass."

"Are you thinking of keeping this apartment locked until you have the toxicology results?" I asked.

"Not sure I could even if I wanted to. The owner of the house, Mrs. Skow, is already after me to release it so she can rent it out again. And I don't know what kind of pressure we'll be under from the Feds. We're dealing with a foreign citizen, and a pretty famous one, who died under mysterious circumstances. They could come in and seal everything off. I want to get whatever I can before I lose control of the situation."

Alexei's bedroom was spare, with little furniture aside from a bed and dresser. No pictures were hung on the walls, which were covered with a maritime-themed wallpaper of small, navy blue boats sailing in vertical stripes. His closet and bureau were packed with clothing, mostly what you would expect a young man to have, in addition to three skating costumes in vividly colored stretch material and adorned with spangles. Only a pile of unopened fan letters on his night table, and a wastebasket full of those he'd already read, held any interest. Mort decided to take both sets of letters back to his office to read, along with the family album.

"See anything else we should take along?" he asked.

"I don't think so," I replied. "What strikes me is that there are things that should be here, but that aren't."

"Like what, Mrs. F.?"

"There's no computer on his desk. I would have expected one."

"Yeah, I would, too. Do you think someone got here before us and took it?"

I bent down to look under the desk. "No. There's no Internet connection here. I think he must have used his cell phone to get and send messages. Did you find one in his pockets?"

"No, but I'll ask the techs in case I just missed it."

"And where are his skates, Mort?"

"Huh?"

"We've been all through his apartment, and I haven't seen a single pair of ice skates. In fact, other than the three costumes hanging in his closet and that album you're holding, there's nothing here to indicate Alexei was a world-class figure skater. Where are his skates? I heard him say he never lets them out of his sight."

"They're probably still at the rink. They have a locker room."

"Maybe," I said. "We can look for them there later. But I

still wonder why he wouldn't keep at least one pair here in his apartment."

"Coffee, Mrs. F.?" Mort asked once we were settled back at police headquarters. "Gladys ordered some Sumatra this time. It's strong, but I like it."

"No, thanks, Mort, but you go ahead."

Mort left me with the letters while he went to get himself a mug of coffee. He returned with a plate of cookies as well. "Maureen baked these to bring to the doc's, but she burned them," he said, setting the plate on his desk. "She scraped off the black parts. They're not bad. I told her they taste like barbecued cookies."

"Thanks, Mort, but I think I'll pass."

We slipped on latex gloves to prevent our fingerprints from contaminating the papers, and spent the next thirty minutes reading Alexei's fan mail. There were a few letters from children starting skating, but more from older admirers, almost all female, and several bearing Cabot Cove return addresses.

"This one has a Cabot Cove postmark," I said, slitting an unopened envelope with a dull knife Mort used as a letter opener, "but no return address. It also isn't signed, but I think I know the reason."

"Why are you frowning?" Mort asked.

"Evidently not all his mail is from admirers," I said, scanning the message, which was scrawled in black crayon on the back of a slip of paper torn off a pad of business forms. At the bottom of the form, it said: "Thank you for your business." The note on the reverse was not as warm. I read it aloud: "'I've told you before. Keep your Commie hands off Christine Allen. She's too good for you. Manhandle her again and you'll live to regret it.'"

I looked up at Mort. "'You'll live to regret it,'" I repeated. "Sounds like a threat to me."

"From Cabot Cove?"

"Yes."

"Better keep that one as evidence." He held open the plastic bag, and I dropped the message and envelope inside.

The phone rang, and Mort leaned over to see who was calling. "It's the doc," he said, pushing a button to turn on the speakerphone. "Hey, Doc. Mrs. F. and I were just talking about you. How was that stew?" He winked at me.

"Best I've ever made, if I say so myself."

"Nicely aged, huh?"

"If you ask politely, I'll let you have some leftovers. It's supposed to be better on the second day."

"Sure you're not conducting a laboratory experiment in your refrigerator? Seems I heard that old stew is the perfect medium for bacteria."

"I'm still alive, aren't I? And considering some of the meals I've been served in your house, that says a lot."

"That's enough, gentlemen," I said. "Was there a reason for your call, Seth?"

"Yeah, Doc. Got anything new?"

"Mebbe," Seth said. "Thought you'd want to know that Olshansky's death was definitely a drowning."

"That's kind of the way I had it figured," Mort said, wincing.

"Does that mean the circumstances surrounding his death are still inconclusive, Seth?" I asked.

"Not exactly."

"What do you mean?"

"His fingers and hands. I paid particular attention after you mentioned them, Jessica. There were cuts on the bottom of his fingers, consistent with him pushing up on the grating."

"So the grating was down when he was in the pit?" Mort put in.

"That appears to be the case."

"Anything else?"

"Ayuh. The tops of his fingers were badly bruised, the little ones crushed."

"How would that happen if he's pressing up from below with his palms?" Mort asked.

"He could have pushed his fingers between the gaps in the metal to get a better grip on the panel," I replied. "Seth, do you think someone might have stomped on his fingers as he was trying to lift the grating up from underneath?"

"That would be a reasonable explanation for the injuries. I had the staff take additional photos before I sent in tissue samples from the fingers, and also from the cut on his nose that you noticed. I'll have the specimens examined to determine if there's microscopic evidence of metal or other fragments."

"Can you give me a preliminary report, Doc?" Mort asked.

"What the devil do you think I'm doing right now?"

Mort's eyes sought the ceiling, and he shook his head.

"Okay, okay. Don't get your knickers in a twist. It's just that I need the report in writing for it to be official. I got a lot of people asking."

"I'll dictate it before I leave here and have the hospital's Medical Records send it over to you."

"That'll be fine, Doc. Thanks for letting us know."

I heard Seth harrumph. "Jessica?"

"Yes, Seth?"

"Do you think I should dump out the rest of the dish?"

"I know you hate to see food go to waste, Seth, and so do I. But I wouldn't want you to get sick. Yes, I think you should discard the stew."

"Well, I suppose I'll trust your judgment, which I might add has not been especially solid lately."

After that comment, he disconnected the call.

Chapter Fifteen

The first forty-eight hours following the announcement of Alexei's death had been a madhouse, with camera crews from national networks as well as local stations sending their satellite trucks into town, their cameras capturing reporters posing in front of the Cabot Cove Ice Arena and waxing poetic about the skater, or taking panning shots of the growing mound of flowers in tribute to Alexei that littered the snow outside the main entrance.

Press had camped out in front of the Allen house demanding a statement from Christine, who had gone into seclusion. Mr. Allen had negotiated a single pool interview in which he allowed her to make one short, tearful statement as multiple cameras clicked furiously around her. Then, with an arm protectively around his daughter's shoulders, he escorted her back into the house, drew the blinds, and waited for the press to melt away. Unfortunately, like the snow, the media lingered in hopes of snatching a candid shot of Alexei's partner that no one else would have.

The Russian news crew was everywhere in town, having hired a Russian-speaking assistant professor of political science from the University of Maine at Orono to act as translator. They managed to learn about the screws that had been strewn on the ice and other unfortunate incidents that had occurred at the rink, and word around town was that they had cobbled together a story of a vast Western conspiracy to keep Alexei from returning to Russia, and at the same time to ensure he would never again be the skater that he once was.

It seemed that by now everyone in town had learned of Alexei's death, and theories ran rampant. I hadn't been back to the arena since Friday, and headed there to see what the staff was saying. It took a while because there was a line of cars snaking in and out of the parking lot as if the building were a drive-by tourist attraction.

Inside, I was surprised to find the place almost empty. A steely-eyed Marisa Brown sat behind the reception desk holding a copy of the *Cabot Cove Gazette*, whose front page featured a photograph of a smiling Alexei Olshansky beneath the headline TRAGIC ACCIDENT ENDS OLYMPIC DREAMS. Under his head shot were two other photos, one of Christine Allen, the other of Alexei's former partner Irina Bednikova.

"Look at that," Marisa said hotly. "Irina's all dressed in black like she knew she was going to have to attend a funeral."

The photo had been taken at Blueberry Hill Inn, the bed-and-breakfast owned by my friends Craig and Jill Thomas. Indeed, Irina was draped head to toe in black; the only spot of light was her tiny white dog, Pravda, into whose furry head she'd buried her face. I was sorry that Irina's first notification about Alexei's death had come from the press, who, despite her bodyguards, mobbed her in front of the inn until Jill came out to chastise them and take a sobbing Irina inside.

It was impossible to reach everyone who needed to know about Alexei before information about his death was broadcast. Fortunately, the State Department had alerted our ambassador in Russia, who personally brought the sad news about her only son to his mother. What a terrible task that must be. I was thankful that a seasoned diplomat might know how to deliver the harsh blow without inflicting more pain than necessary.

Eldridge Coddington had insisted that Mort allow him to reopen the rink after two days, and Mort had acquiesced with the stipulation that the Zamboni garage remain off-limits. Just to make sure, he sent two of his deputies to keep curiosity seekers out of the crime scene, but he needn't have bothered. The hockey rink was dark, and only a few of the regular customers circled the other ice.

Mort had called in Maine's state police to arrange for the services of its dive team to examine the pit before it was pumped out. While he hadn't made a public announcement, he was convinced that what we had was a murder, and the dive team was among the forensic specialists needed to comb the Zamboni garage for clues. Who knew what could be sitting six feet below the surface? Mort feared that letting the water out could disturb a crucial piece of evidence, perhaps even see it disappear down the drain along with the water.

"Why do you think she came here, Mrs. Fletcher?" Marisa asked, pointing to Irina Bednikova's picture.

"To try to lure Alexei back to Russia, so she could be his pairs partner again."

"I wish she'd succeeded," she said. "Then we wouldn't have this mess. People keep asking me questions, taking pictures, leaving flowers, yak, yak, yak, everything Alexei. That's all I hear. I'm sick of it. Sick of *him*." She stopped and looked around, realizing someone might misinterpret what she was saying, but no one else was nearby.

"Look, I'm sorry he's dead. Really. I know I said I didn't like him, but I'm sorry he died. He was pretty young, too. I never knew anyone that young who died before. It's really weird. I just saw him on Friday, and now he's never coming back again. Am I awful that I didn't like him? Why couldn't he have been nicer? I never said anything bad about him, at least not to his face."

Lyla, who had been listening in on our conversation, took Marisa by the shoulders and turned her around. "I think you need to take a break," she said. "Go lie down on the sofa in my office."

"I'm not tired."

"Go! I don't want to see you for ten minutes."

"Do you have a minute to talk?" I asked Lyla when Marisa had closed the door to the coach's office.

"I guess so. I've never seen this place so empty. There's

barely anyone here skating, even though the parking lot is full." She shook her head. "They're all outside watching the press or waiting for something to happen."

"That's just a temporary novelty," I said. "The skaters will come back."

She glanced at the door and rubbed the back of her neck. "Not if they're afraid to come inside where someone died. They'd better get over that fast or we'll go out of business again."

"Lyla, may I ask you a few questions about Alexei?"

"Why not? Everyone else has."

"Last week, when the Russian camera crew was here, why did Alexei get so angry when the reporter brought up his former partner?"

"They didn't part on good terms. Irina's been bad-mouthing him ever since. It's been all over the Internet and on the skating blogs. She was a star at home, the center of attention, and now she's not. Instead of the talk dying down as it usually would, she continued to fuel the fire."

"What did she say?"

"There was nothing attributed directly to her, but I knew Irina was behind all those nasty comments being passed around about Chris."

"What kind of comments?"

"At first, there were ugly rumors circulating that if Chris's father hadn't paid off Alexei, she couldn't have attracted a partner on her own, that she's not good enough. It's just not true. Then the rumors said Alexei was getting back together with Irina, and Chris was begging him to stay."

"It all sounds very dramatic, like a daytime soap opera."

"You're not far off. The other day, someone wrote that the only reason Chris and her father moved East was to get away from a stalker. Another blogger said her father was divorcing her mother so she wouldn't stand in the way of Chris's career. Chris was very upset by that one. I don't know where they get these things." Lyla linked her hands behind her neck, looked down, and sighed. "Anyway, these kinds of rumors happen all the time. Skating is a tight community; there's a lot of gossip, jealousy, and backbiting. But it can be devastating when you're the victim of it. Plus, it wasn't very good publicity for Alexei and Chris starting out together."

"So Brian Devlin allowed the Russians to film to give them a positive story to cover."

"That was the idea. In Russia, Irina and Alexei were followed by paparazzi. They were a very volatile couple, always arguing in public, angry at each other, constantly in the press. Sometimes that could translate into passion on the ice. The judges love to see that. But it makes a lot of work for the coach. Their last coach spent half his time trying to get them to skate without killing each other."

"Doesn't sound as if it makes for efficient practices," I said.

"It sure doesn't. Brian had a lot of reservations about bringing Alexei over. But Mr. Allen was convinced he was the right partner for Chris. Heaven only knows why. The combination of a black skater with a white skater means that you're taking a chance."

"Why is that? Do you think some judges would have been prejudiced against them?"

"Judges are human beings. The scoring system in competitions has always been controversial. You're bound to find some prejudiced judges. Why stack the deck against the pair to begin with?"

"It didn't seem to hurt a German pair who were successful," I said. "They were an interracial couple, and they went on to win the world championship."

Lyla sighed. "There are always exceptions."

"Maybe Chris and Alexei would have been an exception, too," I said.

"We'll never know now."

I left Lyla at the desk and wandered past the rows of fifty-cent lockers toward the concession stand, where Joe the security guard was getting a cup of coffee. I looked around. Mort and I hadn't found Alexei's skates in his apartment. They must be somewhere here at the rink. Surely, the staff and elite-caliber skaters like Alexei and Christine wouldn't be expected to put in quarters in order to have a place to stash their possessions.

"Hi, Mrs. Fletcher. Feeling better?" Joe asked when I came up to him.

"Oh, yes, much." I thanked him again for having driven me to the ER and asked where the skaters in training had lockers.

"Behind the new hockey locker room," he replied. "Used to be the old hockey locker room. All the coaching staff and special students have lockers back there, if they want to use them. Most don't bother."

I thanked Joe and pulled out my cell phone, dialing Mort's number as I walked toward the new area. I told him about the special locker room.

"See if you can find his locker. I'll be there in a little while," he said. "I'm on the phone with the leader of the dive team."

Walking past the hockey locker room, I came upon a door marked STAFF. It was locked. Retracing my steps to the front desk, I caught Lyla as she was donning her jacket and gloves.

"Why do you need to see Alexei's locker?" she asked when I requested the key to the staff area.

"The sheriff is gathering his personal effects to send home to his family," I said. It wasn't entirely untrue; I didn't want to raise any eyebrows if I admitted that Alexei's possessions might yield some understanding of his death.

"I don't ever use those lockers since I have an office here, but Marisa has a master key," she said.

"Wonderful," I said.

"Stay here. I'll get it for you."

She returned a few minutes later with the key on an oversized key ring. "Return it to Marisa when you're done," she said.

When I unlocked the door marked STAFF, I found myself in a small anteroom that had two doors leading from it into separate areas labeled MEN and WOMEN. Obviously, Alexei's locker would be in the section reserved for men—which posed a question for me. Did I dare enter that area and perhaps embarrass myself, not to mention whoever might be there, possibly undressed? I put my ear to the door and focused my hearing on the other side. Nothing. I took a breath, knocked on the door, waited a moment, then put my hand on the brass plate and pushed it open. The hinges squealed, but I had hesitated for nothing. The room was empty. It was much smaller than I anticipated, and pretty run-down. Clearly, this was an area of the ice arena that Coddington hadn't gotten around to renovating. Eldridge had spent his money on places the public would see but had held back when it came to staff accommodations and, according to Devlin's complaints, behind-the-scenes amenities for his students.

A row of lockers was on my left. Scarred wooden benches ran their length. At the far end was a door that led to the showers. I listened intently again. No sound of running water. I peeked in. The shower section had been added when the new hockey locker room had been built. The tiles were gleaming; it looked as if it had never been used.

I walked back along the lockers and read names on pieces of white tape affixed to the doors. Most of the lockers were open, but a few weren't. I found what I was looking for. The black writing on the tape said *AO*, which had to be the initials for Alexei Olshansky. An old padlock was inserted through the hole in a flange on the door that lined up with an identical one on the locker. Where was the key? Mort and I hadn't found any keys in our cursory search of Alexei's apartment. Could the key be at the bottom of the pit?

I turned at the sound of a squeak to see Mort Metzger coming into the room.

"Did you get the report from the dive team?" I asked.

"Yeah. We won't get forensics on the trace evidence back for a while, but they found his cell phone, his gold chain, and his keys. I asked to get a list of the last calls he made. That should come through fairly quickly and give us some leads to follow," he said. "Which one of these is his locker?"

"It's right here," I replied, "but it's padlocked."

"No problem. I think I've got a bolt cutter in the trunk of my cruiser."

Mort returned moments later. "Someone walked away with my bolt cutter, but these should do the job." He held up a screwdriver and a hammer. Positioning the blade near the shank of the lock, he gave the top of the screwdriver a few good whacks with the hammer. Seconds later, he placed the open padlock on the bench and pulled open the door to Alexei's locker.

"With those skills, you could have been a first-rate safe-cracker," I said.

"Sometimes it's the simplest tools that are the most efficient," he replied. "Let's see what we got."

Alexei's apartment had been relatively neat, but his locker was a lot messier, and I had a hunch it was a more accurate reflection of the way he usually lived. Workout clothing, emitting the expected scent of having been worn during strenuous exercise, hung from hooks on either side of the narrow, metal closet. A towel taken from a prominent hotel was balled up on the shelf above. As Mort pulled out each item and dropped it into an evidence bag, I made a note of it on a pad of paper.

There was a pair of skates in a plastic skate carrier on the floor of the locker. Tossed in on top of the carrier were envelopes and scraps of paper. Mort opened a second evidence bag, this one considerably smaller than the one that held Alexei's clothes. We scanned what was written on the papers before Mort deposited them in the bag. Some were postmarked Moscow and written in Russian, probably letters from his mother or friends back home. I was about to give up hope of finding anything helpful when the final slip of paper fell out of Mort's hand and landed at my feet. Without picking it up, I read it:

garage—5:30—friday

The day he died, and the approximate time of death according to Seth's initial estimate.

"Do you think that's his handwriting?" Mort said as he added the note to the evidence bag.

"I don't know, but it should be easy to verify," I said. "The more difficult question to answer is: Who was he meeting?"

"Maybe that turkey with the gun Jeremy found sitting on the Zamboni. He said someone had pointed him out as the guy who was interested in buying the rink."

"Did you call Eve to find out if it might have been her client?"

Mort nodded. "I left a message on her guy's answering machine, but he hasn't returned my call yet. You think he's still in town?"

"Probably not, especially if he's guilty," I said.

"I don't know, Mrs. F. You never can tell what crazy people will do. I'm going to run these back to the station. Need t anywhere?"

"No, thank you. I think I'll poke around a little longer, if you don't mind."

"Suit yourself. Thanks for the call about these," he said, hefting the two bags. "Worse comes to worst, they'll go back home to his mother."

Mort took the evidence bags out to his cruiser while I returned the staff locker room master key to Marisa and bought myself a hot chocolate at the concession stand. Sipping the sweet drink, I contemplated the myriad questions floating around my mind.

Why had Alexei changed his mind about skating Friday afternoon? And whom had he met in the Zamboni garage, a place he rarely if ever visited before his death? The last slip of paper we'd found indicated that he'd arranged to meet someone there late in the afternoon on that fateful day. Was it Eve's client Harvey Gemell? And if so, why would Gemell want to kill Alexei? How would he have gained by the skater's death? *What would anyone have gained by killing Alexei?*

The hot chocolate provided a welcome calm. But I had some questions for Eldridge Coddington. I left the table and main hall and climbed the stairs to the second floor, pausing at the windows overlooking the hockey rink, which was hosting lessons on one end of the ice and hockey-stop drills on the other.

The gym was locked, as was the dance studio Brian Devlin had sneered at the first time I'd wandered upstairs. But Eldridge Coddington's office door was ajar. I heard his end of a conversation but couldn't tell if he was on the telephone or talking with someone in person.

"I swear you're setting me up, but I've half a mind to sell it to you so you can reap the lawsuit along with all the other headaches this place has been giving me."

I heard a soft murmur; he had someone with him.

"Why does he want it? That's what I want to know. Nothing but one crisis after another. The utility cost is sky-high. When the temperature outside drops, I keep the windows open overnight so I don't have to pay to keep the ice frozen. Does he have any idea what it takes to run a business like this?"

Another murmur.

"You tell 'im he'd better come talk to me directly. I don't want the mayor and town council falling down on me like a brick wall if he wants to raze the place and build another shopping center. I have to live in this town. What's that? No, you can't stand in for him. You're not going to own the place once he puts down the money, are you? You let me take the measure of the man, and then I'll think about it. But that's all I'll do. Don't take this as a commitment. Now let me get back to work."

Someone opened the door, and I heard a voice I recognized. "You won't be sorry, Eldridge. I so appreciate your seeing me today, especially after this Grand Guignol."

"What the heck's that?"

"Horror show."

"Certainly is. Can't believe he sent you to see me in the wake of it," Coddington muttered. "The man must have a stone stomach."

"*Au contraire, monsieur*. He is *très sympathique*."

"For the love of Harry, woman, speak English."

"I'll call you as soon as I hear from him."

Eve Simpson stepped into the hall and closed Coddington's door behind her.

"Hello, Eve," I said.

"Oh, Jessica, what a surprise." She smoothed down the front of her wool skirt and looped her handbag over her arm. "Are you here to talk to Eldridge?"

"I thought I'd stop in and say hello."

"Terrible news about Alexei," she said. "So *tragique*, even though Loretta told me she'd heard he wasn't a very pleasant young man. Well, I have to get back to the office. Nice running into you."

"Wait, Eve," I said, taking hold of her arm as she tried to brush past me. "Is Harvey Gemell the only person interested in buying the ice arena?"

"So far as I know. Eldridge never mentioned anyone else. Oh, dear, you haven't heard something I don't know, have you?"

"Was Gemell here on Friday?"

Eve smoothed her hair. "I'm not certain. I don't keep track of his whereabouts."

"Come on, Eve. I saw you escorting a man around the rink last week. Wasn't that Gemell?"

"I thought that was you on the ice. Are you feeling all right, Jessica?"

"Perfectly fine, Eve. Was that Gemell you were with?"

"Yes. Nice looking, isn't he?"

"That was Wednesday. Was he still in town Friday afternoon?"

Eve squirmed a bit. "Really, Jessica—"

"Please, Eve. It's important."

"Probably not, but I actually don't know. He wasn't supposed to be. He told me he was going to leave on Friday morning. He doesn't know anyone else in Cabot Cove. There wasn't any reason for him to stay."

"So you think he's back in Connecticut now?"

"Oh, I'm sure he is. I spoke with him this morning."

"Mort would like to speak with him. Would you ask him to call the sheriff's office?"

"Why does he want to talk to Harvey?"

"Mort needs to know if Harvey was at the rink on Friday, and if he was, if he noticed anything out of the ordinary."

"All right. He should be calling me later today. I don't want to call and have him think I'm badgering him. You know how men can be. I'll give him your message."

"Thanks, Eve. Oh, by the way. Do you know whether Mr. Gemell carries a weapon?"

"What?"

"A weapon. A handgun."

"That's ridiculous. Sometimes you ask the oddest questions. *Ciao*, Jessica."

I waited for her to reach the staircase and disappear from view, then knocked on Coddington's door.

"What is it now?" his gruff voice sounded through the wooden panel.

I opened it. "May I come in?" I asked.

Coddington shook his head. "May as well. Everyone is conspiring to keep me from working today. I should go home, put my feet up, and watch the Bruins lose another game instead of messing around in here. Can't be any worse for my indigestion than sticking to this desk."

"Eldridge, are you really ready to sell this arena?

He gave a big sigh. "I'll give it to you, Jessica. At least you come right out and ask. No pussyfooting around. That's what everyone in this town wants to know, and not a spleeny one of them has had the nerve to put the question to me directly. Why not?" His voice rose. "Am I such an ogre?" He tapped his fingers on the arm of the chair. "Bunch of gorbies trying to steal my dinner."

"Who, Eldridge?"

"Those real estate people."

"You mean Eve Simpson?"

"Her and her greedy boyfriend. Thinks if she reminds me of the string of accidents been happening here, I'll throw up my hands and chuck it all. Like I haven't hit a skid of bad luck before. Underestimate me. They all do. I see what's happening here."

"I'm glad to hear you say that, Eldridge, because—"

"Course, I never had anyone die here before," he said, interrupting me. "But he was hanging around in an unauthorized area, now, wasn't he? The foolish tourist. I told Jeremy to find a lock for that grate. Doesn't have to be anything special. We must have dozens of them in some drawer that we pulled off the old lockers. Don't need to use the pit anyway. Just plow the stuff out into the parking lot is the way I'd do it."

"Then why don't you do it?"

"We're too close to the reservoir is why. Town decided

the ice from the rinks might flow downhill and pollute the water, so we had to connect to county sewers. Cost me a pretty penny. But what choice do we have now with the cops locking up the garage?" He chuckled. "There's so much snow out in the parking lot, the town'll never know if we add to it."

"Eldridge, were you here anytime on Friday?"

"Thought you might get around to asking that. Friday is the day I visit my wife's cousin in the Waterview nursing home, outside Portland." He stared off, thinking quietly for a moment. "Bella was real close to her cousin Phoebe and asked me to look after her. I've been as faithful to her as I was to my Bella. Never miss a Friday. Bring her a coupla Charlene Sassi's almond pastries. She likes that."

"What do you think will happen to the figure skating program without your star attraction?"

"Not up to me. That's Devlin's problem. He'll have to get another pair in here or maybe play it safe and coach singles instead. But I'll wait to install all those fancy fripperies he wants, see if he can still make a go of the program."

"Have you spoken with him about it?"

"Haven't even seen the man since last week. Not my favorite fellow; that's for certain."

"How did you happen to find him?"

"He came on Allen's recommendation. He wanted him. Wanted to get his daughter out of San Francisco. Some trouble there."

"How did Mr. Allen find *you*?"

"I advertised. Put the word out in one of those skating logs or whatchacallit—Jeremy did that for me. Said that we had ice and wanted to expand the program. Allen calls me up and we made a deal."

"Is he your partner in the rink now?"

"We're talking." A little smile played around his lips. "We'll see how it goes. I might get ready to retire some day. Didn't tell that to Eve Simpson, though. Don't want to get her hopes up."

By the time I got downstairs again, Lyla had left. "She got hit with a puck, you know," Marisa said. "Those things are hard as rocks. She fixed her hair so you can't see the bruise, but she started looking peak-ed, turned a bit green, and said she had to go home. Mr. Devlin drove her."

"Is he coming back after he takes her home?"

"Didn't say."

A woman carrying a big flower arrangement approached the desk. "These are in memory of Alexei Olshansky," she said. "Can I leave them here?"

Marisa looked at me as if to say, *I told you so.* "We have two baskets here already," she said to the woman. "Wouldn't you rather enjoy those flowers at home where they'll remind you of him?"

"I can't. My husband will start asking questions. Please let me leave them here." She started to tear up.

"Sure, sure," Marisa said. "Just push over that basket to the right."

After the woman had left, Marisa confided to me, "You should see Lyla's office. Her desk is covered with flowers."

I wanted to ask Marisa some questions, but the phone rang and I could tell by her end of the conversation that she was going to be talking for a while. I buttoned up my jacket, pulled on my gloves, and walked outside to look at the makeshift memorial that was filling the space at the foot of the stairs into the building. Several people took pictures of those admiring the flowers, most of which had been pushed into the snow that had piled up when the front stoop was shoveled clear. Some of the mourners had poked holes in the snow so the flowers stood up as if they were in individual vases, making the area look like a florist's display. Ribbons around the stems fluttered in the breeze, and there were condolence cards either pressed into the snow next to the flowers or scattered at the base of the pile.

One flower caught my eye. It had been sprayed with black paint, as had the back of the note that was attached to it, a note that looked like it had been torn out of a store's order pad. I plucked it from the flower and turned it over. The message was written in black crayon:

Happy you're dead, you Commie creep.

Chapter Sixteen

"What do you think, Mrs. F.? Looks like the same writer to me," Mort said when I'd delivered both the note, and the flower it had been wrapped around, to the sheriff's office.

"I agree," I said, "and both notes are written in black crayon on the same type of paper."

Mort slipped the new note into yet another evidence bag and clipped it to the one containing the message we'd found among the fan letters in Alexei's apartment. "I think it might be time to find out if there are any fingerprints, other than ours, on those papers," he said.

I knew that any prints the lab came up with would be run through Maine's Bureau of Identification. If no match was found, they could be sent to the FBI's Integrated Automated Fingerprint Identification System, or IAFIS. Of course, if the writer of these two notes had never committed a crime, or had his or her fingerprints taken for any other reason, IAFIS wouldn't be of any help.

"We're probably talking about a guy here, don't you think?" Mort asked.

"It seems reasonable, but I wouldn't rule anything out just yet," I said. "A handwriting analyst could give us a better idea."

"A handwriting analyst would be perfect," he said, "but that service will have to be provided by the state police, or maybe the Feds. I don't have the resources to bring in experts."

"Can you put in a request to one of those agencies for a handwriting expert?"

"Sure, but it'll take a while. In the meantime I've got to keep the investigation moving."

"With good, old-fashioned legwork?"

"Right."

"It's been successful before," I said, smiling. "Have you interviewed Irina Bednikova yet?"

"Was about to go out to Blueberry Hill Inn before you stopped by."

"Do you mind if I tag along?"

"I don't," Mort said, "but I don't know how she'll react. After all, it's an official call."

"I'll understand if you don't want me there, but I've met her before. She might be more forthcoming with a familiar face nearby."

Mort weighed my argument. "She might. Sure. Let's go."

The snow on the front lawn of the Blueberry Hill Inn had been trampled into slush by reporters and photographers, spoiling the usually picturesque scene the old Victorian home presented. Although the first wave of press excitement had subsided, there still were several people camped out in vans across the street waiting to capture a comment or candid picture of the three Russians who were staying there.

"Hey, Sheriff Metzger, what's happening?" a reporter from a Bangor TV station yelled out as Mort and I exited his car.

A couple of other members of the media suddenly surrounded us. Mort tried to wave them off, but they were persistent. He held up his hand and said, "I don't have any statement to make at this time. When I have something to report, I'll hold a news conference."

"What's Mrs. Fletcher doing here with you?" a reporter asked.

"She's been involved with this from the beginning and has been very helpful. That's all I have to say for now. Excuse us."

Jill and Craig Thomas came through the front door as we stepped up onto the porch. "Happy you're here, Sheriff," Craig said. "These media vultures are driving us crazy."

"They're relentless," said Jill.

"I don't envy you," I said as Craig and Jill led us into their home, which also functioned as one of Cabot Cove's nicest inns.

"We're here to talk to Ms. Bednikova," Mort said.

"So you said when you called," Craig acknowledged. "We told her you were coming. She didn't seem happy about it, but I'm sure she realizes that she doesn't have a choice."

A man appeared from the kitchen. He was short and slender and wore a brown tweed jacket and a pale green shirt over a brown turtleneck.

"This is Professor Simmons," Craig said. "One of the Russian TV crews has hired him as a translator. He's staying with us."

We shook the professor's hand and asked if he would be willing to serve the same function for us. While Irina spoke some English, emotions might overwhelm her and make it more difficult for her to express herself. Allowing her to answer questions in her native language would help Mort's interview go more smoothly. Not only that, but it might keep Irina from falling back on her limited English to avoid answering those difficult questions that she may have thought were too personal or cast her in a bad light.

"I'm happy to be of service," the professor said pleasantly. "I'll do anything I can to help. Dreadful what happened to Mr. Olshansky. I understand he was a wonderful figure skater with a great future."

"He was a very talented athlete," I said. "It's always heartbreaking when a young person's life is prematurely cut short."

"I'll go get Irina," Jill said and disappeared up the stairs.

I wondered if Ms. Bednikova would be accompanied by her two bodyguards. She never seemed to go anywhere without them. I didn't have to wait long to find out. They came lumbering down the stairs followed by their ward, who was dressed in a close-fitting silver metallic pants suit.

She descended the stairs like a movie star in an old Busby Berkeley musical motion picture, her dog, Pravda, wearing a matching doggie coat, nestled in her arms.

"Good afternoon," Mort said.

"Good afternoon," she responded in a voice dripping with tragedy. She held Pravda with one arm as she dabbed at the corner of one eye with a hankie in her free hand, although I didn't see any trace of tears.

"This is Mrs. Fletcher," Mort said. "She's working with me on the investigation of Mr. Olshansky's death."

"We've met," I said.

Irina looked as though she was about to collapse at the mention of Alexei's name, and sagged against her brother, Maxim. I wondered whether the second guard was also a relative.

"I know this must be tough on you, ma'am, but I have to ask you some questions," Mort said.

"Why don't we all go in the living room," Jill suggested. "You'll be more comfortable there."

I have to admit that the presence of the two large Russian men was unsettling. While they were humorless, their broad faces set in a perpetual scowl, they appeared to be making an attempt to fit in with their surroundings. They were dressed in American sports clothes. Each wore a long-sleeved polo shirt, their broad shoulders straining the seams. Their slacks were khaki, and on their feet were the kind of caramel-colored hiking boots I knew were popular with the students at Cabot Cove High School. Irina sat demurely in the center of a green and yellow floral-pattern couch, the men flanking her. She seemed almost lost in the midst of their bulk. Mort and I took chairs across a burl-wood coffee table that Craig had created from a tree that had fallen on his property during a storm. Professor Sim-mons stood at the end of the couch ready to provide trans-lations should the need arise.

Mort held a clipboard on his lap and wrote down each of their names. The second bodyguard was called Boris Abelev. He handed Mort a business card. I looked over to see what it said, but it was written in Cyrillic script, the Russian alphabet. Mort tucked it in his pocket.

"I suppose we should start with some basics," the sheriff said. "I need to know the whereabouts of all three of you on the Friday that Mr. Olshansky died."

Irina looked left and right at her protectors, her wide eyes and raised eyebrows indicating that she didn't under-stand the question.

"Where were you the day he died?" Mort put it more simply.

The professor translated for her.

"What day this was?" she asked in her thick Russian accent.

"Last Friday," Mort said.

She wrinkled her face as though trying to remember. Fi-nally, she said, "I was here this day. No, I shop, too. I buy things for Irina." She held out a hand and admired her long fingernails, which had little flowers painted on them.

"What about later in the day?" Mort continued. "Say, be-tween four in the afternoon and eight that evening?"

Again, her expression was exaggerated.

I turned to Craig Thomas. "Do you recall whether Ms. Bednikova was here during those hours last Friday?" I asked.

Craig shook his head. "Jill and I were in and out all day last Friday. I'm afraid I have no idea what Ms. Bednikova was doing."

Irina's brother spoke up. "Irina with us all day," Maxim said in what sounded more like a growl.

Mort ignored him and asked Irina, "Did you spend time with Mr. Olshansky on Friday?"

Again, the question was translated for her.

"*Nyet*," she said firmly. "I try to see him but no find him. He is like little child in hiding game." She sniffled and dabbed at her eyes again with her hankie, then waved her hands in front of her face. "Now he is no more, my poor Alexei Nicolayevich Olshansky."

There was a pause while Irina composed herself; her tears didn't strike me as being especially genuine. After a few seconds had passed, I asked, "Would you please tell the sheriff why you came to Cabot Cove, Ms. Bednikova?"

Simmons translated.

"I come—I come to bring Alexei home to Russia where he belong. Why he did come to skate with American girl, who is not as good as Irina? He leaves alone his mother in Russia. She cries all the time to have him come home. He is Russian, not American. Russian skaters, we are the best in the world, I tell him before he go. Now he will come home as dead man."

"But we know you were at the ice rink on Friday evening," Mort said. "There are witnesses. Are you telling me you didn't see Olshansky anytime on Friday?"

Simmons's translation inspired a stream of infuriated Russian. "She says she hasn't seen Olshansky once since she arrived. She has been hunting for him without success."

"Ask these guys if the same is true for them."

"*Da!*" Maxim said, not waiting for the question in Russian. Boris simply nodded.

"We are together always," Irina added, throwing her hands up dramatically.

As Mort's questioning progressed, I silently grappled with a memory that slipped from my grasp. It was something I needed to follow up on. It had been nagging at me all day. I couldn't quite put my finger on it. It was there; yet it wasn't. Finally, it came to me just as Mort was preparing to wind down the session. It was a snippet of conversation that I'd overheard the previous week between Alexei and his coach. Devlin had referred to a scandal that involved Alexei back in Russia. But it was what Alexei had said in response that niggled at me, that the same could possibly be said about Devlin. What had he meant by that? Was there something in Devlin's background that he didn't want known? Could it have had a bearing on Alexei's death?

How much did anyone know about Brian Devlin aside from his reputation in the figure skating world? There had been nothing written about him since arriving in Cabot Cove that touched upon his personal life. He had mentioned during his talk to the chamber of commerce that he had been an army brat and had ended up at Nellis Air Force Base in Nevada. I also knew from the little I'd heard that he'd spent much of his professional career at a famous skating center in Hackensack, New Jersey. And word was that he never married.

Another fragment of thought came, went, and then returned. The newspaper clipping found in Alexei's apartment was about the death of a man in Colorado Springs. Why had Alexei elected to keep that particular clipping? We knew Alexei had spent time in Colorado Springs as a young boy. Another clipping we'd discovered in his apartment had shown him as a ten-year-old in the Broadmoor Skating Club's winter ice show.

Colorado Springs is another famous skating center. Was there a connection between Alexei and Devlin going back to Colorado Springs? It would be interesting to find out that they'd known each other before Mr. Allen had paid to bring Alexei to the states. I didn't know if it was so, but I intended to do some digging into the possibility of a linkage between those items at my first opportunity.

"Well, I don't have any more questions for these folks, Mrs. F.," Mort said. "What about you?"

"Irina, you told Evelyn Phillips that Alexei had a cousin in the United States whom he'd visited as a boy," I said.

"Do I know this Evelyn Phillips?"

"The newspaper editor, Mrs. Phillips. At the rink, last week."

"That is right," she said after the professor had translated my question. "He come here to States when little boy. He learn English here, but now—but now he speak no more English. He speak no Russian. He speak no nothing no more. My poor Alyoshenka. My poor Dasha." She threw herself on Boris and wept. This time the tears were real.

"Who is she talking about?" Mort asked Simmons.

"Alyoshenka is a Russian nickname for Alexei," the translator replied. "Dasha is a girl's nickname. I don't know who that is."

"Who is Dasha?" I asked Maxim while Irina and Boris consoled each other.

"The sister of Boris—Dariya. She is fiancée to Alexei."

"Fiancée?" I said.

"He promise marry to her," Boris shouted, banging a fist on the wooden table.

"Okay. Okay. Take it easy," Mort said. "Nothing to get excited about." He stood and announced, "Thanks for your time, Ms. Bednikova. Sorry to have upset you. I may have some more questions, so I suggest you not leave town until I say it's okay."

"We go when we want go," her brother said.

Mort stared him down and said, "No, you go when I say so. Understood?"

"We call embassy," Maxim said.

"That's your choice," Mort said. "Good-bye, Professor Simmons. Appreciate your time and help."

Members of the press camped on Jill and Craig's front steps fired a barrage of questions at us as we made our way to Mort's marked vehicle. He waved them off as he'd done when we'd arrived, then started the engine, and we drove away.

"Well, Mrs. F., what do you think?" he asked.

"It's hard to say, Mort. She certainly had ample reason to be angry at Alexei for abandoning her as a skating partner and coming here to the United States to skate with an American woman. Did you happen to notice the length of her fingernails?"

"Can't say that I did."

"Long and pointed," I said. "I'm thinking, of course, about that scratch on Alexei's nose. It could have been caused by a number of things, but I couldn't help thinking about it while watching her hands."

"I gotta say, I can't picture her pushing him into that freezing pit of water."

"Because she's a woman?" I asked.

"Yeah, I suppose so."

"It wouldn't take brute strength to push him in," I said.

"On the other hand, those two goons are plenty strong. They could easily have dumped Olshansky into the pit and held down the grate. If Alexei broke his promise to marry the one guy's sister, it could be a motive."

"I suppose it's possible, but an awful lot of engagements have been broken without resulting in violence," I said.

"I guess you have a point. Care to come back to the station house with me? We got a new coffeepot, makes much better brew."

"Thank you, no, Mort. I want to get home. I have some things to follow up on."

"About the case?"

"Yes."

I told him about Alexei's remark and my curiosity about Devlin's past.

"Might be interesting, Mrs. F., but I doubt if it has anything to do with his death here."

177

"You're probably right, Mort, but I think I'll follow up on it anyway."

"Keep me posted. I'm going to stop at Sassi's for some doughnuts. I'll drop you off on the way, unless—"

Back in my home office, sitting in front of my computer, my address book and atlas nearby, a fresh cinnamon bun from Sassi's Bakery on a plate, I picked up a pencil and wrote down the names of the people I wanted to research online. Alexei Olshansky topped the list, followed by Brian Devlin, Irina Bednikova, her two bodyguards, Boris's sister Dariya, William Allen, and his daughter Christine. I had confirmed with Charlene Sassi that Eldridge Coddington had indeed stopped by Friday morning for his usual almond pastries to bring to his late wife's cousin at the nursing home, so I left him off the list—for the moment.

I tapped the end of my pencil on the pad. Who else? What was the name of Eve Simpson's client again? Oh, yes, Harvey Gemell. At the bottom of the list I added Deval Holdings. That was from the clipping we'd found in Alexei's apartment. It was the name of the company in Colorado Springs headed by the man who'd died in his speeding Alfa Romeo.

Chapter Seventeen

I've been blessed in many ways, including having had the opportunity to travel extensively. Not only has this allowed me to experience many wonderful places, but it's also brought me into contact with a wide variety of people from all walks of life. Of course, being the author of mystery novels has meant spending a considerable amount of time with law enforcement. As every reader of murder mysteries knows, it's imperative that an author be as accurate as possible when it comes to depicting police procedures. The same holds true for novels involving the legal system. Not only have I thoroughly enjoyed spending time with men and women who devote their careers to keeping society safe, but also I find that their insight and willingness to share their knowledge is refreshing and extremely helpful.

I reviewed my list. In addition to people who had been in Cabot Cove when Alexei was killed, I added the names of contacts to call in various parts of the country. It turned out to be a fairly lengthy list, and I was happy to settle in the peace and quiet of my home office and get started.

The first thing I did was to access Google and look up the name of the company headed by the man who had died in the automobile crash years ago. There wasn't a lot of information, but what I did discover was a sad story. The alleged suicide victim, Paul Valery, had been on the receiving end of numerous lawsuits from investors in his company and had been at the helm of the firm when it closed its doors, leaving them with no way to recover their money. Most of that same information had been in the brief obituary Alexei had saved and kept in his album.

One article I found went into greater depth as to why Deval Holdings had gone under. It claimed that Valery had been running what amounted to a Ponzi scheme, paying off early investors with money contributed by latecomers, who ended up with nothing when it was found there were no legitimate profits to distribute. Valery denied the allegations, but a prosecutor believed he had enough to go forward and was preparing a variety of charges against him, including fraud. Apparently Valery couldn't face the prospect of being convicted and going to jail. He chose a different way out.

I found it interesting that Valery had been born in the former Soviet Union. Was this man related to Alexei? Was he the cousin Alexei had been visiting in Colorado Springs as a young boy? There was no one to ask because both men were dead.

The clipping in Alexei's apartment had mentioned few survivors, but among them was Valery's son, who had been in business with his father. His name was Peter. I did a search for Peter Valery and found that he'd moved from Colorado Springs to Danbury, Connecticut, where he'd gone to work for a nonprofit organization, All-for-One. I looked up the phone number for that organization, dialed it, and asked the woman who answered to be connected to Peter Valery. He came on the line a minute later.

"You don't know me, Mr. Valery," I said. "My name is Jessica Fletcher. I'm calling from Cabot Cove, Maine."

"The mystery writer?"

"Yes. I'm hoping you can help me with some information. We've had an unfortunate death here in Cabot Cove. It involved a well-known Russian figure skater."

"Oh, yeah. I saw something in the papers," he said. "Are you writing a book about it? I don't know what kind of help I can be."

"Oh, no, I'm not asking about that. Actually, my interest is in your late father and whether he might have had some relationship with the victim, Alexei Olshansky, when he was a youngster visiting the United States and skating in Colorado Springs."

His tone up until this point had been friendly and open. Now I sensed a tightening in his voice. "Just because I come from Colorado Springs doesn't mean I'm associated with figure skating," he said coldly. "My father never knew anyone like that, Mrs. Fletcher."

"I can certainly understand that," I said, "considering the age difference. It never would have occurred to me to call you about this except that Alexei kept a newspaper obituary about your father's death. Naturally, I wondered why he might have done that if he didn't know your father. The

obituary was one of only a few things he had in his posses-
sion. I found that interesting, if not strange."

He paused for what seemed a long time before saying,
"Let me be honest with you, Mrs. Fletcher. I have absolutely
no interest in figure skating. As a matter of fact, I want nothing to do with anyone involved with that so-called sport."

I hadn't expected such a vehemently negative comment.

"Might I ask why that is, Mr. Valery?"

"It's a long story and not a very pleasant one."

"I certainly don't mean to drag up unpleasant memories,
sir, but Alexei died under suspicious circumstances. While
the authorities here in Cabot Cove haven't made an official
statement, I have no doubt that he was murdered."

My blunt declaration created another pause in our conversation. He broke it by saying, "He was being coached by
Brian Devlin, wasn't he?"

"That's right," I said. "Do you know if Mr. Devlin spent a
period of time in Colorado Springs? Might your father have
known him?"

I didn't expect his answer.

"Mrs. Fletcher," he said sternly, "you've just touched a
very sore spot with me."

"I'm terribly sorry," I said. "I certainly had no intention
of doing that. But since I've already introduced the subject,
I might as well ask why the name Brian Devlin raises such
unpleasant associations for you."

"Devlin killed my father, Mrs. Fletcher. Is that reason
good enough?"

"My understanding was that your father died in a car
accident."

"Some accident," he said, the combativeness gone from his voice.

"I'm sorry to bring up a painful topic, Mr. Valery, but could you explain what you mean when you say Devlin killed your father?"

"I suppose that you assume I'm accusing Devlin of shooting my father, or sticking a knife in him. It was nothing like that. Devlin and my father were business partners, if you could call them that, in Deval Holdings."

"I wasn't aware of that," I said. "I didn't know that Mr. Devlin had been involved in anything during his professional career other than figure skating."

"He shouldn't be. All he knows is to teach kids how to skate. He should have stuck to what he knows best. My father learned that lesson, only it was too late by the time he found that out."

"What sort of business activities were your father and Devlin in?"

"I guess you'd call it real estate, only we weren't a real estate company in the usual sense. We bought up distressed properties and used legal loopholes and government funding to improve them to the point that we could sell them at a profit. It was a good business—at least it was until Devlin got involved."

"I'm afraid I'm not very good at complex business matters. How did Mr. Devlin get involved? Did it have to do with figure skating, or with an ice arena and training facility?"

"No, what happened was—excuse me, please."

Someone had entered his office, and I could hear their

conversation, although not clearly enough to hear what was being said. After a few minutes he came back on the line. "Look, Mrs. Fletcher, I'm at work and this is too long a story for the phone. I have a suggestion for you."

"What's that?"

"I have to travel to Portland tomorrow on agency business. I wasn't sure I could do it because of the nasty weather in Maine, but it looks like it's not going to snow again soon."

"Yes, the weather has improved considerably."

"I can make a side trip to Cabot Cove to spend a little time with you if that would fit into your plans."

"I'll make myself available," I said. "You say you'll be here tomorrow?"

"That's right. I could be there by early afternoon."

"I'll look forward to meeting you." I gave him my phone number and address, and we ended the conversation.

I would have preferred to hear the story of Devlin's involvement with Valery's father's company while I had the son on the phone. But after hanging up, I realized that meeting Peter Valery in person might be to my advantage and could result in a fuller understanding of Devlin's background.

I went back to my computer, and this time I Googled Brian Devlin. There was, as I expected, quite a bit about him, but nothing that hinted at any involvement he might have had with any real estate company, much less Deval Holdings. I knew, of course, that he had been in Nevada when his father mustered out of the service, and I included "Nevada" with his name in my search. That resulted in only a few items, each of which talked of his launching a figure skating career. I tried other combinations of words to attempt to link him to something other than ice-skating, but to no avail.

Time to shift gears.

I picked up the phone and called a number in San Francisco that I resurrected from my telephone directory. Years ago when I'd visited northern California as part of a conference on crime writing, I was introduced to a fellow panelist and police detective, John Molito. Detective Molito headed a special task force within the San Francisco Police Department that focused on unusual, high-profile crimes. He was a bear of a man with a full inky-black beard and a hearty, knowing laugh that testified to his appreciation and understanding of the human condition. The last time we had been in contact, by telephone, he'd told me that he was about to retire from the force and open his own private investigation agency. I called his home number and was pleased that he was there, not off providing services for a client.

"What a treat this is," he said in the big, booming voice that I remembered so well.

"I wasn't sure that I would catch you at home, John."

"Business has been slow, Jessica. No, I suppose that's not quite accurate. I recently decided to slow down a bit and, what's the expression—smell the roses?"

I wondered whether an illness or the economy was behind his decision but, of course, didn't ask. I didn't have to.

"Not really my choice, Jessica," he said. "My cardiologist told me that if I didn't I'd be permanently put out of business in a casket." He laughed. "I took on an associate, which leaves me time to putter around the garden and catch up on reading for fun."

"I hope my books are on your list."

"Of course they are. How have you been? Get much snow up your way? I saw a storm in New England on the Weather Channel. Did it reach you there in Maine?"

"Nothing we couldn't handle, John. We're used to it. I'll tell you why I called, and I hope that what I'm asking won't prove too much of a bother."

"If it's something I can help you with, I'm happy to do it."

"We've recently had a tragic death here in Cabot Cove, John. A Russian figure skater named Alexei Olshansky."

"Figure skater, you say? Never heard of him, but then again I don't follow that sport. I'm more a football kind of guy. What happened to him?"

"He drowned in a six-foot pool of water used to melt ice that's been scraped off our skating rink."

"Not a very nice way to go."

"No, it's not. At this juncture our local sheriff hasn't made it official, but the death is suspicious; there's no doubt about that."

He chuckled. "I don't know your sheriff, but I do know you, Jessica. If you say it's suspicious, I'll put my money on your interpretation. What do you think happened? Murder?"

"That's exactly what I think, John. Alexei came here from Russia to pair up with an American skater, Christine Allen. Why she chose him is a long story; actually, it was her father, a wealthy man, who made the decision to bring

Alexei over from Russia and to arrange for them to train here in Cabot Cove. We have a newly renovated ice arena that the owner is trying to turn into a world-class figure skating training center."

"I assume the stakes can be pretty high in figure skating, with all the television coverage and such."

"They don't get as many sponsors as football players, but yes, elite skaters are often asked for endorsements and can make a great deal of money, although the preparation it takes to reach that level is expensive. I don't know that those conditions would have been a factor in Alexei's death, though."

"No? Then how can I assist you?"

"I'm calling because Alexei's partner, Christine Allen, came here from San Francisco. She'd been training there, but her father evidently felt that she needed a change of scenery."

"Local girl makes good. I always enjoy those stories."

"She's a talented skater, but I'm not sure what the future holds for her now that her partner is dead."

"You say her last name is Allen. What's her father's name?"

"William. William Allen."

"African-American businessman? Banker?"

"That's right."

"A controversial figure out here," Molito said. "I don't know a lot about him except that he's ruffled a few feathers over the years, not the kind to suffer fools gladly, that sort of thing. If I remember correctly, he was once charged with assault, some dustup with a business associate or a competitor. I don't think the charge stuck. He walked."

"Interesting," I said. "He came here with his daughter and is renting a house in town. I'm told that Christine's mother stayed home with her younger child."

"Okay," he said, "we've established who we're talking about. I take it there's something you'd like me to do on this end."

"Actually, I was hoping to get some background on an incident that allegedly occurred with Christine when she was in San Francisco. The story has it that her father decided to bring her all the way across the country to get away from a stalker. I'd like to know if there's any truth to that rumor, and if so what the circumstances were."

"I wouldn't have come across anything like that, but I can check it out easily enough. How fast do you need the information?"

"As quickly as you can come up with it, provided that doesn't put too much pressure on you."

"You know, Jessica, I don't mind a little pressure; in fact, I think I could use some. Frankly, I'm bored to tears. Give me a day and I should have everything you need."

"That's great, John. I can't thank you enough."

"A signed copy of your latest book would be nice compensation."

"Consider it on its way."

I sat back and enjoyed the feeling of satisfaction that washed over me. With only a few searches under my belt, I'd already been able to dig deeper into what actually happened to Paul Valery, whose obituary Alexei had kept. And through the good offices of my friend in San Francisco, Detective Molito, I was tracking down the truth behind a rumor. Before that, I'd been, as Seth would put it, dazzled with confusion. Now I felt that I had least taken some tangible steps that hopefully would lead to a resolution of Alexei Olshansky's death.

I was thinking about that when the phone rang.

"Mrs. F.? It's Mort."

"Hello, Mort. I meant to call you. I wanted to let you know I've been looking into Brian Devlin's background and expect to unearth a few findings that might interest you."

"Happy to hear them, Mrs. F., but you might be interested in what I'm going to do. I plan to announce that Olshansky's death was not accidental."

"What's led you to that decision, Mort?"

"Doc Hazlitt's autopsy report. It's all down here in black and white."

"What did he say?"

"Well, you know about the bruises on Olshansky's fingers. Preliminary tox report is negative. No drugs or alcohol in his system, making it less likely he would have fallen. Doc also said that the circumstances surrounding the death point in the direction of murder."

"I have to say, Mort, I simply couldn't accept the possibility that this physically fit young athlete could have lost his balance, tumbled into the ice pit, and then not been able to get himself out."

"Well, the good doc agrees with you—and so do I."

I was pleased, of course, that my initial impression had been validated, but I certainly wasn't about to gloat over it.

"So what are these things you say you're looking into?" he asked.

"It's just preliminary right now, but Brian Devlin may have had some questionable business dealings. I've also put in a call to an old friend of mine in San Francisco, a retired detective who now has his own agency. I wanted to follow up on the rumor that Christine Allen was being stalked while she was living there."

"Anything concrete so far?"

"My friend is going to get back to me tomorrow. In the meantime, Mort, have you learned any more about the man who threatened Jeremy with a gun?"

"No. That guy Gemell never called me back. Thanks for reminding me."

"I asked Eve Simpson about him," I said.

"I've been too busy to get the Connecticut cops after him."

"Eve thinks it's ridiculous that anyone would think that he carried a gun, but she said that she would pass along the message to have him call you."

The minute I said it, I knew what Mort was thinking, that I was stepping on his toes and treading in his investigative waters, so I quickly added, "I'm not sure if she'll remember, so it probably makes more sense for you to call him again."

"I intend to do that the minute we get off the phone. By the way, Mrs. F., Maureen wants to know if you have plans for dinner."

I hesitated before answering. It sounded as though I was about to receive an invitation to the Metzger home, and I wanted to leave myself an out in case his wife was in one of her frenetic kitchen moods and whipping up an experimental dish. Thankfully, Mort didn't put me in the position of having to ask what was on the menu.

"Maureen has been playing all day with a new Mexican recipe, scallops cooked in some kind of chocolate sauce. I never heard of scallops being cooked with chocolate, but she thinks it'll be terrific."

"I appreciate the invitation, Mort, but I've fallen behind on my correspondence and bill paying. Please tell Maureen that the dish sounds yummy."

I don't mind a white lie now and then.

Chapter Eighteen

I'd been truthful when I told Mort that I had fallen behind in my correspondence and bill paying and had decided to focus on those tasks. But after less than a half hour of responding to e-mails and writing a few checks—I've never become comfortable with the idea of paying bills online—I got up from my desk and paced my office. My research and phone calls had given me a sense that I'd made a modicum of progress in the Olshansky case. I suppose that his death being officially labeled a murder only bolstered my need not to lose momentum.

Restless, I glanced at the clock on the wall: four thirty. I went to the window and looked out. It was already dark. Even so, I decided that a brisk walk was in order to clear my mind. I slipped into my down winter jacket, put on boots, and was about to head out when the phone rang.

"Mrs. Fletcher?" a young woman's voice asked.

"Yes?"

"It's Marisa, from the ice arena," she said, her voice wavering.

"Hello, Marisa. What a nice surprise."

She burst into tears.

"What's wrong, dear? Are you all right?"

"Did you hear what they're going to do?"

"No, I don't think I've heard anything new," I said. "Are they going to close the arena again?"

"I wish!"

"You do? Why don't you tell me what the problem is and—"

"I can't talk on the phone. Someone will hear me. They're all looking at me. Can I come see you? Would you mind?"

"Of course I wouldn't mind. Or I'll come to where you are. You sound very distraught."

"It's horrible," she said.

"*What's* horrible?"

"What's happened."

It was obvious that I wasn't going to elicit any useful information from her on the phone.

"Do you have a car? If not, I can call a taxi and—"

"I have my car."

"Good. Here's my address." I gave it to her slowly and included directions from the ice arena.

With my plans suddenly changed, I removed my boots and jacket and went to the kitchen, where I put up water for tea, opened a package of cookies, and awaited her arrival. Fifteen minutes later she knocked at my door, and minutes after that we sat at my kitchen table with steaming cups of tea in front of us, Red Zinger for her, English breakfast for me.

"Now," I said, "let's hear what has you so upset."

"It's—it's Jeremy."

"What about Jeremy? Has something happened to him?"

She reached for a cookie, nibbled on it, took a sip of tea, and said, "He's become a monster."

"That sounds ominous, Marisa, but you'll have to be more specific."

"It's all because of Christine."

"I thought this was about Jeremy."

"It's about both of them, Mrs. Fletcher. I hate them."

"That's a harsh thing to say, Marisa. From what I had gathered, you and Jeremy were making wonderful progress as a pairs team. I'm sure that Alexei's death has set everyone on edge, but I'd hate to see it get in the way of you and Jeremy realizing your potential as skaters."

She moaned. "That's just it. We don't have any potential. We don't have a future anymore as a pairs team," she said. "Jeremy has seen to that."

I sat back and took a few seconds to take in the pretty young woman sitting across from me. At that moment she projected a combination of profound sadness and abject anger. It was clear that something traumatic had happened between her and Jeremy.

"I don't understand, Marisa. Why is Christine the cause of whatever problem it is you're having with Jeremy?"

"She . . . I mean, he . . ." She took a deep breath and waved her hands as if to clear her thinking. "I'm so mad I could spit. Now that Alexei is dead, Chris wants Jeremy to become her partner."

"Are you sure? Did Jeremy tell you this?"

"He's been hinting around, but I couldn't believe it. Just before I called you, Mrs. Fletcher, he pulled me into Lyla's office at the arena and told me he was going to become Chris's partner. He was so excited. And the stupid idiot thought I'd be happy for him. How could she do that to me, after all the things I did for her, defending that jerk, Alexei, when he was shoplifting at Nudd's, and not telling on him?"

"Well, I'm not sure that protecting Alexei at that time was the wisest thing to do, but let's put that aside. Surely, Jeremy can't make such a major decision like that unilaterally. What about Christine's coach, Brian Devlin? Has she discussed it with him? Or Mark, who's been coaching you two? Don't they have something to say about this? Jeremy can't just decide to replace Alexei as Christine's partner."

"I'll bet that Mark will be furious, but his opinion doesn't matter. Mr. Devlin is the top coach at the arena. What he says matters most. I don't think that he'll care one way or the other just as long as he keeps getting paid."

"What about Christine's father?" I asked. "He has some very strong opinions as to the type of partner his daughter should skate with. He spent a lot of money to arrange for Alexei to come here from Russia. I'm sure Jeremy has lots of potential, but he has a long way to go before reaching Alexei's skill level and reputation. I somehow can't conceive of Mr. Allen buying into this."

She came forward in her chair, her forearms on the

table. "You don't understand what's been going on down at the arena, Mrs. Fletcher. There's nothing but backbiting and scheming. Jeremy has been after Christine ever since she arrived. He's mad about her; he'd sell his soul to get close. You can't get much closer than being a pairs partner. Mr. Allen looks like a mean man. He struts around like he owns the place, but everybody knows that Christine twists him around her little finger. If she wants to skate with Jeremy, her father will go along with it."

Her comment that Jeremy was mad about Christine and would sell his soul to become close to her was troubling. If that were true—and allowing for overstatement on her part—did it mean that he was willing to *kill* to achieve that goal? That contemplation was chilling.

Marisa seemed to read what I was thinking because she said, "I hate to say it, but I wouldn't put it past Jeremy to have gotten rid of Alexei in order to get what he wants."

"That's a pretty shocking statement, Marisa. I hope you aren't accusing him of that."

"But it's possible, isn't it, Mrs. Fletcher? I mean, look at it. Jeremy is the one who has the most to gain with Alexei out of the way. Frankly, Jeremy scares me. He has a mean streak, a bad temper when things don't go his way."

"This is the first I'm hearing about that."

While listening to her, I thought back to comments that had been made at the arena about Alexei's treatment of Marisa. According to her—and Jeremy, too—Alexei seemed to take pleasure in deriding her both personally and professionally. Yet here she was insinuating that Jeremy might have murdered Alexei because he had something to gain.

But had the Russian skater's behavior toward her been sufficiently harsh to have prompted *her* to strike out in a fit of pique and push him into the ice pit? I hated to even consider that possibility, but the fact was that at this juncture, anyone involved in the arena couldn't be ruled out as a suspect.

Was Marisa simply an overly dramatic adolescent reacting to having been hurt? Or was she being shrewd in coming to me in order to point a finger at someone else? I didn't like thinking that about her, but I'd learned over the years when dealing with murder that no possibility should be left off the table.

"Why are you telling *me* this, Marisa?"

"I had to tell someone, Mrs. Fletcher, and you seem to be the sort of person who would understand. I know that you're famous and all that. Everybody says you'll probably know who killed Alexei before the police do. Maybe I shouldn't have bothered you today, but I was ready to explode after Jeremy told me he wouldn't be my partner anymore."

"Did he tell you what he *intended* to do, Marisa, or did he say that he'd already *done* it?"

She shrugged. "I guess he said he planned to do it. But that's as good as doing it, isn't it? I mean, if he plans to do it, he will."

"Not necessarily," I replied. "He might simply have been expressing a desire, but that doesn't always translate into it becoming a reality. As I said before, it's not his decision to make alone. Did he say that Christine had agreed to become his partner?"

She shook her head.

"Well then," I said, "I suggest that you put what he said in perspective. Christine might not want him as a skating partner, and her father will certainly have something to say about it. And I'm not so sure that Mr. Devlin would want to coach Jeremy until he's at the level Christine has already achieved. I understand why Jeremy's announcement upset you so, but I suggest that you step back and not assume anything until everyone else has weighed in."

She picked up another cookie, took a bite, and said, "I suppose you're right, Mrs. Fletcher. It's just that I want so much to become a champion skater. You put so much into it and you feel like you're getting somewhere, and then someone throws a rock in your path. It's going to take so many years to make it in singles competition, and I'm not sure I'll ever be as good as the world gold medalists. But I know that I can be great in pairs. Maybe I should try ice dancing."

"I'm sure you'll figure out the right thing Marisa. You know how competitive the sport is and the years of dedicated practice and training it takes. I have no doubt that if you apply yourself you'll achieve your goal, whichever way you decide to go. But in the meantime, I suggest that you put aside what Jeremy has told you and wait to see how things develop."

The conversation, and the tea and cookies, had done their job. She was considerably calmer than when she'd arrived and actually had a smile on her pretty face when she left the house.

I was glad that she had come to me and that we'd had the conversation. It was evident that if I were to play a productive role in solving Alexei Olshansky's murder, I was going to have to learn everything I possibly could about the potential suspects, and that included everyone who worked at the arena.

I tried to get back to answering correspondence and paying bills, but my mind was too clogged with other thoughts of murder and potential murderers. I looked at the pad on which I'd written the names of those I was researching. Then I added six more:

Jeremy Hapgood
Marisa Brown
Lyla Fasolino
Eldridge Coddington
Mark Rosner
Luc Beliveau

I hoped I had included all the possible suspects. Of course, there was always the remote possibility that Alexei had been killed by someone with no connection to him or to the arena, but that was so unlikely that I discarded the notion.

I was pondering this when Seth Hazlitt called.

"I thought you might be at Mort's for dinner," he said.

"He invited me, but I declined," I said. "Too much to catch up on here."

Seth chuckled. "Sure your decision didn't have to do with scallops in chocolate sauce?"

I joined in the laughter. "I take it that you were invited, too."

"Ayuh, I was. Somehow, Maureen's latest culinary adventure didn't appeal. So, you're free for dinner."

"I suppose I am."

"I'm cooking roast duck," he said, "and would be pleased to share it with you."

I hesitated and looked at the pile of bills that needed to be paid and the stack of correspondence awaiting a response.

"I love duck," I said, "but only if Mort and Maureen don't find out that you and I had dinner together. I'd hate to hurt their feelings."

"It'll be our little secret, Jessica. Seven?"

"Seven it is."

Chapter Nineteen

In addition to being a wonderful physician—especially when it comes to diagnosing difficult cases—Seth Hazlitt has worked to become a very good cook. He's developed a special knack for things like roast duck, preparing it so that it's moist on the inside and perfectly crisp on the outside. This night was no exception. The salad he whipped up, which included walnuts and cranberries along with fresh endive, was a perfect match for the rich, succulent taste of the duck with orange sauce, and I left the dinner table thoroughly sated.

"That was splendid," I said as we settled in his den with after-dinner drinks. "Chef Hazlitt hasn't lost his touch."

"Much obliged for the compliment, Jessica. Now, fill me in on what's going on with that Russian skater's death."

"You mean that Russian skater's *murder*," I said.

He looked at me quizzically. "And where did you hear that, Jessica?"

I hesitated answering because I didn't want to reveal that

Mort had shared Seth's autopsy findings with me. I needn't have been reluctant.

Seth said, "So our outstanding sheriff passed that information along to you, did he?"

"He did mention it, Seth. He knows how much I've been involved with the goings-on at the arena and didn't want to keep me in the dark. He meant well."

"Sheriff Metzger always means well, Jessica. I would have told you tonight myself, but no harm done. Now that Mr. Olshansky's death is officially a murder, how does that fit with the conclusions you've come to?"

"You don't sound as though you're pleased that I've come to *any* conclusions, Seth."

"It's not my place to second-guess you. I learned long ago that when my dear friend Jessica Fletcher decides to stick her nose into what it is basically police business, it is useless to resist."

"I'm not sure that I agree with your characterization that I 'stick my nose' into police business, but I suppose it's one way of putting it. You certainly will agree that the circumstances brought me into the picture. I was there when the body was discovered, and I've accompanied Mort during some of his interviews. I've also taken some steps on my own to try to help him with the investigation."

"There! See? So what have you uncovered, Detective Fletcher?"

I ignored his sarcasm and gave him the details of my conversation with Peter Valery. "He says Brian Devlin is responsible for his father's death."

"Does he have anything to back up that accusation?" Seth asked.

"I don't know yet, but I'm meeting with him tomorrow. He's coming to Portland on business and plans to stop here."

"A little out of his way, isn't it?"

"He didn't seem to mind. He did say that Devlin and his father had been in business together."

"What sort of business?"

"Something to do with real estate. I really don't know much more than what I've told you. I'll fill you in if I learn anything new. I also spoke with an old friend, a detective now retired from the San Francisco Police Department. I doubt if you've heard the rumor that Christine Allen had been the victim of a stalker back in San Francisco. Lyla Fasolino told me it was on the Internet. I'd like to know more about that, and I'm sure Mort would, too."

"You're probably right, Jessica. Mort has always been quick to give you credit when you've helped him with a case. But it seems to me that—"

He was interrupted by the ringing of his private, unlisted home phone.

"Oh, hello, Evelyn," he said, wincing for my benefit. "No, you're not interrupting something important, Evelyn, probably nothing as important as why you're calling me at home." The edge in his voice was apparent. "Is that so, Evelyn? What? As a matter of fact, I was just discussing the case with Jessica. I'll put her on the line with us." He pointed to an extension, which I picked up.

"Hello, Evelyn," I said.

"Seth said you were discussing the Olshansky case, Jessica. Anything I should know about? You know I have a lot of connections. I could probably help out with research."

Seth and I looked at each other and smiled.

"No, Evelyn," I said, "I have nothing new to tell you."

"All right. Keep secrets. I always find out in the end." She turned her attention to Seth. "I need a quote from you, Dr. Hazlitt."

"A quote about what?"

"About the conclusion you came to after the autopsy, that Olshansky was murdered. The headline I'm running is 'Russian Skater Murder Victim.'"

"Where did you learn about the autopsy findings?" Seth asked.

"A good reporter tracks down the news, Seth. I spoke with Sheriff Metzger, and he—"

"Then I suggest that you get a quote from our sheriff," Seth said.

"I already have, but I need one from the acting medical examiner, who happens to be you."

"I think it would be inappropriate for me to comment at this stage, Evelyn. The sheriff's office is your best source of information."

She sounded huffy. "I'm disappointed in you, Seth Hazlitt. The murder of the Russian skater is the biggest news we've had in Cabot Cove since Walter Motley burned his house down using a blowtorch to take the paint off his dining room wall."

"I appreciate that you have a job to do, Evelyn," said Seth, "but I still have no comment, at least not at this moment."

She gave up trying to wheedle something from Seth and tried me again. "You've been involved in this case since the beginning, Jessica, and don't say that you haven't. The people of this town have a right to know what's going on, especially when it involves a murder at a public facility."

I shrugged at Seth before saying to Evelyn, "You know as well as I do that certain aspects of a murder case are not made public until the investigation has been completed."

"Will you be at the press conference tomorrow?" she asked.

"What press conference?" Seth and I said in unison.

"At the ice arena. Sheriff Metzger is conducting it. I suppose you don't consider the *Gazette* to be as important as the other media that will be there to cover it, but—"

"That isn't true, Evelyn, and you know it," I said. "The *Gazette* is a fine community paper, and I've always been a big supporter of it."

"No matter," she said, her pique evident in her voice. "I just think it's strange that the medical examiner who decided Olshansky was murdered won't be there to explain his findings to the public."

"Now, see here," Seth said. "I've already provided a written report of the autopsy's findings. I don't need to conduct a class in postmortem examination, do I?"

"Sorry to have bothered you," Evelyn said stiffly. "Have a good night."

Seth and I returned the phones to their cradles.

"Sometimes I lose patience with that lady," Seth said. I started to say something in her defense, but he cut me off. "I know, I know—she is a good reporter and editor, and I'm fond of her personally. But I think she should back off a little."

Evelyn Phillips might have been a little aggressive, but she was a good and fair journalist. What was more important to me at that moment was the news that Mort Metzger intended to hold a press conference the following morning. Had he come up with new, useful information about the murder that he would announce at the conference? If so, he'd obviously decided to not share it with anyone until making it public. I couldn't blame him, of course, and I appreciated how much he'd already shared with me. Still, I was a little disappointed that I hadn't known about it.

"Will you go to the press conference, Seth?"

"Nobody asked me. Besides, I have a full slate of patients in the morning. What about you?"

"I won't be there, either. I'm meeting with the fellow who's driving in from Connecticut tomorrow, and waiting for a phone call from my detective friend in San Francisco. Plus, I still haven't caught up with my correspondence and finances."

Seth drove me home. We sat in my driveway and chatted about a few things, none of which had anything to do with murder. As I was about to get out of the car, he placed his hand on my arm and said, "I know you don't like me to tell you what to do, Jessica, but keep in mind that there's a murderer down at the ice arena, someone who won't take kindly to anyone out to identify him—or her."

"I appreciate your concern, Seth. I promise not to get myself in too deep."

"Glad to hear it," he said. "Pleasant dreams of scallops doing the backstroke in chocolate sauce."

Chapter Twenty

I wished Seth's parting words hadn't invoked the image of scallops swimming in chocolate sauce. That vision dominated my dreams and became even more unpleasant when the scallops and chocolate sauce were in the ice pit from which Alexei Olshansky's body had been pulled. Alexei was in the dream. He was covered with chocolate and struggled to keep his head above the murky mix of ice water and chocolate, eventually losing his battle and disappearing beneath the surface.

I woke up in a cold sweat and out of sorts. The sunny weather of the previous day had given way to low-hanging gray clouds, and I could smell more snow in the air. Hopefully, it would hold off until Peter Valery had completed his drive from Connecticut.

He wasn't due in Cabot Cove until early afternoon, and I reconsidered my decision not to attend Mort Metzger's press conference at the ice arena. Evelyn Phillips had said that it was scheduled to begin at ten o'clock. Because of the time change between Maine and San Francisco, I didn't expect to hear from Detective Molito until noon my time, or even later. I'd had good intentions of devoting the morning to catching up on personal matters but decided that putting it off one additional day wouldn't matter.

My taxi dropped me in front of the arena at quarter to ten. A couple of TV remote trucks were parked close to the entrance, their satellite dishes jutting up into the lowering gray sky. Mort had positioned two uniformed deputies at the door to check press IDs as people passed through. The media was invited but not the public. I wasn't sure I agreed with the decision to ban everyday citizens from attending, but it obviously wasn't my call to make. I only hoped it wouldn't keep me out.

Mort must have called in additional staff from the state police. An officer I didn't recognize stopped me at the door and examined my private pilot's license, which I carry for identification since I don't possess a driver's license. For a moment, I thought he was going to deny me access, but Mort, who was standing nearby, nodded at the deputy, and I entered the arena, where a podium and microphone had been set up in the concession stand's seating area. The picnic tables had been pushed to one side, and folding chairs were lined up in rows. I spotted the Russian television crew that had had a run-in with Coach Devlin the previous week. Seated with the Russian reporter was Irina Bednikova, flanked by Maxim and Boris. There were two dozen reporters and dignitaries scattered throughout the area, including Mayor Jim Shevlin and members of the town council. I spotted Eldridge Coddington, sitting two rows behind

Richard Koser and Evelyn Phillips from the *Gazette*. I took an empty seat next to her.

"Good morning," she said. "I thought you said you weren't coming."

"Changed my mind."

"Looks like someone else changed his mind," Evelyn said as Seth Hazlitt slipped into the chair next to mine.

"Morning, Evelyn," he said.

"Morning, Seth."

"Do you have any advance indication of what Mort will be talking about?" I asked her.

"Unlike some others I could name, he doesn't take me into his confidence," she said, "but I hope it's worth holding a press conference. I already got the ME report, and I have lots of other things I could be doing this morning."

At ten o'clock straight up, Mort came to the podium, tucked some papers under his arm, and held up his hands for silence. The room went very quickly quiet, except for the click and whirr of camera shutters.

"Good morning. Thank you all for coming. As you know, we had a tragic event here at the ice arena, the death of a pretty well-known Russian skater, Alexei Olshansky, age twenty-five. Pending autopsy reports, his death was initially considered accidental. But Dr. Seth Hazlitt, who is acting medical examiner in Doc Foley's absence, performed the autopsy."

"Where is Doc Foley?" a reporter called out.

"In Florida," Mort said, chuckling. "I bet we all wish we could be in Florida with him, huh?"

No one laughed.

Mort cleared his throat and continued. "Anyway, please hold your questions until my statement is complete." He looked down at his paper. "Dr. Hazlitt performed the autopsy and has ruled that Mr. Olshansky's death was a homicide. This finding confirms what I've felt all along." He looked at me for a reaction; I didn't have one.

Mort went on. "This isn't your routine murder investigation. It has what I suppose you could call international implications. The Russian embassy in Washington, D.C., has gotten involved and is putting on the pressure for me to come up with an answer. Our own State Department is pretty interested, too, and wants this case solved today, if not sooner. The Maine State Police are on board, and I appreciate their help. The FBI is asking questions, too, but aren't part of my team, at least not yet. No matter where the deceased came from, this is a local matter, and I want to assure you that my office is pulling out all the stops to get to the bottom of it. We are on this case twenty-four-seven. Everyone who worked at the arena the night he died has been questioned, and I intend to question them all again. Doc Hazlitt has provided a written report of his autopsy findings, which I've had photocopied, and it's available for all you folks from the media.

"I can't get too specific about the details of the investigation, but I promise each and every one of you that we will bring whoever killed Mr. Olshansky to justice. I know that there's a lot of rumors going around town, and plenty of folks are on edge because this happened in our otherwise peaceful town. Well, there's no need for anyone to worry. I'm counting on you media types to get the word out that information from any citizen will be appreciated and kept confidential. If anyone knows anything that might help in the investigation, please notify my office. Along with the autopsy report, I have a press release that includes contact information in case anybody wants to get hold of me.

"On a different topic, there have been a series of incidents here at the ice arena lately that have nothing to do with the murder. I'm pleased to announce that my office has identified the individual behind these incidents and an arrest has been made. I will not be releasing the name of the person now in custody until further questioning of the suspect has been completed."

Mayor Shevlin came to the microphone and read his statement, declaring the city's cooperation with the police department and pledging that the citizens of Cabot Cove had nothing to fear; the police were on top of the situation. Eldridge Coddington added his two cents, saying that he had hired additional security at the rink for the hours it was open, and that while several programs had been suspended at parents' request, they would be reinstated the following week, and there would be no refunds.

Mort returned to the microphone. "Now, I'll take a few questions, but don't ask about details of the investigation. I'm not at liberty to answer them at this time."

I glanced over at Evelyn Phillips, who was busy making notes in a long, thin reporter's notepad. She stopped writing, turned to me, and said, "What do you know about Mort arresting someone, Jessica?"

"Not a thing," I replied. "I'm only hearing about it now."

Our conversation was drowned out as reporters threw

questions at Mort, few of which he elected to answer. They soon gave up trying to get something out of him and turned to Irina, wanting mostly to know what her plans were now that her former skating partner was dead. She answered the best she could, considering the language barrier. Eventually, her beefy brother put a stop to the questioning and the trio left.

"Maxim and Boris are very protective of her," I commented.

"Who's Boris?" Evelyn asked. "The other bodyguard?"

"He's the brother of Alexei's fiancée," I said.

"Fiancée? I didn't know he had a fiancée," Evelyn said, sounding annoyed. She got up and ran after the departing Russians.

It struck me that some significant figures were absent that morning. Christine Allen and her father weren't there, nor were Brian Devlin, Marisa Brown, Lyla Fasolino, Jeremy Hapgood, or Mark Rosner. I mentioned it to Seth. "I suppose there wasn't any official reason for them to attend, but I would've thought that at least a few of them would have shown up, if only out of curiosity."

"They might be here somewhere out of sight, since Mort restricted attendance," Seth said. "Although if I know Eldridge Coddington, he probably gave them all the day off, unpaid, of course."

We waited until the crowd thinned around the podium before approaching Mort, who was gathering up his notes. The autopsy report and press release had already been distributed.

"How'd I do, Mrs. F.? Doc?" Mort asked.

"Just fine," I said.

"Not easy dealing with the media," Seth added.

"No, it never is," I agreed.

We followed him out the front door to his vehicle, and Seth went to get his car.

"Find out anything new, Mrs. F., since we spoke yesterday?"

"No, but I should know more later today. You mentioned in your remarks that you were reinterviewing everyone who worked at the rink."

"Already started the process. Interesting the things you find out the second time around."

I wasn't sure I should ask, but I did. "What did you come up with?"

He looked around to be sure that we weren't being overheard. "Checked into that second bodyguard, not the one who's the skater's brother but the other one, Boris something. Did you know his sister, Dariya, had a baby?"

"Oh?"

"The father of that baby was none other than Alexei Olshansky. So it's not simply a broken engagement. Seems to me that Boris has a pretty strong motive to kill Olshansky," Mort offered.

I had to agree with him.

"What about this person you've arrested?" I asked.

"I can't say any more about that, Mrs. F., except he's a person of interest. Excuse me. I have to get back to the office. I have Ms. Allen and her father coming in for follow-up interviews."

He got in his car and drove off.

The news that Boris's sister had been impregnated by Alexei Olshansky was, of course, confirmation of yet another rumor, this one provided by Christine. Both of the big, hulking Russian bodyguards had reason to be angry with Alexei—Maxim because Alexei had abandoned Irina as a skating partner, and now the other man, Boris, whose sister had a child out of wedlock with the murder victim.

Seth pulled up in his car, and I climbed in.

"It's eleven," he said, "a little late for breakfast and too early for lunch, but I wouldn't mind a snack at Mara's. How about you?"

I still had an hour before it was likely that Detective Molito would be calling. "As long as I'm home by noon. I'm expecting a phone call," I said.

"I have to make a fast stop at Charles, but we should get you home in time, no problem."

The sky was leaden and the wind whipped up a chop on the water in the bay. By the time Seth and I walked from his car to Mara's, the cold had gone right through me, and I looked forward to a bowl of whatever soup she was featuring that day. The restaurant was busy, but we managed to find an available table away from the draft created each time someone came through the door. It appeared that Mara was shorthanded this day. She scurried between tables and behind the counter while two young female waitresses, who'd worked there a while, helped the owner keep up with taking orders and delivering the food.

Mara waved to us in acknowledgment and held up her index finger to indicate that she'd get to us shortly. When she did arrive, I said, "Looks like you could use an extra hand."

"Are you volunteering, Jessica? If so, I'll put an apron on you."

I laughed. "I'm almost tempted to take you up on it. What's the soup today?"

"Roasted tomato. It's terrific."

"I'm sure it is if you say so. I'd love a bowl, and some bread, please."

"Coming up. You, Doc?"

"I'll have a short stack of the blueberry pancakes."

"Seth, what happened to your diet?" I asked.

"Put the maple syrup on the side," he said.

Mara took a black grease pencil from behind her ear and wrote our order down on her pad. "You folks go to that press conference this morning?"

"As a matter of fact, we did."

"Anything exciting happen?"

"No. Go on. You don't have time to chat with us."

Friends stopped by our table while we waited for our order to be delivered. Despite the growth that Cabot Cove has experienced over the years, it still remains a close-knit community, particularly for those who have been there a while, including Seth and me. Jack Wilson, the town's leading veterinarian, joined us for a few minutes; so did Susan Shevlin. It occurred to me as I chatted with them that I was in the unusual situation of not actively writing a book at the moment. I'd delivered my most recent novel to my publisher a month ago, and while I had a contract for two more, I was taking a break from writing. But I'd started to develop a plot for the next one and was thinking about that when Mara arrived with my soup and Seth's pancakes. By that time, the crowd had thinned out a little, and she took a moment to sit and catch her breath.

"You would think it was high tourist season," she said through a laugh. "Seems like there is no tourist season anymore. They show up every time of year, including the dead of winter."

"Which is good for you, Mara."

"Good for business, that's for sure," she said. "The problem is I'm never sure how to staff the place. When I think it might be slow, they come pouring through the door, and when I bring on extra people in anticipation of a big crush, it's slow as molasses."

"Where is that new young fellow you introduced me to?" I asked.

"Tommy? I don't know. He didn't show up today, which is unusual. He's been as punctual as a Swiss watch until this morning. I hear there's flu around."

"Same as every winter," Seth put in.

"He must've gotten sick and forgot to call in," Mara said.

I sighed. "I'm sure that's the toughest part of running a business, hiring the right people."

"You're right, Jessica. I try to be understanding with all my help, and people *do* get sick. I would've appreciated a phone call, that's all." She stood. "Enjoy your soup. Doc, are you sure you don't want me to make that a long stack instead of a short one? Take me a minute to get you the extra pancake."

"No, thanks, Mara. This is fine. I'm dieting."

With an effort, I refrained from saying anything about Seth's diet and did exactly as Mara had suggested—enjoyed my soup and the warm, crunchy bread from Sassi's Bakery, where Mara buys most of her baked goods.

Mara put the check on the table upside down as she always does. "My treat," I said to Seth, "as thanks for the ride." I turned it over to see what I owed. "Oh, my."

"What's the matter?"

"What does this look like, Seth?"

"Mara's usual scrawl. She could've been a doctor."

"No, I mean the pencil she used. What does that look like?"

"Looks like a black crayon to me. Finish your soup. We have to be going."

Charles Department Store was busy when we pushed through the front door. One of the clerks walked past us with a stack of shoe boxes in her arms. A shipment of Ecco ballet flats had arrived. Several women were trying on the new spring colors, even though it would be months before the ground was dry enough to wear them outside.

David waved at Seth. "Got your package ready for you, Dr. Hazlitt."

"Great. Did you get in that wok you were telling me about?"

"We did, and I'll be happy to show it to you. Would you also like to see Martin Yan's latest cookbook?"

"Ayuh. I would," Seth replied. "I won't be but a minute, Jessica."

"Go on," I said. "We have a little time."

I greeted Jim, who was packing up the holiday ornaments that had been on sale the previous week.

"Last chance to pick up one of these beauties, Jessica,"
he said. "They won't come out again until next September."

"No, thanks, Jim. I have all I need."

"Shame what happened down at the rink."

"Yes, it was," I said.

Jim lowered his voice. "You know I hate to speak ill of
the dead, but Olshansky was a bit of a problem. A couple
of these walked out of here with him, once or twice." He
indicated the ornaments.

"I'm sorry to hear that."

"We didn't say anything. After all, he was a big skating
star, kind of, and we wouldn't want to tarnish his reputation, or set off an international incident. But I heard from
some of the other merchants that he did it with them, too."

"Did you let the sheriff know?"

"We don't bother Mort with small stuff. He's got enough
on his plate right now."

"You should let him know anyway."

"Maybe we'll do that when things calm down. By the
way, he left something here to be repaired and I don't know
who to give it to."

"Who? Alexei?"

"Yes. I'm not looking to be paid, understand? It only
took our jeweler two minutes to fix his gold chain, but I
don't want to hold on to it. It may have sentimental value to
his family. In any case, it's not ours."

"Why don't you give it to the sheriff, Jim. He's collect-
ing Alexei's belongings to ship home to his mother. And

while you're there, tell him about the shoplifting. He'll want to know."

"Good advice, Jessica. We'll do that."

Seth dropped me off at home at five minutes to noon, and I got to work reading and answering e-mail messages. I was in the midst of that when the phone rang.

"Jessica? John Molito."

"Hello, John. How are things this fine day in San Francisco?"

"Splendid. Perfect weather. I see that you aren't so fortunate. The weather channel shows another storm heading your way."

"I'm sorry to hear it."

"Jessica, I had a friend at the PD dig back into the stalking case that you mentioned. It did involve the skater, Ms. Allen."

"How serious was it?"

"Evidently serious enough for Ms. Allen's father to file a complaint with the department. A couple of detectives who work Internet cases tracked the stalker down. He wasn't very good at concealing his identity or whereabouts. They traced his e-mails and cell phone calls pretty easily and picked him up at home. According to the lead detective, the kid was a congenital liar; you couldn't believe anything he said. He denied knowing who Ms. Allen was, but his bedroom was plastered with photographs of her. He was sort of a computer nerd, heavy into fantasy video games and stuff like that. Anyway, they brought him in and called her father."

"And he filed charges?"

"No, he didn't. The detective I talked with said Mr. Allen declined to press charges but told him to put the fear of God in the kid."

"Did it work?"

"Hard to say. The stalking stopped, so I suppose it did, at least for a while. They followed up on the kid. He was gone, had moved from the area."

"Can you give me his name?"

"If you keep it between us. Since he wasn't charged, his record is clean."

"You have my word."

"That's good enough. His name is Thomas Mulvaney."

"Do you know where he moved?"

"No. Once he was gone, and there were no additional complaints, the case was closed."

"What about his parents?"

"The investigating officer spoke with his mother. Nice, normal, middle-class family. Dad's a dentist. Mom's a schoolteacher. Who knows why some kids go kerflooey?"

"Well," I said, "I really appreciate this information, John. Oh, did this Thomas Mulvaney ever stalk anyone else?"

"Not that we know of. He had sent a couple of nasty e-mails to a male skater Ms. Allen was training with, you know, telling him he wasn't good enough for her, that sort of thing, nothing threatening."

"I don't suppose you have a description of him?"

Molito laughed. "I was waiting for that," he said. "Again, between us, I have a picture taken of him when they brought him in, not an official mug shot—he was never formally charged—but they popped a few shots for the record while he was being interviewed. Want me to e-mail it to you?"

"That would be wonderful, John. I really appreciate this."

"My pleasure. When are you heading out this way again?"

"Soon, I hope. You know how much I love San Francisco and the entire Bay Area."

"Love to see you again, Jessica. Stay in touch."

We ended the call and I turned to my computer, where I accessed my e-mail. There it was, a message from him with an attachment. I clicked on the small icon representing the attachment. The screen came to life, and I was staring into the face of Christine Allen's San Francisco stalker, Thomas Mulvaney—aka Tommy Hunter, the young man who waited tables at Mara's Luncheonette.

Chapter Twenty-one

Thomas Mulvaney, Mara's new waiter, stared at me from the screen as I tried to gather my thoughts.

When he hadn't showed up for work that morning at the luncheonette, I'd entertained the question—but only fleetingly—that he might have been the person Mort had arrested as a suspect in previous incidents at the ice arena. Now the likelihood of that was significantly greater.

Had this fresh-faced young man come to Cabot Cove in order to continue stalking Christine Allen? Was he the one who'd drilled a hole in the wall of the women's locker room and who had been seen lurking in that area on other occasions? These were logical conclusions to come to, and if true, Mort had identified the right person as being behind those incidents.

Molito had said that Christine's stalker hadn't been particularly clever in covering his tracks. By taking a job as a waiter at Mara's—which placed him in the public eye on a daily basis—he'd continued his reckless behavior. I

seemed to remember that Mara once mentioned that neither Christine nor her father had been to the luncheonette
since arriving in Cabot Cove. Of course, they might not
have recognized Tommy even if they had. Detective Molito had indicated that they'd never confronted the stalker,
perhaps never even bothered to learn his identity. Mr. Allen
had simply told the police to use the arrest to scare him into
not doing it again. Obviously, this young man hadn't been
sufficiently frightened to stop his reprehensible acts.

Our sheriff was currently handicapped while questioning Tommy. He didn't know anything about the young
man's previous life in San Francisco, and I was duty bound
to pass along what I'd learned as quickly as possible.

I placed a call to headquarters but was informed that
our sheriff was away on official business until later that afternoon. I didn't know if he'd completed his questioning of
Tommy and had released him, or if the young man was being held in one of the cells at headquarters. Either way, it
couldn't hurt to wait a few hours to alert Mort to what I'd
learned about Tommy's days in San Francisco. I wanted to
tell him in person and not pass the information through a
third party or leave it in a voice mail.

Several years ago, I attended a seminar in New York
City, at which an expert on stalkers and stalking had made
a presentation. It was part of a three-day conference hosted
by the New York City Police Department for members of
the media and writers of books in which law enforcement
played a role. I'd been privileged to be invited and had
brought home with me a number of papers and pamphlets
on stalking, provided by the speaker, plus my own notes

taken during the presentation. I looked for them now, riffling through a file drawer until I found the material, and quickly perused their contents. According to the presenter, almost ninety percent of stalkers were male; eighty percent of them were white, and about half were between the ages of eighteen and thirty-five. They were, for the most part, of above-average intelligence and shared characteristics such as jealousy, narcissism, obsessive-compulsiveness, and an inability to distinguish between fantasy and reality. Another common trait was the tendency to fall in love instantly with the object of their fanciful obsessions.

The material also contained a long list of things that stalkers tended to do, and I read it with great interest. Obviously, their focus is on the person they're stalking—repeated phone calls, constantly showing up where the object of their obsession is, showering their target with unwanted expressions of their love, and a host of other upsetting activities. But as far as I knew, Tommy had not made direct contact with Christine since coming to Cabot Cove, although he had just missed seeing her and Alexei when Evelyn and I had encountered him at the rink. He could have been there at other times as well. Mr. Allen was still concerned about Chris's e-mail messages, so Tommy "Hunter," as he styled himself, may have been up to his old tricks.

Molito told me that while in San Francisco, Christine's stalker had contacted a male skater with whom she was training, accusing him of not being worthy of partnering with her. Two similar notes had been written to Alexei, one while he was alive, the other after his death, the latter having been wrapped around a flower left in front of the ice arena. Both had been written with what looked like a black crayon. Mara and her staff used black grease pencils, often used as china markers—which on paper looked like crayon—to write down their customers' orders. If Tommy Mulvaney was the writer of those notes, it said to me that he was more dangerous than the average stalker.

There was no doubt that anger, perhaps even rage, was behind the messages. Had Tommy's obsession with Christine Allen shifted to a warped need to attack her skating partner? Could his anger have morphed into a desire to kill the man he viewed as his rival for her affections? Had Thomas Mulvaney murdered Alexei Olshansky? If so, not only did Mort have in custody the person who'd been behind the incidents at the arena; he also had Alexei's killer in hand. It was a lot to think about.

I made myself a light lunch and was going through that day's mail when the phone rang.

"Mrs. Fletcher? It's Peter Valery."

"Yes, Mr. Valery. Are you calling from Cabot Cove?"

"Yes. I'm only a few blocks away. I didn't want to just arrive without calling first."

"That was thoughtful of you. I'm here. Please come by."

He was a nice-looking middle-aged man, prematurely balding and on the pudgy side. He wore a suit and tie, appropriate for his later business meeting, but hardly an outfit I would think comfortable when setting out on a long drive. I suggested that we sit at my kitchen table but gave him the choice of more comfortable seating in my living room. He opted for the kitchen, which made serving tea and a pineapple upside-down cake I'd picked up at Sassi's Bakery easy.

"I think you've arrived just in time," I said. "They're forecasting snow for this evening."

"I'd better not linger too long, then," he said. "I'd like to get to Portland before the storm comes."

"I promise not to prolong the questions I have. Let me get right to the point. You told me on the phone that Brian Devlin was in business with your father back in Colorado. I was hoping you could tell me how that came about."

Valery sipped his tea and thought for a moment. "My dad and Devlin got involved because my father, as smart a guy as he was, was also incredibly naïve when it came to judging people. He'd gone to Las Vegas for a business meeting and was introduced to Devlin by some guy, Harry or Herbie-something."

"Might it have been Harvey? Harvey Gemell by any chance?"

"It sounds right, but I couldn't swear to it." He fell silent.

"I'm sorry I interrupted you. You were talking about Devlin."

"Right. Brian Devlin bragged to my father about his skating successes, all his medals. The truth was that Devlin may have been successful as an amateur, but at the time he wasn't much of a success as a professional. That came later. In Las Vegas, he was resting on his laurels, banking on his fame to open business doors."

"Your father followed figure skating?" I asked.

"My father was a sports nut, Mrs. Fletcher. He bowed down to anyone involved in athletics, probably because he didn't have an athletic bone in his body. If you live in Colorado Springs, it's hard not to learn *something* about figure skating. So Dad knew a little about it, but not a lot. Devlin claimed to be wired in with a group in Las Vegas that had political connections. He told my father that there was a large tract of land just outside the city that was ripe for the picking if you knew how to handle the deal. The key was to make a valuable piece of property look less valuable, pick it up for a song, paying off the right people along the way, and develop it into a multimillion-dollar complex."

I could see what was coming next. Peter's father gave Devlin a large sum of money, allegedly to be used to pay off politicians in return for gaining access to this valuable piece of property. And, of course, the money never reached the politicians, instead finding its way into Devlin's pocket and the pockets of others who might have been in on the scam. I was right; that's exactly how Peter described what happened next.

"Didn't it become evident to your father at some point that things weren't going the way they were supposed to?" I asked.

"Sure. He sensed that things were going wrong but kept thinking that if he pumped more money into the project, it would eventually pay off. He started raising money in Colorado." Valery shook his head. "Amazing how many people are willing to suspend disbelief when big money is at stake. Greed is a powerful motivator, Mrs. Fletcher, and it can blind even the smartest of us. My father was not an innocent here; too trusting maybe, but willing to stretch the law or circumvent it altogether. Even so, he didn't deserve the hosing he got from Devlin and company. There's lots of detail I could go into, but I don't want to belabor it. The money my father put up, and raised from family, friends, and business associates, never got where it was supposed to go, nor did it result in the tract of land coming into my father's hands. My grandmother's retirement savings. My mother's inheritance. My uncle's business. When my dad went bust, all his investors lost everything they had put into the project. People stopped talking to him. A few of them sued, and when the state of Colorado decided to bring fraud charges against him, he lost all hope, became a broken man, a shell of himself. That's why he took his life."

His eyes became moist, and I knew that he was fighting to stay in control of his emotions. I made an excuse to go to the sink to allow him a few private moments. When I returned to the table, he'd pulled himself together and smiled. "I suppose I overstated it on the phone," he said, "when I claimed that Devlin killed my father. The reality is that Dad was responsible for his own problems. Combine his naïveté with greed and a willingness to cut legal corners, and you have the perfect storm for failure. But that doesn't let Devlin off the hook. He was the consummate con man who knew a patsy when he saw one."

"A tragic story," I said.

"It was for everyone involved," he agreed. "It did one positive thing for me, though. It sent me running as far away as possible from anything having to do with business. I'm really happy working for a nonprofit organization where the bottom line isn't everything."

"Mr. Valery, I asked you on the phone if your father knew the Russian skater who was murdered here, Alexei Olshansky."

"I don't know if he knew him personally. The Olshansky name is familiar to me, however. After you called, I spoke with my mother. She recognized the name immediately. My dad was from Belarus. Immigrants from the same region tend to stick together when they come over here. We had a lot of Russian-American neighbors when I was growing up. I remember a bunch of them showed up at Dad's funeral." He suddenly narrowed his eyes and cocked his head. "I can't help but get the feeling, Mrs. Fletcher, that you think Brian Devlin might have been involved in some way with this skater's murder."

"I don't know anything of the sort," I said, "but Devlin was Alexei Olshansky's coach. As such, he is as much a suspect as everyone else involved in Alexei's life. I don't have an official role in the investigation, but I have been doing some, let's say, exploring of my own in the hope that what I come up with will be of help to our sheriff. As I mentioned to you on the phone, Alexei had kept a copy of your father's obituary. I found that strange, which is why I called you."

"Makes sense, I guess," he said, glancing at his watch.

"I don't want to keep you too much longer," I said, "but I'm surprised that your father ended up taking the full brunt of the fallout from the land project. From everything I've been able to find online, Brian Devlin was never a party to any of the lawsuits, nor of the criminal action brought against your father."

"That's right. Devlin was pretty shrewd when it came to covering his tracks. My father's company was based in Colorado, and the money he persuaded people to invest also came from that state. When the criminal action was brought against him, he tried to implicate Devlin, but the prosecutor wasn't interested in dragging in someone from another state. He had a bird in hand. Dad's attorney made inquiries and discovered that Devlin had left Nevada. We could have had him traced, but it was already too late to benefit my father. My mother just wanted it all to end. So, Devlin got away untouched but, from what we later learned, left a trail of gambling debts behind him. After all that, he didn't get rich. That gives me some solace. Not a lot, but some."

Peter Valery declined a second piece of cake, finished his tea, and announced that he was leaving. I walked him out to his car, where we both looked up into a sky saturated with snow that would soon fall.

"Thank you so much for taking the time to help me understand," I said.

"I didn't mind doing it, Mrs. Fletcher. Gives me some closure, too. Now someone else knows what a con man this guy is." Then, through a wide grin, he said, "Besides, it isn't every day that I get to meet a famous writer. Would it be imposing too much if I—?"

I read his mind. "Just wait a minute," I said. I went inside, pulled a copy of my latest published novel from a carton, sat at the desk, and inscribed it to him:

For Peter Valery—
Thank you for opening my eyes.
With sincere best wishes.

I signed it and rejoined him in the driveway.

"I appreciate this," he said.

"Not as much as I appreciate you making this detour. Travel safe."

I watched him drive off, returned to the house, and spent a half hour typing up notes based upon our conversation. When I was finished, I called my local taxi company and told them that I needed a ride.

Chapter Twenty-two

I tried Mort's cell phone, but he didn't pick up. A call to headquarters elicited the information that he wasn't expected back until later.

"Is there any way I can reach him?" I asked.

"Afraid not, Mrs. Fletcher. He must be out of range. Is this an emergency? Can someone else help?"

"No, thanks, but please leave a message for him to call me on my cell phone as soon as possible."

"Shall do, ma'am."

Marisa Brown answered when I called the ice arena and asked for Brian Devlin.

"He's not here, Mrs. Fletcher."

"Do you know where I can reach him?"

"At home, I guess."

"Thanks, Marisa, I'll try him there."

To say that what Peter Valery had told me during our brief conversation was surprising would be a gross understatement. "Shocking" would more aptly describe my reaction. If what he said was true—and I had no reason to doubt him—Devlin had fallen back on coaching only when his financial finagling had failed so badly that it caused his partner to commit suicide. What was even more startling was that Harvey Gemell, Eve Simpson's potential buyer of the ice arena, was possibly involved with Devlin's scam to defraud Peter Valery's father. Did Gemell tell Eve that he had a connection with Devlin? If he had, she'd never acknowledged it in our conversations. Not that she was obliged to tell me about it; the larger question was whether Eldridge Coddington was aware of it. I doubted that.

My meeting with Peter Valery had kindled many provocative questions, and the only person who could answer them for me, aside from Harvey Gemell, was Brian Devlin himself.

I decided not to call Devlin. It would have been too easy for him to brush me off on the phone. Mort Metzger had gathered the addresses and phone numbers of all the staff at the ice arena the night that Alexei Olshansky's body was discovered and had given a copy to me, so I knew where Devlin lived. Surprise was the element needed here. I would simply drop in on him, provided he was home, and trust that he would feel obligated to invite me in.

Fifteen minutes later I was on my way to where Devlin had established his living quarters. When the cab was a few hundred feet from the house, I asked my driver to stop.

"Something wrong?" he asked.

"No, but let's just wait here a minute."

My reason for hesitating had to do with what was occurring on the porch of Devlin's house. The skating coach stood there with none other than Harvey Gemell. It appeared that Gemell was leaving, and I wanted to wait until he was gone. The men shook hands. Gemell came down from the porch, got into a black Mercedes, and pulled away. Devlin looked up and down the street before reentering the house.

"I don't know how long I'll be," I told my driver, "but I'll call when I'm ready to be picked up."

"My cell phone is on, Mrs. Fletcher."

"Good. Thank you."

As I climbed the steps to the porch, I was aware that someone was peeking through a gap in the curtains. I ignored it and rang the bell. I heard movement inside. A few seconds later Devlin opened the door, and judging from his expression, he wasn't happy to see me.

"Hello, Mr. Devlin," I said with a smile. "I'm sorry to barge in on you this way but—"

"Who is it?" a woman's voice asked from behind him.

I looked past Devlin to see Lyla Fasolino emerge from what I assumed was the bathroom. She was wearing an oversized, red terry cloth bathrobe.

"It's nothing," he said, and waved her back into the room from which she'd come. "What can I do for you, Mrs. Fletcher?" he asked, arms crossed over his chest, his expression stern and unwelcoming.

"I was wondering whether you would give me a few minutes of your time."

"What's the occasion?"

"It has to do with Alexei Olshansky."

"His death was tragic. What more can I say about it?"

"To be honest," I said, "I've come across some information that I think Sheriff Metzger will be interested in having. I believe it bears directly on his investigation of the circumstances surrounding Alexei's death."

"That's great, but what does it have to do with me?"

"If you would allow me to come in for a few minutes, I'll be happy to explain it to you."

I could see the wheels spinning in his brain. Surely, his curiosity about what I'd just said would compel him to want to know more. I was counting on that. My assumption was right.

"I only have a few minutes, Mrs. Fletcher," he said as he opened the door fully and stepped aside to allow me to enter. "I have to be somewhere else."

"I'll try not to keep you," I said, crossing the threshold. Lyla was standing there, this time fully dressed in a scoop-neck sweater and jeans, one hand casually curved around the back of her neck. But there was something different about her. Perhaps it was her red face.

"Hello, Lyla," I said to her. "I'm sorry if I interrupted you."

"I was just leaving," she said, grabbing her coat from a hook by the door. "I'll see you at the rink," she said to Devlin. "We can finish our discussion later." She tossed a quizzical glance at him as she walked past us and out the door.

"We were having a meeting," he said.

I was tempted to ask what sort of "meeting" required wearing bathrobes, but I thought better of it.

As though it suddenly occurred to him that it was in his best interest to be gracious, Devlin asked if I wanted a drink, a beer, or coffee. I declined.

"Sit down, please," he said, indicating the sofa. "I apologize for rushing you, but I don't have much time. I'm due at the arena, and I'm already running late." He made a show of looking at his watch as he perched on the edge of a chair.

"I'll try to be brief, Mr. Devlin."

"Please, call me Brian."

"All right, Brian. Does the name Paul Valery mean anything to you?"

There was no need for him to answer; his expression was revealing.

"I've met so many people over the years," he said. "I . . . I can't remember all of their names. Who was he?"

I noted that he used the past tense in asking about Valery. I responded in kind. "He *was* a real estate developer from Colorado Springs who lost everything in a fraudulent land deal in Nevada."

Devlin shrugged.

"I spent time with his son, Peter, earlier today. He told me that you and his father had been involved in that land deal."

"He must be mistaken," he said in clipped tones. An angry scowl crossed his face before he schooled his features into a more neutral expression. "You know the name 'Devlin' is hardly uncommon. It must have been someone with the same or a similar name. You can't honestly be suggesting that I'd be involved in some fraudulent deal."

"I'm honestly reporting what Mr. Valery's son told me, Brian. Was he wrong?"

He didn't respond.

My cell phone vibrated and rang. I looked at the screen. Of all times for him to return my call, this was the most inconvenient. "Excuse me," I said to Devlin. "Can I call you back in a few minutes, Mort?" I asked.

"I'm back in my office, but I'll only be here for the next hour," he replied.

"I'll get back to you as soon as I can." I clicked off the phone and returned my attention to the coach.

"Was that your sheriff?" Devlin asked, rocking back and forth in his chair.

"Yes."

"I thought I recognized his first name. What's his last name?"

"Metzger."

"Right, right, Metzger. I hope you don't mind my saying that he comes off like a real bumbler to me."

"He's anything but, Brian. He's a former New York City policeman. They're known to be pretty sharp, wouldn't you agree? And Mort has done a wonderful job in Cabot Cove. Don't let his demeanor fool you. He's a first-rate lawman."

Devlin looked at his watch again.

"My apologies for keeping you," I said. "I believe you were saying that you have no recollection of anyone in Colorado Springs named Valery?"

"You're talking about a long time ago, Mrs. Fletcher," he said, which said to *me* that he had, indeed, known Peter Valery's father. Buoyed by that tacit admission, I pressed on.

"I couldn't help but notice when I arrived here that Harvey Gemell had been visiting you."

If my mention of Paul Valery's name had caused Devlin to become ill at ease, the name Gemell increased his apparent discomfort fivefold. I expected him to bring the conversation to an abrupt end and order me to leave, but instead he mustered a bit of bravado.

"So?" he said, cocking his head at me. "Am I not allowed to talk to people?"

"I assume you're aware that Mr. Gemell is considering buying the ice arena from Eldridge Coddington."

"Sure, I'd heard that," he said. "He had some questions on how the facility is run, and if I intend to keep my program there. Nothing could be more natural for someone interested in investing in it. Do you question that?"

"Under normal circumstances, Mr. Gemell's interest in the Cabot Cove Ice Arena wouldn't raise any eyebrows— except for the fact that I've been told that it was he who introduced you to Paul Valery in Las Vegas."

It was time for Devlin to do what I'd expected him to do a few minutes earlier. He ended the conversation by saying, "I don't know much about you, Mrs. Fletcher, except I understand that you're a successful writer. I suggest you stick to murder mysteries—fiction seems to be your strength— and keep your nose out of other people's business. Who are you to be digging into my background and making accusations that are totally false? You have some nerve coming here with your imagined scenarios. That may work when you're writing one of your books, but it has no place in my life. Now, excuse me. I have more important things to do."

I'd wanted to press forward and follow up with more questions, but it was obvious that wouldn't happen during this visit. I stood, straightened my skirt, zipped up my jacket, and said, "I need to call for a taxi. I don't drive."

He looked at me as though I might be from another galaxy. "You don't drive?" he said. "I hope you don't expect me to ferry you somewhere after the accusations you just aimed at me."

"Not at all," I said. I pulled out my cell phone and pressed the speed dial for the taxi driver's cell phone. He answered immediately and said he'd be there in five minutes.

"Thank you for your time, Brian," I said. "I know that you haven't found this pleasant, but I remind you that one of your pupils has been murdered at the very arena where he trained with you. You may not think it's my business, but I was there the night they dragged Alexei from the ice pit, and I intend to do everything I can to help Sheriff Metzger solve the case. Again, thank you for allowing me to stop in unannounced."

The minute I got into the taxi, I called Mort Metzger at his office.

"Mort? I have to see you. It's urgent," I said.

"Sure, Mrs. F."

"Do you still have in custody the person you claim was behind incidents at the ice arena?"

"Yeah. In fact, I intend to question him again in about an hour."

"I assume you're talking about Thomas Mulvaney."

"His name is Thomas all right, but his last name isn't Mulvaney. It's Hunter."

"I'm not surprised that he changed it, considering his background."

"What are you talking about, Mrs. F.? What do you know about him?"

"Quite a bit. I've learned a few things that I think that *you'll* want to know before you question him."

"Can't wait to hear what it is," he said.

"And I can't wait to tell you."

Chapter Twenty-three

Mort offered me coffee when I arrived, as he always does, and I declined, as I usually do. There was a time when he was fussy about his coffee and researched good blends and fancy pots. But the busier he got, the less effort went into the beverage, and eventually his became like all other station-house brews—terrible. For some reason, every police precinct or station house in the country makes awful coffee. It's as though cops are taught while going through the police academy how to take perfectly good ground coffee beans and turn them into acrid mud.

Mort poured himself a cup. "You're sure? It's Sumatra."

"Another time, thanks," I said. "I've had my quota for the day." I took the chair opposite his. "Did you get anything from Alexei's cell phone?" I asked.

"The phone itself was ruined, but we got a list of his calls from the telephone company. Nothing really helpful. A few calls from the rink, but we can't tell who he spoke with."

He took a sip of his coffee, winced, and put it down. "Okay, Mrs. F., what's this information you've come up with about the kid I have back there in one of the cells?" He tipped his head toward the jail.

"First, Mort, may I ask what led you to bring him in for questioning?"

"We got a call from one of the security guards at the ice arena. The kid was hanging around the door to the ladies' room, trying to catch a peek inside, I guess. Apparently they'd caught him at it before, and this time they were willing to press charges. One of my deputies headed over there and brought him in."

"What has he told you?" I asked.

"Not much. He's like a little boy. Just sits there and pouts, won't answer any questions. The name on his California driver's license is Hunter, says he's twenty-one, but I doubt it. The license looks like a forgery. We're checking with Motor Vehicles out there. But you said his real name is something else."

"That's right. His real name is Thomas Mulvaney. He's been working as a waiter at Mara's as Tommy Hunter."

"I knew I'd seen him somewhere around town. How long has he been at Mara's?"

"Not very long. He told me he's originally from the 'flatlands of southern Nevada,' but there are no flatlands in southern Nevada. He's from San Francisco. He was accused out there of stalking Christine Allen, the young woman who was Alexei Olshansky's skating partner."

"How did you find that out?"

"I have a friend out there who used to be with the PD." I

didn't want to reveal John Molito's name; I didn't want him accused of breaking department rules. Mort was wise to my fudging. He didn't ask for a name.

"So this Tommy's a real foul ball," Mort said.

"He told Mara his parents were killed in a car wreck, but I'm not sure we can trust anything he says. He's troubled, that's for certain. I think he's the one who wrote those nasty notes to Alexei Olshansky, the one found in Alexei's room, and the other that was with flowers outside the rink."

Mort's eyes widened. "Then that means there's a pretty good chance that he killed Olshansky."

"It certainly doesn't rule him out as a suspect," I said, hoping Mort wouldn't jump to premature conclusions.

"It'll take a lot more to make a solid case against him," he said.

"You say he won't answer any questions," I said.

"That's right, Mrs. F. Clammed right up like a losing tout at the track. Refuses to say a word."

"I wonder if he'd speak with me. I was introduced to him at Mara's and he seemed friendly enough."

"If he won't talk to me, an officer of the law, I doubt if he'll talk to you."

"Well, sometimes someone who is less threatening might be able to get through."

"I didn't threaten him," Mort said, looking offended.

"Of course you didn't, but as you pointed out, you're in uniform. That alone can be intimidating, especially to a young boy. Why not let me take a shot at him?"

Mort rubbed the back of his neck. "Okay," he said, getting up and coming around the desk. "Come on, I'll take you back to the squawk-and-talk."

Tommy was led into a relatively comfortable interview room, at least when compared to most police interrogation rooms I've seen. His face expressed surprise to see me. I greeted him with a big smile and extended my hand, which he tentatively took. Fear was etched into his eyes, and I felt sorry for him. No one, of course, including me, would dismiss his activities as a stalker, but that didn't mean that I couldn't respond to his vulnerability. He sat on one side of the table; I took a chair opposite him. Mort leaned against the wall with his arms crossed.

"Sheriff Metzger thought you might be more at ease talking with someone other than a member of the police," I said.

"Are you a lawyer?" Tommy asked.

"No. If you remember back to when we were first introduced, you found out that I write murder mysteries. I know you said you didn't read much, but maybe I can get you interested in books. I'll be happy to give you one of mine."

"Would you sign it to me?"

"If you like."

He started to say something but held back, his eyes darting to Mort and then to the floor.

"Would you prefer that Sheriff Metzger leave us alone, Tommy?"

He nodded and managed to say, "I think so."

I looked to Mort, who shrugged and left the room, but not without saying, "We'll be keeping an eye on you, Mrs. F."

I enjoyed a distinct advantage over Mort because I knew more about the young man's stalking history. I decided to try to catch him off guard with that knowledge and began by saying, "I know that you're a fan of Christine Allen's."

His eyes took on life that hadn't been there before.

"She's my girlfriend. We've been best friends for years."

"You have?"

"Yeah, but her father doesn't want us to be together." He caught himself. "Hey! How do you know about . . . about me and Chris?"

"I have some friends in San Francisco, Tommy. They told me about the trouble you had there."

"See? It was her father. She wants to be with me," he said. "I know she does. He told the cops I was planning to hurt her, but I would never hurt her. She knows that. We're going to run away. We're going to pretend that I abducted her. Like a princess, you know, in the storybooks."

My mind flashed back to first time I'd seen Tommy. It was at Charles Department Store, the night Irina Bednikova had come in. He'd been buying duct tape and white rope used for hanging laundry. It was possible his abduction fantasy about Chris included tying her up. I shivered at the thought.

"I'm sure you wouldn't want to hurt her," I said to him, "but you can understand why she would be upset having someone pay too much attention to her."

"I just want her to know who I am," he said. He slumped back in his chair and seemed more relaxed.

"We'll talk more about Christine at another time," I said, "but—"

"We're going to get married," he said, absently. "And I'll be the only one she skates with."

I decided to change direction and become more specific in my questions. I had no idea how long Mort would allow me to be in there with him and didn't want to be removed before I had a chance to ask what I considered to be the most important ones.

"Tommy, did you write notes to Alexei Oshansky, the Russian skater who was killed?"

His relaxed demeanor changed. He sat up straight and looked around the room as though seeking a means of escape.

"Did you?" I repeated.

"He doesn't deserve to have her," he said.

"But he didn't deserve to die, either."

He'd referred to Olshansky in the present tense, as though he were still alive.

"I didn't hurt him."

"I didn't say you did, Tommy. I just asked whether you had written notes to him."

"I don't know what you're talking about."

"We have those notes, Tommy, written on Mara's order pads and with the same grease pencils you use at the luncheonette. Comparing your handwriting to the writing on the notes won't take very much." I didn't say that Mort wasn't prepared to pay for such a service just yet. But the thought alone might convince Tommy he was caught in the net. "I would like to help you, Tommy, but I can't if you aren't honest with me. Sheriff Metzger naturally wonders whether you had anything to do with Alexei's death."

I waited for a response.

"Did you have anything to do with it, Tommy?"

"He didn't deserve to have her," he said again.

"You aren't doing much to help yourself," I said.

"Chris and I saw him," he said.

"Alexei?"

"Uh-huh."

"When did you see him?"

"That night."

"The night he died?"

"Uh-huh."

"Chris was at the rink with you."

He nodded. "I saw him go in where they keep those big machines."

"The Zambonis?"

"The big machines."

"Did you go in with him?"

He shook his head.

"Did you see someone else go in with him?"

He nodded.

Before I could follow up, he jumped to his feet, wrapped his arms around himself, and trembled. "I don't want to talk anymore," he said.

He went to the door and pounded on it. Mort immediately opened it and said, "I think we'd better end this, Mrs. F."

He was right, of course. I'd had no idea how troubled Tommy was. It was shocking to witness the change in him from when I'd first met him at Mara's. There he'd been friendly and open. Now he'd closed himself off from the world, wrapped up in his fantasy and totally unaware of the trouble he was in.

"You almost had him going there, Mrs. F.," Mort said as we settled back into his office.

"You heard him say that Chris was at the rink the night Alexei died. She had denied that."

"Yeah, but who knows if she was there for real or only in his imagination."

"He said he saw Alexei go into the Zamboni garage the night he was killed," I said, "and that he saw someone go in with him."

"Shame he clammed up after he said that. Maybe he actually saw the murderer."

"Or, in his mixed-up mind, was referring to himself in the third person."

"I hadn't thought of that. Thanks for getting the info about his being a stalker back in Frisco."

"I have more information for you, Mort."

"I'm all ears."

"It's about Brian Devlin and the man Eve Simpson says is interested in buying the ice arena. I went by Devlin's house before coming here and—"

Chapter Twenty-four

I went directly home from Mort's office, started a fire in the fireplace, made myself a cup of soup, and settled in for some serious thinking. I left the lights off and enjoyed the peace the darkened room and roaring fire created, the flames tossing flickering shafts of orange light onto the ceiling and walls.

That day had been an eye-opener for me. While I'd not ruled out anyone as a suspect in Alexei Olshanky's murder, I hadn't focused on specific people. But Tommy Hunter's emergence on the scene as not only Christine Allen's San Francisco stalker, but also a troubled young man with anger festering inside of him, cast a deserved spotlight on him as the potential killer. It certainly could be said that he had a motive—get rid of the man who, in his befuddled mind, was a rival suitor for Christine.

But there was Alexei and Christine's coach, Brian Devlin, who turned out to have had more in his background than figure skating and coaching. Not only had he been a gambler in Las Vegas—and not a very successful one, according to Peter Valery—but he'd also been implicated in at least one dubious business deal that entailed purposely sabotaging the value of a piece of property in order to buy it at a fire-sale price. Never mind that the plan also involved bribing politicians and presumably anyone else who could help the scheme along. Peter Valery's father had paid dearly for choosing the wrong business partner. That Harvey Gemell had been the one to introduce Devlin and Valery, coupled with my having seen Gemell leave Devlin's house that afternoon, sent me on an entirely new train of thought.

Was Devlin working with Gemell to devalue the Cabot Cove Ice Arena and to push Eldridge Coddington into selling it to Gemell at less than its worth? Could Devlin have been behind the incidents that had beset the arena? If that imagined scenario proved true, how far would he go to taint the arena's reputation and compromise its value? Was murder an option?

But surely, I reasoned, killing someone in order to create a negative image of the arena was beyond the pale. Only someone demented, and desperate, would resort to such a heinous act. Brian Devlin might be desperate, but he wasn't demented.

Could Devlin have had another motive for killing Alexei? The Russian skater's comment to Devlin that hinted at something shadowy in the coach's background had stuck with me. Alexei had been in Colorado Springs; his extended Russian-American family there had known Paul Valery. Might he have learned about the financial problems and legal action that had caused Valery to take his own life?

There had to be some connection between the skater and his time spent in Colorado, and Devlin's role in Valery's shady Las Vegas business deal.

It was hard to imagine that Christine Allen would have killed her pairs partner. From what I'd observed at the rink, they got along nicely, both on the ice and off. Of course, that didn't mean that there was an absence of tension between them. Alexei had a reputation for being cruel to certain people. Marisa Brown had been the object of his nastiness on occasion and was vocal about it. Jeremy Hapgood was equally open in his dislike of the Russian skater and had been on the receiving end of many of Alexei's verbal barbs. But, according to Marisa, Jeremy had a much more powerful motive to get rid of Alexei. He wanted to be Christine's pairs partner. Would he have killed Olshansky in order to achieve that opportunity? People have been killed for lesser reasons, for a pair of sneakers or an imagined insult.

Although I had no idea how it might fit into the scheme of things, having learned that afternoon that Devlin and his assistant coach, Lyla Fasolino, were evidently more than professional colleagues added another dimension to the scenario. I had no reason to believe that Lyla had anything but a cordial working relationship with Alexei, nor was there a hint of any romantic interest between them. But then again, I hadn't been aware of her relationship with Devlin. If Lyla was two-timing Brian with Alexei, it could change the whole picture. Jealousy ranks right up there with greed as a motive for murder. But lacking any knowledge of an affair between Alexei and Lyla, I put aside that notion of a love triangle as having a possible bearing upon the murder.

Despite the assorted conjectures that rose in my active mind, the dark room and crackling fire conspired to make me sleepy. A good night's rest had eluded me since finding Alexei's body in the pit, and I decided that there was nothing more to be accomplished by staying up and continuing to analyze motives and suspects. After banking the fire, I went upstairs, undressed, put on my pajamas, and curled up in a recliner, my favorite spot for reading. I had a new novel but had to struggle to stay awake, no fault of the author. Finally I surrendered to the inevitable, closed the book, turned out the floor lamp, and was padding toward the bathroom when the phone rang. I glanced at my digital alarm clock: 10:20.

"Hope I'm not calling too late, Mrs. F."

"Another few minutes and you would have been," I said.

"Glad I didn't wake you. Thought you'd want to know since you sat in today on my questioning of Tommy Hunter that I'm holding him as a suspect in the murder of Alexei Olshansky."

"You feel you have enough evidence to do that, Mort?"

"I can't hold him any longer without charging him, Mrs. F. Legal Aid has assigned him a lawyer. The way I see it, he had motive and means, and he admits he saw the victim go into the Zamboni garage the day he was killed. Like you said, maybe he was talking about himself when he says he saw somebody follow Olshansky into the garage. That means he was there. And I have the threatening notes he wrote to the victim. Seems like a pretty strong case to me. Of course, I'm pretty sure he'll file an insanity plea."

"Have you run it past the district attorney?" I asked.

"First thing in the morning. Just figured now that the murder is solved, you can put it out of your mind and enjoy a good night's sleep."

"That was thoughtful of you, Mort," I said, deciding not to question him further. "Good night."

His call had abolished any sleepiness I'd been experiencing. I returned to the chair, turned on the light, and tried to get back into the novel. A half hour later, my eyelids drooping, I decided once again to call it a night. No sooner had I climbed beneath the covers when the phone rang. I debated letting my answering machine pick up but succumbed to the need to know who was calling at that hour.

"Mrs. Fletcher?" a male voice asked in almost a whisper.

My first thought was that it was a crank call, and I waited for the heavy breathing. But the caller dissuaded me of that possibility.

"Mrs. Fletcher? It's Jeremy Hapgood at the ice arena."

"Jeremy?" I said.

"I know it's late, but I have to talk with you."

"Can't it wait until morning?"

"No, ma'am. Marisa told me that she spoke with you about what's going on here at the rink."

"Yes, she did. Is this about that?"

"It's about Alexei Olshansky's murder. I told her she got it all wrong."

I was now fully awake. I sat up against my headboard and blinked away any vestiges of fatigue that remained.

"You have my attention, Jeremy," I said, concealing a yawn.

"Can you come to the rink?" he said.

"Now? Isn't it closed?"

"Yes, but it's better that no one else be here."

"You can come to my house if you'd like," I offered.

"No, it has to be here. I want to show you how Alexei died. Marisa said that you can be trusted." He paused. "Look, if you're not interested, I'll just—"

"Don't you think this is something you should share with Sheriff Metzger?"

"I'm sorry I called," he said.

"No, wait," I said. "I'll come and meet with you. You say we'll be alone. What about security guards?"

"They go off duty once the rink is closed."

I remembered Coddington saying the same thing at the press conference.

"The back door, at the rear of the parking lot, will be open."

When I didn't say anything, he said, "Are you coming?"

"Yes, Jeremy. I'll be there as soon as I can."

He hung up.

I got out of bed, splashed cold water on my face, got back into my clothes, and went downstairs. It was a few minutes after eleven. I looked outside through my front window. It had started snowing again, but only feathery flakes, the deceptive prelude to a heavier snowfall.

I picked up the phone and called Mort's cell number. There was no answer. I tried police headquarters.

"This is Jessica Fletcher. Would the sheriff happen to be there?"

"No, Mrs. Fletcher. This is the night dispatcher. I think he's on his way home. Can I help you?"

"Would you please see that he gets a message the minute he reports in?"

"Sure."

"Tell him that Jessica Fletcher has gone to the ice arena and would like him to meet her there."

He wrote down the message and repeated it to me.

"Perfect," I said. "Oh, and please tell him that it's extremely important that he come to the arena."

"Shall do, Mrs. Fletcher."

Next I phoned Maureen.

"Is Mort home yet?" I asked.

"No. He was going to stop down the highway for some Chinese food. I expect him home in a half hour or so. Did you try his cell?"

"I think he's out of range," I said. I repeated the message I'd left with the night dispatcher. "It's very important, Maureen. Promise me you won't forget to tell him."

"You have my word, Jessica."

Dimitri runs my trusty cab service, which has been providing me with dependable transportation for years. "I need a taxi to the ice arena," I told him.

"It's closed, Mrs. Fletcher."

"I know, but I'm meeting someone there. Do you have a driver available?"

"He'll be there in ten minutes."

I sensed that my driver wasn't pleased to be called out on a frigid night at the start of a snowstorm, but he didn't tell me that. He drove me to the arena, where I instructed him to drive around to the back of the building.

"Sure this is where you want to come?" he asked.

"Yes. I'm meeting someone inside."

"Do you want me wait for you?"

"I have no idea how long I'll be."

"That's okay," he said. "I have a book to read." He held up one of mine. "I was almost to the end when Dimitri called."

"Well, thank you, then. I'll take you up on your offer. I hope I won't be long."

He watched me as I walked to the building and tried the door, which was unlocked, as Jeremy had said it would be. I turned and waved. He waved back, then drove to the edge of the lot and parked under a streetlamp.

I paused inside the arena to get my bearings. A strange thought crossed my mind at that moment. I thought of so many movies I'd seen in which the heroine willingly places herself in a dangerous situation, while the audience is silently pleading, "Don't do it!" This was no movie, and I'm no heroine, and there was no one at home to consider my having come there alone in the middle of the night as foolhardy, if not plain stupid. Why hadn't I waited for the sheriff to call me back? I had no idea how long it might take for Mort to get my message. Only the taxi driver knew where I was, and he was absorbed in reading one of my books. I pulled out my cell phone and held it in my gloved hand. I didn't want to miss Mort if he called me back.

The lights that illuminated the Olympic-sized rink had been turned off, but a crescent moon shone through the giant glass windows on one end and bounced off the white ice, giving half its surface an eerie blue glow. The rest lay in shadows. The cavernous interior was bone-chillingly cold. I pulled the collar of my jacket closed and without removing my gloves awkwardly pushed the jacket's top button through its loop with one hand. The sound of dripping water somewhere inside echoed off the concrete walls. I breathed in the damp air; violent shivers ran up my spine.

Tempted to whisper in the empty silence, I took a deep breath instead and called out, "Hello? Jeremy? Are you here?"

The words reverberated in the icy atmosphere. There was no response.

"It's Jessica Fletcher. You told me to meet you here. *Where* are you?"

Nothing.

I took a few tentative steps on the rubber mat that carpeted the area around the rink. Skaters had been complaining about wrinkles in the flooring that rose to trip them if they weren't watchful. I blinked several times, trying to accustom my eyes to the gloom, and reached out, pressing my fingertips onto the narrow ledge formed by the boards ringing the rink and the tall plastic panels on top that kept errant hockey pucks from beaning unwary spectators. Moving slowly, following the contours of the oval arena, I reached a part where the Plexiglas barrier ended and I could grip the flat railing of the boards with my gloved hand. Ahead of me were the bleachers, steel benches rising nearly to the roof to accommodate hockey fans, and perhaps, one day, to hold an audience for a major figure skating competition.

I peered across the ice to the Zamboni garage's doors, squinted, and leaned forward.

Something or someone was there, a dark shape slumped on the skating surface.

"Hello?" I called again. "Jeremy? Is that you? Do you need help?"

No movement that I could see, and still no answer. I rummaged in my pocket for my keys, which had a tiny flashlight attached to the ring. While the beam would never reach the other side of the ice—its light barely penetrated the dim blue shadows—it was a great help when trained on the floor, allowing me to step over the lumps in the rubber that might have pitched me onto my knees if I hadn't seen them.

I found the gate in the boards that admitted skaters to the ice and lifted the latch. Not stopping to think, I stepped out onto the slick sheet and let go of the board. I took two steps and slipped, arching painfully to keep from tumbling backward. The cell phone flew from my hand. I heard it hit the ice and skitter away. I gasped and felt my stomach rise, the blood rush to my head, and adrenaline surge through my veins before I was able to regain my equilibrium. Breathing hard now, I paused, shivering, as much from the shock of nearly falling as from the cold. I squinted in the dark, straining to see where my phone had landed, but I had no time to search for it; whoever was on the ice needed my help now.

Cautiously, I tipped my body forward, reaching my arms out in front of me, and slid first one foot and then the other, advancing slowly. If I took a tumble, I wanted to land on my stomach to avoid cracking the back of my head on the hard ice as had happened during my initial skating attempt. I had to assume that the dim figure splayed on the ice was Jeremy Hapgood; as far as I knew, he was the only person inside the arena at that hour. I felt a sense of urgency and, without reconsidering, continued across the vast expanse of ice in his direction.

It seemed an eternity before I reached my goal and warily squatted down, dropping to my knees—next to Jeremy. I grabbed his oversized down jacket and tried unsuccessfully to raise one arm to turn him over. On the ice next to him was the remote control device he'd demonstrated to Mort Metzger, the contraption that controlled the ice-cleaning machine.

I tugged off my gloves and felt around his head, attempting to locate where a pulse might beat in his neck. I let out a breath of relief when I detected one, albeit faint and irregular. A dark stain of blood had already congealed under the cheek touching the ice.

I shook a shoulder and managed to dislodge the side of his face glued in place by the blood. "Jeremy," I said. "What's happened to you?"

My mind was a jumble of conflicting thoughts, but one took precedence. I had to get help—and get it fast. I looked back across the ice and dreaded the return trip. My cell phone was somewhere over there. I'd come close to falling a number of times on my way to Jeremy; the rink looked like a hundred-mile-long Siberian frozen lake.

I drew a deep breath, managed to get to my feet, and had taken only one step when the screeching rattle of a garage door opening sounded behind me. Startled, I whirled around to see the huge Zamboni lumber up the ramp onto the ice like some prehistoric monster emerging from its dark lair.

I bent my knees to maintain my balance on the ice and waved my arms. "Over here," I shouted. "We need help."

The roar of the engine was deafening in the empty arena as the machine slowly turned in my direction, blinding me momentarily with its headlights. One foot went out from under me, and I painfully fell back onto my knees. The machine continued coming straight at me and Jeremy, the razor-sharp blade cutting the top layer of ice, the long brush smoothing out the wash of cold water that formed the new coating. How could the driver not see us?

But questioning why he hadn't spotted Jeremy's prone body on the ice, and me frantically waving and yelling, wasn't doing us any good. The Zamboni continued to bear down on us; the lights of the huge machine were in my eyes and prevented me from seeing who was in the driver's seat. My voice was drowned out by the increasing roar of the engine as it closed the gap between us. I attempted to stand again, but the soles of my boots couldn't find any purchase on the ice. I tried crawling, but my knees slipped away.

It was then that I remembered the remote control unit that now lay beside Jeremy. I grabbed it and started flipping switches, trying desperately to remember what he'd told Mort while demonstrating it for him. I looked up. The Zamboni was about to crush us both; its long, razor-sharp blade would slice us to ribbons. Despairing, I pushed every button. The Zamboni's whirring engine was deafening. Then, as the machine loomed over us, it whined, its forward motion stopped with a jerk, and the engine shut down, a wave of water pulsing forward to dampen my knees.

I'd been holding my breath for the past few seconds. Now I let it out, and my body, which was as tense as a steel rod, relaxed along with the whoosh of exhaled air. I looked up from where I sat on the ice and saw a figure climb down from the high seat. It took a moment for me to see that it was Brian Devlin. As he approached, he said, "Good God, Mrs. Fletcher. What are you doing here? I never saw you. This could have been a horrible accident."

I stared at him in disbelief. I had no doubt that he'd aimed the Zamboni directly at us.

He reached down to help me to my feet. "Is that—"

"Yes," I said. "It's Jeremy Hapgood. He needs a doctor immediately."

"What happened to him?" Devlin asked. "I didn't know that anyone was here."

"We can discuss that after we've called for an ambulance. I lost my cell phone."

"Here. Use mine."

With trembling fingers, I dialed 911. I told the operator who answered that there was a badly injured man at the ice arena who needed help immediately and was assured that she would dispatch someone right away.

Devlin reached out and plucked his cell phone from my hand. Across the ice, mine began to ring. There was no way I could reach it in time to answer the call without Devlin's help. He didn't offer it.

"Jeremy asked me to meet him here tonight, Brian," I said. "He said he would show me how Alexei died."

Devlin knelt down beside Jeremy. "How would he know anything about it?" he asked. "Unless he was about to confess to you." He pushed Jeremy onto his back and slapped the younger man's cheeks. "C'mon, buddy," he said. "Wake up."

"I doubt if that was Jeremy's reason for calling me. He had no reason to confess because he didn't kill Alexei."

"You sound pretty sure of yourself, Mrs. Fletcher."

"What I'm not sure of is why you would be here at this hour driving the Zamboni. You're a coach. Coaches are not responsible for keeping the ice clean."

My cell phone rang again. Again Devlin ignored it.

"I spoke with Jeremy less than an hour ago," I said. "He called me at home from here. Yet within that hour he ends up close to death out here on the ice. As far as I can tell, you're the only person here aside from him. Are you telling me that you have no idea what happened to him?"

Up to this point Devlin had been conciliatory, feigning concern for me and Jeremy. But my questioning changed his demeanor. He got to his feet, his face set in a scowl, jutted out his chin, and said, "I've really had enough of your accusations, Mrs. Fletcher. I resent your tone and your innuendos that I might've had something to do with Alexei's death, or tonight with whatever happened to Jeremy. I'm leaving." He turned his back to me and began sliding toward the gate.

"You're not even waiting for the ambulance?" I said, incredulous. "You attacked Jeremy, didn't you, Brian?" I called to his retreating back. "And you intended to use the Zamboni to make it look like an accident?"

He stopped and retraced his steps to me.

I added, "And you wouldn't have hesitated including me among the victims."

He forced a crooked smile. "Oh, you aren't content with accusing me of killing Alexei, are you? You're also saying that I wanted to kill Jeremy and you. You don't know what you're talking about, Mrs. Fletcher, and you haven't from the beginning."

"Very clever, Brian. A bit of misdirection. No, I'm not saying that you killed Alexei Olshansky, because I know that you didn't. But you were willing to kill others to shield the person who did."

We were interrupted by loud banging at the rear entrance. Mort burst in through the door, shouting instructions to his deputies. Instantly, the rink was flooded with light, leaving us blinking in the glare. Then two EMTs arrived, carrying a portable gurney.

"Where is the injured person?" one of them asked.

They had a lot of trouble keeping their footing but eventually managed to remove Jeremy from the ice and carry him out to the waiting ambulance, its rotating emergency beams combined with those of the police cruisers lighting up the dark parking lot. I followed the EMTs, stopping only to retrieve my cell phone, and was grateful to step onto the terra firma of the rubber mats.

"I think it's time I left," Brian said, walking past me toward the exit.

"What's your rush, Devlin?" Mort said. "I'd like to hear what happened here tonight."

"Why don't you ask Mrs. Fletcher? She seems to have all the answers, even if none of them are right."

"It was Lyla who pushed Alexei into that pit, Brian, wasn't it?" I said.

I expected a vehement denial. Instead, he was silent.

"You and Lyla make quite a pair, Brian, but not as skaters."

"Mrs. F.? What's going on?"

"Just the attempted murder of Jeremy Hapgood tonight. I would have been killed in that attempt, too, if it wasn't for Jeremy's love of electronics and the remote control he built for the Zamboni."

Mort looked confused, and I can't say that I blamed him.

"She's making it up, the way she does in her books," Devlin told our sheriff.

"I'm not making up anything, Mort. While you're questioning Mr. Devlin about what happened here tonight, you might also get him to tell you what he knows about Alexei Olshansky's murder."

Mort confronted Devlin. "You have anything to say about that?"

"I'll tell you this, Sheriff. I didn't kill Alexei."

"That's true, Mort," I said, "but he knows who did."

Mort looked even more confused than ever.

"Don't listen to her," Devlin said.

At that, a female voice said from the shadows, "She's right, Sheriff. I pushed Alexei into the pit."

We all turned to face Lyla Fasolino, who stepped into the light.

"Don't say another word," Devlin said.

"No, Brian. It's no use. I want to stop lying. We were going to be found out sooner or later. She was going to make sure of that." Lyla walked to his side, then fixed me in a hard stare. "How long did you know?"

"It became evident to me this afternoon," I replied.

"What tipped you off?" Mort asked.

"A chance visit to Charles Department Store," I said to Mort. "You and I assumed that the golden chain recovered from the bottom of the ice pit belonged to Alexei. But he'd dropped his off to be repaired and never picked it up." I turned to Lyla. "Where's your gold chain, Lyla? You were never without it. But you're not wearing it now—and you've been rubbing a bruise on the back of your neck for days. When you struggled at the edge of the pit and scratched his face, Alexei ripped off your chain and it fell into the water. I think I know why you killed him, but I'm sure the sheriff would rather hear directly from you."

"You don't have to say anything, Lyla," Devlin said, putting his arm around her.

"They may as well hear the truth, Brian," she said, looking down and rubbing her neck where the bruise must have healed by now. "I don't know how he found out, but Alexei knew about a disastrous business deal that Brian had been involved in years ago. He threatened to go to Mr. Coddington about it. Brian owes money to a lot of people, some of them not very nice people. He was working on a new way to pay off his debtors. I pleaded with him not to get involved with this guy, but he wouldn't listen to me. Alexei said he wanted a piece of the action himself to keep his mouth shut."

"What guy? What action?" Mort asked.

I answered for her. "I believe that Brian entered into a

partnership of sorts with Harvey Gemell again. He was a party to the first deal that resulted in a man's death. Gemell was trying to buy this arena at a bargain-basement price—with Brian's help—by arranging for a series of disruptions and accidents, intended to pressure Coddington into throwing up his hands. I don't know how Alexei came into that information, but in the end it cost him his life." I turned to Lyla. "Please correct me, Lyla, if I have some of the details wrong."

She offered nothing additional.

Devlin dropped his arm from Lyla's shoulders and stepped away from her. "Okay," he said, "you know who killed Alexei. But I had nothing to do with it."

Lyla gasped.

Devlin cast a final glance at Lyla before striding toward the front door.

Mort pursued him and grabbed his arm. "Where are *you* going?"

"I'm going home. I'm tired of all this. Getting involved in a business deal isn't against the law, is it?"

"It is if it involves fraud, Devlin," Mort said. "Besides, if what Mrs. Fletcher says is true about what happened here tonight, you'll be facing a charge of at least assault, and maybe attempted murder."

Mort signaled his deputies, who took Brian into custody. "If you're tired, these gentlemen will be happy to give you a warm, comfortable bed for the night when they drive you down to headquarters."

When he returned, Lyla was crying. "I was so sure everything was going to go right this time. So much has gone wrong in my life."

"What was it that went wrong for you, Lyla?" I asked. "I thought you had a good life."

"I never made a success of anything," she said, tears streaming down her cheeks. "Sure, I won a few skating competitions, but everything went downhill after that. My pro career was a flop, and I had to come home to Cabot Cove and beg Mr. Coddington for a job. And Brian, too, missed that thrill of victory we had when we were young and competing for medals. I thought, this time, we'll do it together. But I was wrong."

There was a flurry of activity at the door, and I looked over to see my cabdriver waving at me from behind one of Mort's deputies.

"You ready to go home, Mrs. Fletcher?" he called out. "I finished the book. It was great. I never guessed who the murderer was."

Chapter Twenty-five

Had Jeremy Hapgood not recovered in time to relate to Mort Metzger and to me what had transpired at the arena that night, Brian Devlin might have walked away without any charges being filed against him. Here's what Jeremy told us during a bedside interview early the following morning.

"I came to the arena to meet with Mr. Devlin about becoming Christine's pairs partner. He turned me down flat. He told me that I was a second-rate skater who'd never make it in competitions, and that I should stick to driving the Zamboni and hang up my skates. I guess I got hotheaded and started swearing at him. I might have even pushed him. I don't remember. Anyway, this was right before I called Mrs. Fletcher and asked her to meet me at the rink. I had my own theory about how Alexei died. I was sure that Mr. Devlin had done it to shut him up about the coach's past, and I wanted to tell Mrs. Fletcher about it."

"How did you know about his past?" I asked.

"Alexei told me."

"I thought you and Alexei weren't on very good terms," I said.

"We weren't. Only Cabot Cove's pretty small. Sometimes we'd end up at the same bar; he'd have too much to drink and start blabbing, you know, boasting about how he was going to become the greatest pairs skater in the world, stuff like that. Anyway—did you know that his girlfriend back in Russia had his kid?"

I acknowledged that I did know.

"So, one night he starts in on how he knows that his coach was a crook, a guy who'd been involved in shady land deals in Las Vegas, and owed money everywhere, and how he was going to use it against him if he ever gave Alexei a hard time. I put two and two together and figured that Mr. Devlin had pushed Alexei into that pit to shut him up.

"After I called Mrs. Fletcher, I went back to him and told the coach what I knew. It was dumb of me, I suppose, to think I could blackmail—I guess you could call it blackmail—him into taking me on as Christine's skating partner. That's when he hit me. That's all I remember."

"You had a fractured skull, son," Mort said. "The doctors did a good job of stopping the bleeding. They saved your life."

"I'm not sure what kind of life I'll have after all this."

"You'll have whatever life you choose to have," I said.

Out of the corner of my eye, I noticed some movement at the door. "You have another visitor," I said.

"Who?"

"Hi, Jer." Marisa cocked her head at him. "You okay?"

"You must be pretty sore at me for trying to ditch you so I could skate with Christine, huh?"

She stood by his bed and picked up his hand. "I'll get over it," she said.

"Chris is going home to San Francisco, you know."

"I heard. Probably too many bad memories here."

"Yeah. Plus she doesn't have anyone to skate with here. No way her father was going to let me be her partner."

"You would have been a great partner for her," Marisa said.

"Mark Rosner said her father is bringing Wolfgang Meister from Austria to team up with her."

"He's pretty famous. They'll be good together."

"Maybe we'll compete against them someday," Jeremy said. When she didn't answer, he added, "Marisa, I just want to tell you it was wrong of me to desert you."

"We were both wrong," she said, lowering her eyes. "I said some pretty bad things about you I hope you never hear." She glanced at me. "I have to go to work now. I just came up to see how you were."

"Wait!" he said. "I'll forgive you if you forgive me."

"The most important thing is for you to get better so you can get back on your skates. I'll see you later, okay?"

"Do you think she'll forgive me, Mrs. Fletcher?" he asked when Marisa had left.

"Judging from her reaction," I said, "I'd say you two might still have a future as a pairs team—and maybe even more than that. Sheriff Metzger and I are going to go now and let you rest."

"Thanks for the information, son," Mort said. "I'll put it to good use."

"Oh, by the way, I've brought you a present, Jeremy. This saved both our lives." I reached into a shopping bag and retrieved the Zamboni remote control he had designed.

"Thanks, Mrs. Fletcher. Good thing I made it, huh?"

"A very good thing, Jeremy."

"Mr. Coddington said I should show it to the Zamboni people and see if they want to manufacture it. That would be pretty neat."

"It would," I said.

Over the following months, the resolution of Alexei Olshansky's murder restored a sense of normalcy and calm to Cabot Cove, although everyone closely followed the process being played out in our court and what ultimately happened to the players in this sordid affair. Evelyn Phillips's *Cabot Cove Gazette* enjoyed record newsstand and subscription sales, and business at the ice arena boomed.

Based upon my testimony and Jeremy's, Devlin was charged with assault and attempted murder. He pleaded not guilty, and his trial is pending. Lyla was booked on manslaughter charges and offered no defense for what she had done. Nevertheless, her attorney worked out a plea deal; she was sentenced to thirty years but could be released after fourteen for good behavior.

Tommy Mulvaney (aka Hunter) was tried as an adult under Maine's stringent antistalking act. Because Christine's father had not elected to press charges in California, Tommy was considered a first-time offender and was initially sentenced to sixty days in jail for having "engaged in behavior that created a credible threat for the person being stalked." His notes to Alexei constituted, according to the judge, a tangible threat of bodily harm and were taken into consideration during his sentencing.

Contrary to Tommy's claim that both his parents had died in an automobile accident, they were very much alive and traveled to Cabot Cove to stand by their disturbed son during the sentencing phase of his trial. Taking their support into consideration, the judge reduced Tommy's sentence to time served, provided that he would be placed under the care of a licensed psychiatrist and enrolled in an approved abuser-education program. My heart went out to his parents, good, solid citizens who obviously loved their son and would do all they could to help him achieve mental stability.

Eldridge Coddington announced that he was not selling the Cabot Cove Ice Arena and instead committed a sizable amount of new money to upgrading every aspect of it. That he'd successfully enticed a semipro hockey team to call the arena its home venue meant hefty revenues, which may have played some role in his decision. The end result was a much-improved public facility that could be enjoyed by all of the town's citizens—at least those for whom ice-skating had appeal.

Coddington's announcement that the arena would remain in his hands meant, of course, that Eve Simpson had lost out on a lucrative real estate commission from Harvey

Gemell. I bumped into her at Loretta's beauty parlor one afternoon a few days after Coddington's decision was announced in the *Gazette* and commiserated with her on the loss of a potentially large commission. "You must be upset," I said.

"*Au contraire*, Jessica," she said. "I knew something was fishy about Gemell, knew it from the very beginning. He was not the real thing, a *poseur*."

"I thought you'd thoroughly checked him out," I said.

"Oh, I did, and he looked solid on paper. But there was something about the guy that set me on edge. It makes me sick to think that he was in cahoots with that Coach Devlin to try to steal the arena from Eldridge." She wrapped her arms about herself and shook her head with an exaggerated shudder. "I'm only sorry he didn't have to suffer some consequence," she said.

As smarmy as he was, Gemell had left all the dirty work to Devlin. He himself had done nothing to warrant legal action.

"Where is he now?" I asked.

"As far as I know, he is home in Greenwich, Connecticut, planning his next scam." She stood and checked her image in Loretta's mirror. "I'm off to meet a potential client. He's interested in buying a dockside restaurant. Do you think Mara might want to sell?"

"I certainly hope not."

The following winter, the Cabot Cove Ice Arena hosted its first major figure skating exhibition. The stands were filled with admiring fans as a succession of skaters—mostly children and teens—showed off their skills in singles, pairs, and ice dancing, gliding over the ice with finesse and athleticism. I sat with Seth Hazlitt, Mort and Maureen Metzger, Mayor Jim Shevlin and his wife, Susan, and other friends. As I watched the skaters perform their magic, I couldn't help but think back to my first time back on the ice following that fateful night at the arena when Jeremy's electronic device had saved our lives.

When I'd told Seth of my intention to skate again, he'd surprised me by saying, "Mind if I tag along and watch?"

I would have preferred that he not accompany me—his presence would make me more nervous than usual—but of course I said he could come. I didn't want to be rude.

Seth dropped me at the entrance, and I went inside to put on my skates while he parked his car. When he rejoined me, he was carrying a large shopping bag from Charles Department Store. He set it on the floor in front of me.

"What's that?" I asked.

"Don't really know. Why don't you open it and find out."

The bag contained a box, and the box contained a spanking-new skater's helmet in black with JESSICA painted in pink script across the front.

"Oh, Seth, this is so thoughtful, but I'm afraid I'll look silly wearing it. No one else on the ice is wearing one."

"Better to look silly, Jessica, than end up in the ER again. Wear it, please. I don't want to have to carry you out of here."

I didn't have a choice. I put on the helmet. It fit perfectly. "You look like a champion," he said, grinning.

I stepped out onto the ice, and I have to admit, the helmet gave me more confidence. And the first time I executed my left crossover, Seth applauded in appreciation.

An announcement on the PA system brought my attention back to the present: "Ladies and gentlemen, representing the Cabot Cove Skating Club, please put your hands together for the winners of the New England Regional Championships, and the stars of our show, Marisa Brown and Jeremy Hapgood. Brown and Hapgood are coached by our own Mark Rosner. They will be skating to Tchaikovsky's 'Romeo and Juliet.'"

A roar of approval rose from the crowd. I clapped my hands, and next to me Seth Hazlitt gave out a loud whistle. I smiled. Aside from an occasional murder, Cabot Cove, Maine, is a wonderful place to live, and I count my blessings every day.